To Begin Again

Janet Stobie has built an inspiring beauty into this story of a Canadian teenage girl's life and tells it with a consummate poetry, spirituality and rhythm. This is a substantial narrative dealing honestly and in depth with current, complex matters of concern to us all: immigration, cultural difference, our fear of terrorism, suicide, friendship, love and redemption.

It does so by tracing and comparing lives parallel to that of the Canadian teenager. One is her great-great-grandmother who was a Barnardo child; the other, that of a contemporary refugee family. A deep understanding of both emerges.

Janet Stobie's sensitive story offers the reader clear insights into the roots for and relationships between Judaism, Christianity and Islam; into the intimate and inner feelings of an orphan teenager; a young, widowed father seeking to re-build his life; and into the diverse reactions and behaviours of their friends and the community at large. These matters are addressed under the guiding love of God.

This deeply-felt story is current, educational, and written in a brave, honest, and constructive way. I warmly recommend it for teenagers as well as adults who seek inspiration and fulfillment.

~ *Viviana Galleno, professor, Faculty of Business and Law, The Open University, U.K.*

"To Begin Again" is the much anticipated, heart-warming continuation of Renee's and Steve's stories and more. Writing with sensitivity, humour and courage, Jan has interwoven themes of friendship, prejudice, grief, and romance.

Steve and Renee's belief in a loving, guiding God makes it possible for them "To Begin Again".

Storyteller Jan has gifted us with another wonderful, faith confirming, thought provoking, enjoyable read.

~ *Diane Claridge, retired teacher.*

A heartfelt novel, *To Begin Again* chronicles the life of Steve and Renee as they continue to deal with the sudden death of their wife and mother even after three years. This book is an honest, open-hearted account of a father and daughter struggling to build a new life after tragedy. Especially engaging are life's always-changing challenges. It is good to see the values of care and compassion in the midst of this troubled world. Issues addressed in the story are timely and timeless. I would highly recommend it to all who are searching for hope.

~ *Nancy Miller, Editorial Assistant (Retired),*
Roussan Publishing.

To Begin Again:
A Catalpa Creek Story

Other Books By Janet Stobie

Books for Children

A Place Called Home/ Homeless? Who Me?

Spectacular Stella

Elizabeth Gets Her Wings

Short Stories for All Ages

A Child Speaks

Can I Hold Him? (Christmas Stories)

Novels

Fireweed

Worship Resource

Dipping Your Toes in Planning Small Group Devotions

To Begin Again

A Catalpa Creek Story

Janet Stobie

Child's Play
Publications

Child's Play Productions
853 Abbey Lane
Peterborough, Ontario K9H 7T1

ISBN 978-1-7752938-0-4

Ordering Information – Special Discounts are available for large quantity orders by corporations, associations and others. For details contact info@janetstobie.com

Editor: Ruth Walker www.writescape.ca
Graphic Art Work: Cover and Interior Layout by Sue Reynolds, www.piquantproductions.ca
Printed in Canada by Marquis, Montmagny, Québec, Canada G5V 4T1

Visit www.janetstobie.com

9 8 7 6 5 4 3 2 1

Dedication

This story is dedicated to all the people everywhere,
who are doing their best to live God's call to love
and accept our neighbours, regardless of race, sexual
orientation, faith, or economic status.
These ordinary people are God's blessing for us all.
Through them we catch glimpses of the world as it can be.
Through them, God gives us hope and strength *To Begin Again.*

And to the Harrars of this world, who feel so alone
and without hope. Stay strong in the knowledge,
that you are God's beloved child. Your life is precious.
Open your heart to the hope that God offers us all.

The foreigner residing among you
must be treated as your native-born.
Love them as yourself,
for you were foreigners in Egypt.
I am the Lord your God.

(Leviticus 19:34 NIV)

Chapter One

A Chance Encounter

Sunday, September 17

Steve

I jerked awake. A fly buzzed across the ceiling. I yanked the blankets over my head. The buzzing continued. Too hot. I pulled the blankets off. The bloody fly tickled my bare arm. Enough!!! Wide awake now, I hauled my body out of bed. Eight flashed on my clock radio. Too early. Church isn't 'til ten. I groaned and pulled on my robe. The fly made another pass. Swatter's in the kitchen, of course. I sighed and trudged into the hallway, gladly leaving the fly behind.

Downstairs on the kitchen counter, a package of thawed blueberries waited, purple-blue oozing down the cupboard door. Right, pancakes. I promised Renée pancakes. I grabbed the dishcloth. A few swipes and the mess was gone.

Ten minutes later, the pancake batter ready, I called up the stairs, "Renée, time to get up." No answer. I yelled this time. Still nothing. I ran up the stairs and knocked on her bedroom door. "Pancakes in fifteen." Still no response. I opened the door. Her cat, Ebony, looked up at me from an empty pile of blankets.

I checked the bathroom. Empty. Chill out, Steve. She's seventeen. She's an early riser. Probably gone for a walk.

I returned to the kitchen. Her baseball hat, jacket and rubber boots were not at the back door. I looked out the window towards the creek. No canoe. My stomach tightened. I wish she wouldn't just buzz off without a word.

I started cooking pancakes. Each time I added to the stack in the oven, my frustration mounted. The last pancake was bubbling in the pan when I saw her pull up to the dock. She had a frown on her face as she strode towards the house. What's that about, I wondered.

Her cheeks flushed from exertion, she opened the back door. "Glad you're up. *Mmmm*, those pancakes smell good."

I took a deep breath. "Thanks for the note you didn't leave me. Hope you had a good time."

Ignoring my sarcasm, she answered, "It's a beautiful morning. Quite warm in the sunshine and quiet, sooooooo quiet."

"Renée, you snuck out!"

"Oh, Dad, take it easy. I didn't sneak anywhere. I just went for a morning paddle on the creek."

"Don't tell me to take it easy. You—"

"I'm seventeen. I can leave the house without your permission."

"That's not the point. What if the canoe capsized or something? I didn't know where you were."

"I had my cell phone. I can call."

"Not if you lose it in the muddy creek bottom."

She gave me the look I'd seen a lot of lately. "Dad, don't be an idiot. A year from now, I'll be at university. You won't know where I am or what I'm doing."

"A year from now doesn't matter. While you're living at home, you're my responsibility."

"Come on. Allow me a little independence."

I clenched my teeth and started again. "Renée, you need to learn to be considerate of others. You could have left a note."

"Okay, Okay. I didn't. So, don't make such a big deal. Next time I will."

The smell of burning pancake assaulted my nose. "Damn," I said, and moved the griddle over as I flipped off the burner switch. When I turned back to Renée, her nose was wrinkled up in distaste, too.

She smiled. "I love you," she said.

My anger wilted. I took a deep breath. "Love you too."

She reached out for a hug. As I held her close, I thought, I can't see over your head. You're not a little girl anymore. Next year you'll be gone. This house will be empty.

"Put that stinky pancake in the garbage. Let's eat the rest. I'm hungry," she said as she pulled away.

We settled at the kitchen island, pancakes swimming in maple syrup. Within minutes, we had cleared the whole stack.

Renée pushed back her stool. "Thanks, that was good. I got some fantastic pictures this morning. Want to see them?" She picked up her camera, pulled out the SD card and set it on the counter. "Just a minute, I'll get my computer. They'll look so much better on the bigger screen." With a flip of her long black ponytail, she disappeared.

I buried my lingering frustration while I cleared and rinsed the sticky dishes, stowing them in the dishwasher.

In just a few minutes she was back, her computer set up. "Beautiful," I said, as a picture of the morning mist rising from the creek appeared. She pointed to the centre of the screen.

"See the duck family swimming towards me through the mist, the little ones almost fully grown. They look magical."

"Great picture."

"Look at this video I took of our frequent shoreline visitor. I've named him Corny Crane. When I spotted him this morning, he was a one-legged statue, staring at the water. I turned on the video just as his neck snaked out and snapped up a fish. I'll break this into frames. I'm sure there will be some spectacular action shots."

Her excitement reminded me of Serena's enthusiasm and joy. "You're already a gifted photographer, Renée. Someday you'll be famous."

"Or not," she said. "This may just be a hobby. I'm not sure what I want to do. I like to write. I love history. Maybe I'll be an archaeologist. There's so much choice. All I know is that I don't want to work with numbers." She shrugged and half-smiled at me. "Sorry."

"That's okay. You don't have to be an accountant. You're not me and that's good. You'll figure it out."

"Will I? Sometimes I wonder."

"Take your time. You've got your whole life ahead of you." I glanced at the clock. "We best get ready for church. I've got a meeting before the service."

She left to shower. I stood at the window, staring out at the creek. Why such a huge reaction? A gust of wind banged the canoe against the dock. I flinched. My mind went to Serena. She was late getting home that night. Once again that policeman stood in the hallway. "Is Serena Rushton your wife? There's been an accident, head-on collision. I'm sorry sir, she died instantly."

I gave myself a shake. That was more than two years ago. It won't happen again.

Renée

Susie met us at the church door, her curly blonde hair loose from its customary ponytail. I smiled and thought, my best friend may be small but she's mighty. We're sure different. I'm tall and willowy and she's short and curvy. Just proof God loves variety.

"Hey, Renée, want to go to Jake's while our dads are at the meeting?"

"Definitely. Let's go." As soon as we hit the street, I said, "I sure had a creepy experience this morning."

"What happened?"

"I woke up way early and decided to take the canoe down the creek. I needed some pictures for my art project."

"You were canoeing already this morning? Really?"

"Yes, really! Not everyone's a sleepyhead like you. Anyway, I found this neat spot. A tall willow tree had spread its branches out over the creek like a giant hand. My canoe slid easily through the curtain of branches into what felt like a secret hideaway." I reached out and gripped Susie's arm. "You'll never guess who was sitting there. He'd built a campfire right on the riverbank." We stopped walking. She stared up at me in anticipation

"Who?"

"Russell Carding, the kid who stalked me two years ago. He stood up when he saw me. He's huge now, like a gorilla."

"What'd you do?"

"I back-paddled out of there as fast as I could. He yelled, 'Stop,' but I didn't. I turned and tore for home. Look! I've got three blisters on my hands from paddling so hard." I held out my hands, one blister had broken and was bleeding a little.

"Renée, that's more than creepy. That's frightening. What did your dad say when you told him?"

"I didn't."

"What? You didn't say anything?"

"No. He was already upset. He'd wakened early and couldn't find me. His imagination was working overtime. When I got back, he started right in about how I didn't leave a note. If I'd mentioned meeting Russell, he'd have exploded."

"Renée, I think you should have told your dad. You know Russell is dangerous."

"Well, I didn't. It was just a chance encounter. That's all." I started walking again. Hoping to distract Susie, I pointed to Richardson's jewellery store window and said, "Isn't that the necklace Rachel wore to the dance last week? The price tag says $145."

Susie wasn't deterred. "Renée, I'm worried about Russell Carding. What's he doing in Catalpa Creek anyway? I thought he moved away once his probation was served."

"I don't know, and I don't care. He's just weird, and besides, he wasn't stalking me. I surprised him."

"Tell your dad, Renée."

"Give it up, Susie. Let's not ruin our whole time talking about Russell." I looked across the street. "There's Harrar. Hey, Harrar, we're going to Jake's for coffee and doughnuts. Want to join us?"

"Gosh, he's gorgeous," Susie said, as he loped across the street.

"Yes, and tall like Dad, and so… sweet, a good friend."

"Friend?" Susie reacted.

Harrar joined us, and I didn't have to respond.

"Hey! How's it going?" he asked, his cheeks dimpled with his huge smile.

"Hey, yourself. What's up this morning?" I asked.

"Just out and about. Why aren't you two at church?"

"Not until eleven. Our dads had a meeting first," Susie said. "We skipped out."

"Perfect," he answered.

At Jake's, Harrar opened the door and waved us through.

I looked up into his eyes as I walked past. "Do you have plans for this afternoon? I got some neat pictures this morning. You might like to use one for inspiration."

He let the door swing shut behind him, his smile fading. "Sorry. I'm loaded with homework." His gaze shifted to the ceiling. "Could you put them on a flash drive?"

Disappointed, I answered, "Sure." What's with him?

Before I could say anything more, Susie said, "Some of our crowd's over in the corner. Let's join them."

Chapter Two

Attic Treasures

Monday, September 18

Renée

After school Monday, I stopped by Dad's office. Totally immersed in his paperwork, he didn't look up when I stepped through the door, giving me a moment to really look at him. My friends think he's a hunk. Well, I suppose he is kind of cute, with that salt and pepper grey hair, and that dimple that dances when he smiles. He rubbed his forehead as if it hurt. He must have felt me looking at him, for he raised his head.

"Hey, Dad! How's it goin'?"

A smile broke through the worry lines on his face. "Busy. How about you?" He came over for a hug and immediately returned to his chair.

I followed and balanced on the edge of his desk. "Ms. Thompson assigned a whole term history project. I hate those things. It'll bug me for the entire semester."

"What's the topic?"

I felt like snarling at him, *Didn't you hear me? I'm worried about this stupid assignment. I need you to hear my feelings, not ask what's the topic.* I knew that would just start a fight. I took a deep breath and answered civilly, "We're supposed to research the life and times of one of our ancestors and connect what we learn with today."

He leaned back in his chair. “Any ideas yet who you’ll pick?”

Okay, I thought. I can do this. “Mom used to talk about Nana Sinclair, her great-great-grandma.”

As always, a shadow flickered across Dad’s face when I mentioned Mom. “Why her?”

“Nana Sinclair emigrated from England as a young child. Her life might compare with immigrants today—maybe the Syrian refugees.”

“Sounds good.”

“That’s it? Sounds good? What about brilliant, because it is. It’s actually brilliant.”

He reached around me for a folder from his desk. He wasn’t listening. His mind had returned to his work.

Determined to keep his attention, I grabbed the folder. “Any ideas where I’d get some info on Nana Sinclair?”

He sighed and leaned back again. “Let’s see. Text your Aunt Sharon. She’s into all that genealogy stuff. Knowing Sharon, she’ll probably have a whole file on Nana Sinclair.” He paused for a moment, grabbed a pen and began tapping it against his hand. “What about Grandma Rushton’s trunk? She might have kept info on her Nana. It’s in the attic.” His eyes flicked to the clock on the wall. “I lost the entire morning at a committee meeting about the town’s search for a new doctor.”

I winced. “Now you’re losing half the afternoon talking to me.”

He frowned.

“What if Ms. Hamilton phoned? You’d have time for her.” My swinging feet hit the desk hard. He rolled his eyes up to the ceiling. Deliberately, he shoved the cap onto his pen and stuck it in his breast pocket.

“Now Renée, be reasonable.”

“Well it’s true…”

He opened his mouth to speak, then clamped it shut. Looking at the folder in my hand, he heaved a big sigh. "Peace…please."

"I'm sorry. It's just that I feel as if you have time for everyone but me."

"I'm sorry, too."

He took the folder from me and laid it on the desk, putting his paperweight on top of it. Leaning back in the chair again, he said, "I am interested in your project."

"Well, do you have any info about refugee kids? That might be relevant."

"Our refugee family coming to Catalpa Creek has three children, the oldest, a boy, is 17.

"Really…" This is new information. I dumped my anger for the moment. "Maybe I could join your committee for some firsthand experience. I'll bet Susie would, too."

Dad laughed. His eyes sparkled. "If you girls think you have time, you'd be welcome."

"Right…I'll discuss it with Susie." I slipped down off the desk. "What time will you be home for supper?"

"Don't worry about supper. We'll just heat up last night's leftovers."

At the door, I turned around to say goodbye.

Dad's attention had already returned to his papers.

When I got home, Ebony was curled up on the mat at the door waiting for me. Kicking my shoes into the hall closet, I picked him up and cuddled him close. "Love ya, buddy." We headed for the kitchen. I poured myself a large glass of milk and bit into a granola bar. Ebony stretched out his neck for my milk. I lifted his head away. "Yes, you can have some too, my friend." His tongue started lapping with the first drops of milk hitting his dish.

Halfway up the stairs I stopped at the picture of Mom and me, hanging in our rogues' gallery on the wall. "Miss you, Mom. Dad's so busy with work. Wish you were here to help me with Nana Sinclair." Ebony nudged at my leg. "Okay, okay, buddy." I climbed the last few steps to my bedroom.

Comfortable in my old pyjama pants and sweatshirt, my hair wound into a knot, I was ready to face the dusty attic. "C'mon Ebony. Let's go. We're going to your birthplace."

Cool, dank air engulfed me as I yanked open the attic door. A quick tug on the cord of the single light bulb produced an eerie glow that didn't quite reach the corners of the room. I scooped up Ebony onto my shoulder. "I'll never forget finding your whole family up here, that fall after Mom died." I cuddled him into my neck. "You gave me a reason to go on living. It felt like God sent you just for me."

I peered ahead. Partially hidden by a barrier of boxes and junk, Grandma Rushton's Tibetan trunk rested, forgotten in the shadows. Setting Ebony down, I cleared a path. My body scrunched to avoid hitting the rafters, I crab-walked across to the trunk and knelt down on the rough floor boards. *Ooooh* chilly.

Grandma Rushton's gravelly voice spoke clearly in my mind as my fingers traced the delicate forms of the fearsome dragons carved on the sides. "This lovely old trunk is one of my most precious possessions, Renée. Your Uncle David and Aunt Joanne brought it from China before you were born. Their visit was a last-minute surprise. Just before the service on Christmas Eve, they appeared at my church study door. I hugged David so hard, I'm sure he was embarrassed. Tears of joy were still streaming down my cheeks when I started the service. Family is so precious, Renée. Never forget that."

The *scratch, scratch* of branches against the roof woke me from my reverie. I shook myself. Enough of Grandma Rushton. It's Nana Sinclair I'm researching. I reached out and pulled the bronze spike from the trunk's hasp. The alien sound of the metal's scrape echoed eerily in the attic's gloom. What will I find?

Books—Christmas books filled one whole side of the trunk. I remember these. Someday I'll reread them. I loved them when I was little. On the other side lay a stack of boxes, the top one labelled, "Income tax records." Not interesting. I laid it on the floor. Next, "Adoption." I knew what was in that box. Mom had brought it down after Grandma's funeral. We spent hours looking at the official papers and talking about Grandma. I laid "Adoption" down beside "Income tax."

I recognized the larger white box yellowed with age. Even though I knew what it contained, I opened the box. Carefully I lifted out the baby clothes—one tiny white embroidered dress and a yellow woollen coat with matching bonnet. Pinned to the bonnet was the note: "Clothes I wore the day my parents brought me home. August 8, 1945," signed "Eloise Rushton." I shook my head. Grandma you must have been so hot wearing this in August. Lovingly, I refolded the clothes and wrapped them in their tissue paper. Closing the box, I placed it on top of "Adoption." The second last box was filled with Grandma's high school souvenirs. Interesting, but not relevant.

The last box was heavier, deeper. I pulled off the lid and rummaged down through a stack of envelopes filled with pictures. There better be something more than pictures in this one. At the very bottom was a little wooden box, a miniature treasure chest, small enough to fit into my camera bag. Carved in the lid was *Margaret Sinclair*. Yay!!! Thank you, God. A tiny padlock dangled from the hasp. I ran my fingertips along the finely polished wood. Surely there'll be something useful in here. Carefully, I set the box on a pile of old clothes, and stuffed everything else back into the trunk, replacing the spike. With

Nana's little box tucked under my arm, I headed for the stairway. When I pulled the string to put out the light, Ebony came running.

Back in my bedroom, I sat cross-legged by the window, Nana's box in my lap and Ebony beside me. After a full half-hour of jiggling with my nail file, the padlock opened with a tiny click. I straightened my back and paused in anticipation. "Mom, is there something special in here?"

I felt her presence. I took a deep breath. Well, here goes.

Tucked down inside the red satin lining, I found a small, worn leather-bound book. Gingerly lifting it up to my nose, a hint of roses mixed with the mustiness of age flooded my nostrils. Just the perfect size and shape, Nana's book felt like it belonged in my hand. The leather crackled as I opened the cover. Inside I read:

> *September 7, 1902*
>
> *This diary is presented to Margaret Sinclair on her 8th birthday. Keep a careful record of your life, my child. Events, people, things, all will become a part of who you are.*
>
> *Life is precious.*
>
> *I love you. Mama*

Nana's diary. I drew in a deep breath and let it out slowly. The moment felt sacred.

Downstairs, the front door slammed shut in the wind. Dad's home. "Hey, Dad, I've found it," I yelled. "I'll be right down." I closed Nana's box and set it on the shelf beside Mom's candle. "Thanks for the help, Mom," I said.

With the diary held tight in my hand, I bounded down the stairs, two at a time. He was standing in the living room doorway waiting. Already he'd chucked his blazer and loosened his tie. I offered him the precious book. "Be careful. It's old. It's Nana Sinclair's diary."

Dad handled the little book with reverence, his focus so complete, you'd think it was someone's income tax. After a few moments, he asked, "Was it in Grandma Rushton's trunk?"

"Yup." I took the diary back from him. "I can hardly wait to start reading this."

"Whoa there. Let's have supper first. You must be hungry. I certainly am."

"C'mon Dad, just a few pages."

"C'mon Renée, just a little food."

We laughed.

"It's leftovers. If we work together, it won't take long."

"Okay. Then we'll have the whole evening together. Right?"

"Right."

Thanks to the microwave, the leftover casserole was ready in ten minutes. Another twenty, and we had gobbled it all and cleared the dishes into the dishwasher. Dad plugged in the kettle.

Our tea steaming in front us, we sat side by side on the kitchen stools at the island. Nana's diary waited patiently. I picked it up. "It's so old. Feels…" I opened the cover to reveal the presentation page.

As I read it to Dad, he said, "Only eight years old, pretty young for keeping a diary."

The page crackled as I turned it. I looked up at him. "It's been written in pencil. It's almost faded out." I frowned as I struggled to read the faint words. My cell phoned chimed. The text from Susie said, *Mom's bringing me tonight. I'll be there in 30.*

K, I thumbed back. "Susie's coming. I forgot. Let's save the diary 'til she gets here. She'll love this."

"How long do we have to wait?"

"Just half an hour."

"I'll use the time for paperwork."

I groaned. Well, I had his attention for a few minutes, anyway.

He picked up his tea and headed for his study.

Laying the diary on the counter, I went in search of some of our neighbour, Mrs. Logan's cookies. A treat will make our reading more fun. Her cookie tin was empty. Darn. I picked up Ebony. "I'll get you some fresh water, my friend." Think I'll text Harrar. See how he's doing on his art project. Maybe he'll have time to talk. Hope he's already looked at my photographs.

Twenty minutes and no answer. Weird.

Susie rang our doorbell at seven sharp, opened the door and called, "I'm here."

"Good," I shouted back. "I'm in the kitchen." I heard her kick off her shoes.

"What's up?" she asked as she stepped through the kitchen door.

"Look," I said, and held up the little book. "It's my Nana Sinclair's diary. Starts in 1902."

"Neat," Susie said as she took it from me. Gently she stroked the leather binding. "Feels good in my hands. This is history, real history."

"Yup. I found it in Grandma Rushton's trunk. I'm going to use it for my history project. Want to read it with me?"

"Sure, I like history, especially when I can hold it in my hand."

"Let's sit on the couch in the living-room." I picked up the diary and the tea tray. Dad stepped out of his study as we passed and followed us. Wow, he really is interested, I thought. Susie and I plopped down onto the couch.

"Go easy on those springs," he said, and eased his long body down beside me. "I'm not ready to buy a new couch just yet,"

Susie laughed. I groaned and opened the diary, "Let's get to it."

September 7, 1902

Diary, you're my birthday present. I am 8 today. Little Bill ate to much cake at my party. He threw up. Mama wore a beutiful dress when she kissed us good night. She and Papa are going out.

September 10, 1902

Diary, Mama and Papa had an aksidint. Nanny Kelly says they are ded. She's crying. Uncle Bruce came. He keeps shaking his head. He says we can't live with him. I want to stay here with Nanny Kelly? I miss Mama.

I stopped reading. "Her parents are dead…both of them? How awful." Dad said nothing. He must be thinking about Mom. I sure am. An accident – people weren't safe even back then.

"This isn't fun. It's sad." Susie said. "Keep reading, Renée. I want to know what happens to Nana and Little Bill."

September 15, 1902

Diary two ladys in long black coats and bonits came today. Uncle Bruce said we had to go away with them. We could bring only 1 toy. Little Bill brot his bunny. I brot you diary cause mama gave you to me.

The ladys took us to a big old house full of children. They said it's an orfanige. I'm scared.

I pictured Nana and Little Bill standing abandoned in a long, dark hallway. Nana, her little head held high, back straight, like a miniature soldier determined to be strong, clutched the diary close to her heart. Only her eyes betrayed her pain and fear. Little Bill was huddled close to her, gripping his beloved bunny by the neck, its feet dangling at his side. My heart ached. I set the diary down.

"Given away to an orphanage! That's cruel," Susie said.

Dad answered, "When their Uncle Bruce refused to care for them, there must have been no one else. Back then, there was no government-sponsored Family and Children's Services like today."

"What about Nanny Kelly? Why didn't she take them home?" Susie asked.

"She probably had no home herself," Dad said. "Back then nannies lived in. With the death of her employers, she would be searching for another place. She'd have no claim to the children, and no money to care for them."

"That's just horrible," I responded.

He put his arm around my shoulders. "I'll read for a while."

September 28, 1902

Diary, I am hungry all the time. Meen Harold steels our food. I told matrin. She grabed Harold by the ear and told him not to. He leaves me alone but still takes little Bills. I share what I get with little Bill.

I want my mama. If papa were here, he'd beet Harold.

December 25, 1902

Diary, it is Christmas Day. Matrin gave us all a big orange. I told little Bill to eat his right away before meen Harold could take it. I did to.

March 10, 1903

Diary, it is cold here. A man came and told matrin we all had to go to scool. That's good. Maybe the scool will be warm. I like scool. I want Nanny Kelly and Mama.

"Can it get any worse?" Susie asked.

"I hope not," Dad responded.

"Reading this is hard. I've chosen a tough topic," I said. "Poor Nana. Maybe it will get better."

Dad just shook his head, doubt written all over his face. "Shall I continue?"

We nodded.

April 3, 1903

Diary, some men came and moved all of us. Now we are in a workhouse. It's scarier than the orfanige. They get us up at daybreak. I wash clothes till time for school. After school I peel potatos til bedtime. We get a bowl of awful tasting stuf in the morning and at night. This matrin calls it grool. When we work hard we get a piece of bread with it. Poor little Bill is with the boys. I only see him at school.

I found the best hiding place for you Diary. I know you will be safe there. I thot about under the mattres but I have to share my bed with Agnes. She wets it everynight. It's time to tuc you back under that loos florboard under the bed. Agnes will be back soon. I don't want her to find you. Good night Diary.

Dad stopped reading. "I've heard about those turn-of-the-century workhouses in Britain. They were no better than prisons."

I sighed and straightened up in my chair. "I have to compare this to the plight of today's refugees. Could it be any worse today?"

"I'm not liking this," Susie said.

"I didn't know the diary would be like this. Mom and I never talked much about the past. I wish…" I felt that familiar heaviness creeping back into my chest. I shuddered trying to shake it off. "Living without Mom is hard. Poor Nana."

"Time for a group hug," Dad said. "A hug always helps."

After our hug Susie said, "We know Nana didn't die, so I'm sure its going to get better. I'll read now."

May 10, 1903

Diary, I hate this place. Its hot. My hands hurt. They bleed. Matrin says its the lye soap. They will tuffin up. I hate her. I'm always hungry. Mr. Scorly beet me with his cane tonight. Said I'm lazy. My legs are brused. They hurt. I cuit crying. It doesnt help. I have a frend. Tilly came here yesterday. Shes older than me. She calls this awful place Gateshed. I guess cause there are ugly heds carved into pillers at the gates.

"Gosh, this is hard to read. The pencil is really faded." Susie flipped ahead a page. "Oh good, she got a darker pencil."

Not enough food. Mean people. And we get excited about a new pencil that makes reading easier for us? I sighed.

September 7, 1903

Dear Diary, I'm 9 today. Tilly gave me a pencil. She stole it. My pencil wor out. I am tired, I hate this place. I want to go home. Tilly says to give that up. No home now. She promised to be my frend always. She will take care of me.

"I'm so glad she has Tilly," I said. "Guess God sent Tilly to Nana."

Susie responded, "Personally, I think God should have protected Nana's parents in the first place…I'm sorry." Susie's eyes filled with tears. "I don't understand how God works."

"None of us do," Dad answered. "I know God doesn't protect us from bad things happening. I believe God walks with us through them."

"I learned that with Mom, but I don't like it. I'd rather God just fixed the world so there weren't accidents and mean people and …"

"Should we quit reading for tonight?" Dad asked.

"No!" Susie and I said together.

September 10, 1903

Diary, They came today and took a bunch of older boys. Said they were going to the Barnardo home then to Canada, wherever those places are. Next time, Tilly says she will get them to pick little Bill and me and her. Anywhere is better than here.

September 17, 1903

They came for girls this time. They picked Tilly and me. I cryed and pleeded that they bring little Bill too. The man they call Doctor Barnardo herd me. He promised he wud take Bill to his boys home. Tilly and me came to the girls place. It's called the village

"Yay," Susie interrupted.

Dad and I locked eyes and smiled. That's God at work, I thought. Guess it's better than no help at all.

September 20, 1903

Tilly and me are at rose cottage with 23 other girls. Most of them are taller than me so they must be older. Rose cottage is reelly clean and pretty. The matrin cut my hair reel short and took my clothes. She made me get into a tub of hot water and scrubbed me with that awful lye soap.

It was worth it. She gave me a new dress, nickers, stockings and even shoes. She told me I look nice now I am cleen. I feel good. And my tummy is full to the top with bred, cheese, potatos and chicken. I hope little Bill is okay.

Susie turned the page.

Dad interrupted her reading. “I think we’d better stop there. Nana is in a little better place. Renée, you’ll need to do some research on England at the turn of the century. Find out what that workhouse was like. Learn all you can about Dr. Barnardo.”

“Do we have to stop now?”

“Yes. You need to research refugee camps as well, so you can compare them to that workhouse. If it’s worth doing, it’s worth doing well. That was your mom’s creed.”

“Oh, all right.” I closed the book. “Already this is becoming heaps of work. Yuck…”

“Don’t be such a grump. The diary’s neat,” Susie said.

“Sad. That’s what it is. Oh well…Let’s go up to my room to study for tomorrow’s test.” I turned to Dad, “I’ll keep the diary in its box next to Mom’s candle.”

Steve

I watched the two of them run up the stairs, Ebony right behind. Their chatter and giggles disappeared behind Renée’s bedroom door. Good to hear them having fun. Renée’s been sad for a such a long time. I retrieved the paper from the hall table and walked to my study. She’s still moody at times, but that deep, deep sadness seems to have ebbed away. Thank you, God.

Seated behind my desk, I looked first at the paper, then my open briefcase. Nope, can’t work anymore today. I pulled my phone from my pocket. Lee Ann. I'll call Lee Ann. We can go for coffee…My thumbs paused, no, not tonight. She's with her book club.

I sighed. I’m supposed to consider other women. I brought up my contact list and flipped down. Janice Lawson... She’s relatively new in town – blonde and single, reminds me of Serena when that ponytail bobs. I’ve only seen her with our badminton crowd. Might be good to get to know her. It’s just a cup of coffee.

Think I'll invite a third, though. I scrolled back up to "E". I'll call good old Eleanor. She's been my friend forever. Serious Janice and slightly crazy Eleanor. We'll be a safe enough threesome.

The two calls took less than five minutes. I yelled up the stairs to Renée, "I'm meeting friends at Jake's for coffee. I'll be back in an hour or so."

"Okay, don't forget your key."

I chuckled to myself.

Both Eleanor and Janice were already seated in a booth when I arrived. Eleanor, being Eleanor, jumped up to greet me and tripped on her long skirt. *Riiiiippp.*

She stumbled and grabbed hold of my neck. Her curly red hair tickled my nose. Love you, my tall, skinny, flamboyant friend, I thought. There's never a dull moment with you. I looked over at Janice. She was frowning. No sense of humour and that is not a good sign.

"Oh dear, I've torn my skirt," Eleanor said, holding up the hem of that wildly coloured thing. "I bought this in New Mexico. It's one of my favourites."

"Maybe you can cut that part off," I responded. "It's a little long anyway,"

"Oh, is it? Do you think? I never noticed. I just love the way it flows," Eleanor twirled around the coffee shop.

By then everyone in the place was laughing. I slid in beside Janice. She moved closer, till her thigh touched mine. Our eyes met. She snuggled closer still. Not bad, I thought…I drew in a deep breath and frowned. Perfume's mighty strong.

Eleanor flopped down on the other bench. "Hey, you two," she said. "Is it that cold in here?"

Janice pulled away a little.

I swallowed hard. Of course, Eleanor would state the obvious.

Janice spoke up, "Thanks for inviting us for coffee, Steve. I was finding the evening a little long."

She looked directly into my eyes as she spoke. Before I could respond, Eleanor said, "Oh, just turn on the TV. There's always something on the Discovery Channel."

Janice frowned.

I kept a straight face.

Eleanor continued, "Steve, I got the notification today that the papers for our refugee family have been processed. Now we just have to wait on the call telling us when they will arrive."

"The sooner the better," I replied. I glanced sideways at Janice. She opened her mouth as if she was going to speak, then closed it. I tried a change of topic. "I'd like to get to know you better, Janice. Where do you work?"

"I'm an IT consultant for Friber's cell phone company—part of the design team. It's interesting and challenging. What about you, Steve?"

"I'm an entrepreneur," Eleanor cut in, her big grin flashing across her face. "I own *Lights Out*, the candle shop on John Street. My candles are handmade, mostly by me. I love people and love the creativity."

"I'm a boring, old accountant," I said. Keeping my face serious, I added, "Mind you, I know the financial business of almost every resident of Catalpa Creek."

Eleanor countered, "Not mine—Oh, I've done it again," she said. "It's not that I wouldn't trust you with my accounts, Steve. It's just that I already had an accountant when you moved to town."

I grinned and patted her hand. "It's okay. We're still friends."

Without drawing a breath, she carried on, "Now that we know what each of us does, let's get to a more interesting topic.

Did you know that the Catalpa Creek Credit Union was robbed tonight?"

"Robbed?" Janice and I exclaimed in unison.

"Yes, robbed. Tom Long's the detective in charge of the case."

"Detective?" I asked. "When did he get promoted?"

"Just a few weeks ago, when Jim Brillinger retired. Anyway," Eleanor continued, "Tom was at my place when he got the call. I don't know anything more."

Tom and Eleanor, a couple… I didn't know that. Guess I'd better catch up with Tom.

"I moved here to get away from crime and violence," Janice said, a deep frown on her face.

"I don't remember the last time—Oh yes, I do. Steve, have you ever heard anything more about that Russell Carding who was harassing Renée?"

"No, not really. At the trial, he was sentenced to two years probation and ordered to stay away from Renée. She hasn't mentioned him since."

I felt Janice stiffen beside me.

"Is this man still at large?" she asked. "What does he look like?"

Eleanor reached out, her multitude of bracelets jangling, and patted Janice's hand. "Oh Janice, dear." she said. "Russell Carding was just a kid desperate for some love. He was sweet on Renée. He kept calling her and asking her for a date. I think he was pretending to be one of those movie stars and got reality and fantasy mixed up. He's harmless. You don't have to worry about him. Besides, you're much too old for him, anyway."

I grinned as I watched Janice's reaction to Eleanor's last sentence. I wasn't so sure that Russell was harmless, especially for Renée, but decided not to correct Eleanor.

The door of the coffee shop opened letting in a rush of cool air. Tom Long stepped through the doorway, scanned the room and walked directly to our table. "Steve, what are you doing out with my girl?" he said and slid into the booth next to Eleanor, his stocky body shifting the table a bit.

Eleanor blushed. "Tell us about the robbery," she said.

Turning his slow, lazy smile full on her, Tom answered, "I can only tell you what will be in tomorrow's paper. He pulled a gun on the teller at the Credit Union. He didn't speak. Just passed her a note." Tom paused to signal the waitress by pointing to our coffee cups. "The teller followed her training to the letter." Tom wrapped his arm around Eleanor's shoulder and said, "I hope you'd do the same, if a robber came in to *Lights Out*."

"Of course, I'm not an idiot," she said. "My life's worth much more than the few dollars in my till."

"Good," he answered, and kissed her forehead.

I raised my eyebrows. Something good is happening with these two.

Tom continued. "The bank teller emptied her cash drawer into the robber's bag. He grabbed it and ran. The teller pushed the silent alarm. Our squad car arrived within three minutes, but there was no sign of the robber."

"Really," I said.

"Yup, melted into thin air. At this point, that's all we know."

"Did he get much?" I asked.

"Less than a thousand. Tellers don't keep much in their drawers anymore."

"I'll bet she was scared. Who was it?" Eleanor asked.

"I can't say," Tom replied.

"What did the robber look like?" Janice asked.

"We don't know much. Short, in a shapeless overcoat, face obscured by hat and turned up coat collar. That's all the surveillance cameras show.

Eleanor leaned into Tom's shoulder. "Thanks Tom," she said. "Now, let's talk about Don and Dorrie's Fundraiser, 'Sharing the Harvest' this Saturday. Are you going, Janice?"

Janice hesitated. "What's that?" she asked.

"A dance at the arena," Eleanor said. "Raising funds for our refugee family."

Janice turned to me, "Are you going, Steve?"

"Wouldn't miss it. I'm hoping our refugee family will be here by Saturday so the town can meet them." I felt Janice stiffen beside me.

"Oh, really," Janice said. "Guess I could go."

"That's good," Eleanor said. "We want a big crowd."

Janice wriggled over a little closer. "Could you pick me up, Steve? I don't want to go alone."

Ooops, I thought and eased my body away an inch or two to give myself some space.

Eleanor came to my rescue. "Don't be silly, Janice. Steve'll probably have his car full of teenagers. Your apartment is only three blocks from the arena. You can walk. I'll meet you at the door if you're nervous."

Janice moved over close again. She may be attractive, I thought, but she's …

The strains of Habanera emanated from my cell phone. I stood up and pulled it from my pocket. Reverend Linda's name appeared on the screen. "This call may tell us when our family will arrive," I said and stepped away from the table toward the back of the coffee shop. "Hello, Reverend Linda."

"Hi, Steve. Great news. Our refugee family will fly in at five, Wednesday afternoon. Could you meet them with me? My car's in the garage. Transmission went."

"Sure. I'd go anyway."

"Thanks so much."

"May Renée and Susie come? They're interested in joining our committee."

"Sure. Great. It might help the teenager to have someone his own age there to greet him."

"For sure, he's the draw."

She laughed. "They could be truly interested in helping."

"They could be, but you weren't there when I told Renée our refugee family included a seventeen-year-old boy."

"We'll need a bigger vehicle than your Prius. Jeff Brunt offered his Tahoe. It seats nine. There's a rack on the top for luggage."

"I'll call him right now and arrange to pick it up."

"Great. I'll be ready by 3:30 Wednesday afternoon."

"No problem."

"Thanks. God Bless." She tapped off.

I called Jeff and arranged the vehicle exchange. With everything set, I returned to our booth. Conversation stopped as soon as I appeared. The three of them looked up at me.

"That was Reverend Linda. We're picking up our family at the airport at five on Wednesday. We should be back in Catalpa Creek by ten even with a stop for supper. Things are finally moving."

"It's time I got home," Janice said, obviously not sharing our excitement. "I've an early morning tomorrow."

"Bye, Janice," Eleanor said. Tom and I just waved as Janice hurried out the door.

"What's with her?" Tom asked.

Eleanor responded, "I'm thinking she was feeling foolish about being so forward with Steve."

"I wonder if it isn't something else," Tom said. "Not everyone is happy about our refugee family. They're Muslim, right?"

I nodded.

"There could be quite a few who are afraid. There's been so much in the news about the possibility of terrorists hiding among the refugees."

"Maybe we haven't done enough educating. Let's talk with our committee, Eleanor."

"It's a big job your committee has taken on," Tom said.

"Yes, but it's worth it." I looked at my watch, "It's nearly eleven." I picked up my bill and my jacket. "See you Saturday night."

Back home, I took the stairs two at a time. Hey, not even breathing hard. I'm much more fit than I was a year ago. Feels good.

A crack of light under Renée's door told me she was still up. I knocked. "Renée, I've some good news. May I come in?"

"Sure."

When I opened her door, she was hunched over her computer. She swivelled round to face me. "I'm done for tonight. I've been researching Dr. Barnardo and his homes, both here and in England. All kinds of stuff. It's so much more interesting when it's part of Nana Sinclair's life." She looked up at me, a glint of mischief in her eyes and said, "Actually, I was tempted to spend the evening reading Nana's diary. When I opened it…I don't know, it just didn't seem right. I'm pleased you and Susie want to read it with me. I didn't want to spoil that."

She looked like a little girl in her green onesie pyjamas, so vulnerable, so sincere. "I love you, hon. I do want us to read it together. Thank you." I reached out. She came for a hug.

"Now, what's your news?" she said, as she moved back to her chair and propped her feet on the bed.

I leaned on the doorframe. "Our refugee family is arriving Wednesday night. I've been designated as airport taxi. Would you and Susie like to be part of the welcoming party?"

"Sure. I'll check with Susie in the morning. It will help the family to have young people greet them. Maybe Harrar would like to come too."

"I don't think the van's big enough."

"Oh…He probably wouldn't have time anyway. He seems to be extra busy lately."

"Been a long day. I'm tired. Think I'll sack out now. See you in the morning."

"Night, Dad."

Back in my own bedroom, I wandered over to the window seat where my Serena candle sat, lonely and unlit. Well Serena, I guess we've started to live again. I ran my finger around the holder's base. Dust, but not because I don't think of you. I sure needed this candle at first. It helped to light it as a symbol of you. Now, I know you'll always be a part of me.

I put the candle back in its proper place on the shelf above the desk. I still miss you, Serena. I miss talking to you, holding you. God, how I miss your touch.

My mind jumped to the coffee shop and the warmth of Janice's thigh pressed against mine. I pictured her frown...Maybe not.

I finished my nightly routine and stretched out in my bed. "Thank you God for women. Living alone is not easy. And thank you that our refugee family's coming Wednesday. It feels good to help someone. And thanks for Renée and Nana's diary. I'm glad she wants time with me. I am truly blessed. Amen."

Sleep rolled in to wash away the day.

Chapter Three

Our New Friends

Wednesday, September 20

Renée

When Susie and I ran down the school steps at 3:20 on Wednesday, Dad was waiting for us out front. He lowered the van window.

"Hurry up, you two. We don't want to be late. With good traffic, it will take more than an hour to get to the airport. I still have to pick up Reverend Linda."

"Where'd you get this big bomb?" Susie asked as she climbed in.

Dad replied, "Swapped vehicles with Jeff Brunt so we would have room for everyone."

We buckled up.

"Being part of the greeting team for our new family is so neat," Susie said. "It's worth missing riding tonight."

"Sure is. A bit scary too." I said. "They'll be nervous too. More than us."

"For sure," Dad agreed.

We picked up Reverend Linda at the church. "May I move the seat back a bit?" she asked as she folded her generous frame into the seat in front of Susie.

"Go ahead. My legs are short," Susie said.

Once settled, Reverend Linda ran her fingers through her short greying hair and unfastened her coat. Her bright red fingernails glistened in the sun when she reached for the seatbelt.

"Neat nails," I said.

"Thanks. My ten-year-old niece gave me a manicure on the weekend." She held up her hands to admire them. "They're a little loud for me, but they make me smile." She reached down inside her huge bag and pulled out a sheet of paper. "I printed off the details for you and Susie. This is who we've prepped for. I've only one copy so I'll read it to you.

*Family name: **Ahmadi**—Syrian, Muslim*
*Father: **Khalil**, Medical Doctor, political activist*
Worked emergency at hospital in Aleppo.
*Mother: **Nazira,** Nurse, political activist*
cared for tortured political prisoners
*Oldest son: **Mustafa,** 17 years old*
*Middle son: **Hassan**, 12 years old*
*Youngest daughter, **Thuraya**, 8 years old*
*Deceased daughter - **Saliyeh** 20, killed in Syria.*
*Deceased son - **Zahir**, 10, killed by soldiers' gunfire en route to Turkey*

Family was upper middle class in Syria. Khalil involved with freeing political prisoners and speaking out for human rights. Nazira worked to end torturing of political prisoners. Spent last two years in refugee camp in Turkey."

We were all silent for a few seconds before Dad spoke. "Pretty grim family history." Susie and I nodded.

"Puts my life into perspective," I said.

Susie added, "I'm glad I'm Canadian."

We rode on in silence for a while. I touched Dad's shoulder to get his attention. "Can we listen to the radio?" He turned on the radio station. Classical music – oh well, it's good for steadying the nervous system.

Out of the same enormous bag came name tags, bearing just our first names. "I made these," Reverend Linda said. "I've a set for the Ahmadi's as well. First names will be hard enough for all of us to manage." She reached once again into the almighty bag, drawing out a white cylinder. "I've also made a sign in Arabic saying: 'Welcome Ahmadi Family'. It will help them identify us."

I looked at Susie and mouthed, "She thinks of everything."

"Oh, and by the way, have you downloaded the Google Translate app onto your phones? You're going to need it."

"Will do," Susie and I said in unison.

We waited at "Arrivals," excited and nervous. Will they like us? How will we communicate? We huddled together around our sign. I could see and feel the stress building in our faces and bodies. The enormity of our project had descended upon us.

Reverend Linda said, "It's too bad Dr. Siddiqui and Rashimi are in Calgary at a conference this week. Just having them here tonight would have helped us and the Ahmadis.

Maybe they would have brought Harrar, I thought. That would have helped Susie and I, too. Wonder what Mustafa will be like.

The double doors parted. People started pouring through. I spotted our family coming up the hallway. At least, I assumed it was them. They were a group of five in Western dress except for an attractive blue hijab worn by the mother. Four walked huddled together. A tall slender young man, about my age, strode confidently just a little ahead of the rest. My first thought—he's not quite as handsome as Harrar.

Susie jabbed me with her elbow. "He's gorgeous. What's his name again?"

I grinned, “Mustafa .” I watched the little girl let go of her mother’s hand and run ahead to her big brother. “She will be Thuraya,” I said.

“The closer he gets; the better he looks. It’s going to be great getting to know him.”

“Hold on, Susie, you don’t…”

“Look, Renée,” she interrupted. “Isn’t that sweet?”

Mustafa had stopped and waited for his little sister to catch up. She reached up and he lifted her with a big hug.

As soon as they saw our sign, relief flooded over their faces. Mustafa and Thuraya reached us first and greeted us with “Salaam Alaykum” (Peace be with you), to which we replied, “wa-alaykum" (and with you). I was glad we’d done our homework to understand their greeting and the proper response.

The father Kahlil talked excitedly—in French.

Dad waved his hands for him to stop and said, “Lentement, lentement, s’ilvous plait.” (slowly, slowly, please.)

Mustafa switched to English. Although it was halting, it was much better than my French. We soon discovered to our surprise and relief that they all spoke some French and a smattering of English.

On the way home, we stopped for supper at a Middle Eastern restaurant, confident that at least some of the food would be Halal. A young man sitting at the table next to us could speak both Arabic and English. He bridged the awkward silences and helped place orders. God does provide.

At one point, I turned to Mustafa and asked what his school was like in Syria. He repeated the words school and Syria and frowned. Then he said, “last year.” Okay, I thought. He didn’t quite understand. I think he’s told me he was in his last year. Now what do I say? I pulled my phone from my pocket and thumbed “When will you graduate?” into Google translate. I had no idea what Google actually said to him, but he answered “engineer”. I smiled and nodded even though his answer didn't seem to fit my question.

Little Thuraya was easier. When the waitress handed her crayons and a picture to colour, her entire body wiggled with delight. She went right to work, her dark head bent over close to the paper.

The rest of our refugee committee was gathered at the church waiting for us. Reverend Linda did the introductions. The Ahmadis tried so hard to communicate. I could see their faces becoming more and more tired. After about fifteen minutes, Dad shepherded them back into the van. We drove to the apartment that was to be the Ahmadis' new home.

We led them into each room, opening closet doors, turning down bedcovers. They kept smiling and nodding. Nazira clapped her hands in delight when she saw the kitchen, especially the fridge fully stocked with what we hoped were foods they would like. Mustafa walked right over to the laptop sitting on the student's desk in one of the bedrooms. He reached out and touched it gently. "Thank you. Thank you," he said, his voice hoarse with emotion.

It must have been awful to leave all their belongings behind, I thought. We left them to settle in after Dad, through Mr. Google, assured them that at least some of the committee would return tomorrow.

We delivered Reverend Linda, Susie and the big van, gathered up our Prius and came home.

"Done!" Dad said, as he pulled into the garage.

"I'm tired but I'm glad I went. I already like the Ahmadis. I'm happy to be part of this. It feels like we're taking a giant step for world peace."

He followed me into the house, talking as we went. "Yes, it feels good to do our bit. But we may have some backlash here in town. We have to be ready for it."

I picked up Ebony, who greeted us as usual. “What do you mean?”

“When I first talked about bringing a refugee family to Catalpa Creek, some people were upset. They were afraid. They were sure refugees would bring their old country quarrels with them.” He reached out to rub Ebony behind the ears. “The Ahmadi family has had enough problems. They don’t need trouble here.” He locked the kitchen door.

“I’m tired,” I said. “Time for bed.”

“Think I’ll read a while.”

I hugged him goodnight and started up the stairs. At the top step, I turned around and said, “If Mom were here, she’d know how to handle the dissenters. She had a knack for dealing with people who were difficult. I sure miss her.”

“I do too.

Chapter Four

Hotheads

Thursday, September 21

Renée

"Another day of school finished, Hallelujah!" Susie said as we walked home. "This time next year, I'll be at Queen's University studying music."

"Wish I knew what was ahead for me."

"You'll figure it out. Why not just apply to do a B.A. at Queen's? They have heaps of specialties. You can choose one when you're ready. In the meantime, we'll be together."

I sighed. "I just may end up doing that."

"Boy, you're feeling mighty bleak. You sound like going off to the same school as me would be a last resort."

I managed a weak smile.

"Okay, what's making you so dreary?"

"Probably my Nana Sinclair research." I shoved my hands deeper into my pockets as I slouched along. "That Gateshead Union Workhouse was a horrible place. Children were better off starving on the streets than trapped in a workhouse."

"Looks like you've chosen a mighty depressing topic for your whole term project."

We walked past some little kids laughing and shouting as they jumped in a pile of coloured leaves. C'mon Renée, perk up a little, I told myself.

Susie dropped her backpack and joined the kids.

Why not, I thought. I tossed mine beside hers and dove into the leaves, too. I threw a handful at Susie. One of the kids dumped an entire armful on my head. Soon, I was giggling.

Feels good, I thought.

Susie and I gathered the leaves back into a heap. We all jumped in again. It was only minutes before the kids' dad appeared with a leaf bag.

Once the bag was full, we brushed off our clothes. "Thanks," we said. The dad smiled and nodded. We picked up our packs and walked on.

"I feel better now. Guess I just needed to play…I can tell you that Dr. Barnardo was a bright spot for kids like Nana. He gave them a place to live, fed them and established free schools so they could learn a trade."

"Now it's my turn to be dreary," Susie said. "What good was that if there were no jobs? My dad says it's the same with the refugees today. We bring them here and teach them English. But we have too many unemployed people here already."

I pointed to the "Now Hiring" sign in the window of Jacob's Furniture Store. "There's work here in Catalpa Creek."

"Yes, but does it pay enough to support a family?" Susie countered.

"Anyway, Dr. Barnardo ended up sending the kids he trained to places like Canada and Australia, where there were jobs." We walked past Harrar's house. The leaves from the giant oak in his front yard were still intact. Magnificent, I thought.

"Thinking about Harrar?" Susie asked. "He's probably at work. Seems like that's all he does, besides school."

I shook my head. "No, I was just thinking about that tree and Harrar's parents. They came here as immigrants, like the Ahmadis and like Nana Sinclair. The Siddiquis have achieved so much. Half the kids in Catalpa Creek go to Dr. Siddiqui. Mom always said he is an amazing paediatrician. Harrar's mom is the driving force behind the women's safe house. Immigrants are good for our country."

"Especially when they're hot guys like Harrar and Mustafa."

"Right." My mind went to Harrar at school this afternoon. I had stopped him as he was tearing off to work. 'I've been missing you,' I said. He looked sad. 'Sorry, Renée,' was all he said.

The sun slipped under a cloud, and a cold breeze came up. Susie buttoned up her coat. "When are we going to read some more of the diary?"

"How about tonight? I just have to check with Dad."

We stopped at my driveway. "I'll call you after supper. See ya later."

"'K."

I picked up the newspaper from the step. The headline shouted, CATALPA CREEK ROBBERY UNSOLVED! A robbery here…That's weird. Ebony greeted me, as usual. I dropped my knapsack by the hall table, hung my jacket in the closet and kicked off my shoes. "Come on, Ebony, my friend," I said, as I scooped him up. "Let's get a snack and check out the paper."

I spread the newspaper on the kitchen island. Grabbing an apple to munch, I sat down to read. I wonder who the bank robber is. He must be a local to have disappeared so quickly and completely. I turned the page and found a two-page spread with pictures of our refugee family. On-the-street interviews showed Catalpa Creek citizens supporting the Ahmadis. Of course, there was one man worried about suicide bombers. I threw down the paper in disgust. Why did they have to include his opinion?

"Okay, Ebony let's go upstairs and get some homework done. I'll work for an hour, then start supper. Dad took some pork chops out this morning." My phone buzzed, text from Harrar. *Saw you playing in the leaves.* Next came a picture. We hadn't noticed him at all. Guess we were having too much fun. "*Great picture*," I texted back. *I'm sending it to Susie. Any time free Saturday?* No answer. I tried again. *Have I done something wrong?* Ten minutes later he replied, *No.* That was all. Just No. I needed more. I waited. Nothing.

I hugged Ebony close. "What's wrong with Harrar, Ebony?" My furry friend snuggled his head into my neck, purring like a roaring motorboat.

My eyes strayed to Mom's candle. I miss you, Mom. Our house is empty without you. I set Ebony on the bed and peeled out of my jeans, slipped on my yoga pants, and favourite old sweatshirt.

I had finished my math and was opening my chemistry text when I heard Dad come in downstairs. Good, I thought. I didn't want to start this now anyway. I'm hungry.

I bounded down the stairs. "Hey, Dad."

"How was your day, Renée?

"Same old, same old."

"Me too, until Bob Handel called just as I was leaving the office. He's asked our refugee committee to meet him at the Homestead Pub at 7:30 tonight." Dad peeled off his suit jacket and tie and hung them over a chair. Unbuttoning his collar, he said, "That feels better."

I frowned. "What's the mayor's problem?"

"He received an anonymous tip that a number of people will be there discussing how to get rid of the Ahmadis. Bob's hoping to stop trouble before it starts. We'll have to rush supper."

"Let's just have a seafood salad. It's quick and easy." I said, stowing the chops in the fridge. "Besides, I don't feel like cooking anyway."

"Good idea."

"You set the table, Dad. I'll wash the greens.

"Sure. We can talk while we work."

Uh-oh, having a talk usually means I'm in trouble.

"About the fundraiser Saturday night…".

I interrupted trying to distract him from whatever. "A whole group of us from school are planning to go together. You won't have to drive. Susie's parents are driving us. We'll meet the rest at the arena."

"That's good to know, but it wasn't what I needed to talk about," he said as he fidgeted on the stool.

I watched him rub his forehead, draw a deep breath, look up at the ceiling and then back to me. "Okay, out with it. What have I done to upset you?"

"You've done nothing. It's just...I know you're not going to like what I have to tell you. I'm planning on inviting Lee Ann Hamilton to go with me to the fundraiser. We've been to the movies and out to dinner lots in neighbouring towns, but this is different. It's a community affair. Everyone will see us, and you will be there with your friends."

I swallowed the lump that rose in my throat as Dad talked. He wants to bring her to the fundraiser. Everyone will know. My dad and my vice-principal. Yuk!

"I can see on your face, it's not a a good idea, but I have to start living again sometime."

I closed my eyes and felt Mom's gentle touch and voice in my mind. "Easy, Renée. Tell him it's okay. Tell him to go for it." I opened my mouth, but those words just wouldn't come. I felt hot tears on my cheeks. I watched the sparkle disappear from his eyes. Guilt poured in, on top of… hurt, anger…I slammed the salad bowl down on the counter in front of him. "Why—why do you have to have another woman in your life? Can't you be satisfied with your memories of Mom? If you're going with HER, then I'll stay home. I can't." I flung the knife into the sink and stomped off.

Back in my room, I flopped on the bed, a quivering mess of tears and anger. After a few minutes, I took Mom's candle down from the shelf and flipped the switch. Nothing. Dead. I rummaged through my stuff, drawer after drawer. Finally, in the bottom drawer of my desk, I found a package of batteries. My shaking fingers won the battle and the light finally flickered on.

Candle alight, I set it on the window sill and knelt down in front of it. I was sure I heard Mom speaking. "Deep breaths, just take deep breaths." I stared at the candle and focused on my breathing. Gradually my heart slowed. I shifted off my knees to sitting on the floor. "Mom, God, whoever," I whispered. "I was doing so much better. I know I have to get used to the idea of Dad dating. I have to, but I don't want to. Help me God, please." My bedroom door creaked. I looked behind me and saw Ebony's little face appear in the crack. He padded over and settled on my lap. "Ebony, my friend," I said to him, "you bring me peace. Thank you."

I sat there for nearly an hour. I should go down and talk to Dad. What will I say? Leave it and get on with your chemistry, I told myself. My phone chimed. Harrar. *Busy Saturday. Next Saturday? Go Karting? Talk at school.* Relieved I texted back. *Sure.*

As I put Mom's candle back on the shelf, I gave thanks for it. Having this candle to symbolize Mom's presence with me has helped so much, I thought.

I booted up my computer. Better text Susie, tonight's a no-go for Nana Sinclair.

Steve

I sat alone at the island. "Dear God, how do I begin again when every step upsets Renée?" I got up and paced the kitchen. "Okay God, I need some help here." My cell phone buzzed.

Without thinking, I yanked it from my pocket and pressed talk. "Hello," I barked.

Tony's startled reply came back to me, "Is that you, Steve?"

I stuffed my anger down, took a deep breath, and replied, "Sorry. Yes it's me. What can I do for you?"

"I need a lift to the meeting, tonight."

"Sure, I'll pick you up." I glanced at my watch. "I'll grab a bite to eat and be there in forty."

An hour later, Tony and I pulled up in front of the Homestead Pub. The parking lot was nearly full. "Lots of cars. Hope they belong to Homestead regulars."

"Yeah," Tony agreed.

We climbed out of the car. I shortened my long stride to match Tony's as we headed for the pub doors.

A security guard, one of my accounting clients, pointed to the upstairs room. "You here for the meeting?" he asked.

We nodded.

"Mayor Bob's already up there. Maybe he and your committee will bring some sanity to these hotheads. The owner's worried. Police will be here shortly."

"After you," Tony said, as he waved me through the door. In a room above the bar about thirty people, coffee cups in hand were talking quietly. "Well, this looks pretty calm."

I nodded.

In the corner, Bob stood talking with two men. A closer look told me that the big guy dressed in a plaid shirt and jeans was Russell Carding's father, Dennis. This should be interesting. Richard Wallace, who owns the laundromat, strode to the front of the room, his cowboy boots clomping on the linoleum, a toothpick bobbing from his teeth. Richard has lived in Catalpa Creek all his life. If he's in charge, he'll keep things under control. Wrong!

"Okay, everyone, refill your coffee and find a chair," Richard commanded. He shrugged off his leather jacket and laid it on a table. With the sleeves of his plaid shirt rolled to the elbow, he was a typical working man. When people were settled, he said, "Listen up. We've got some worried people in this town. You all know about the, newcomers. Now, I'm all for welcoming people to Catalpa Creek…" He looked a few people in the eye and continued, "Even foreigners."

Uh-oh, I thought. He's not going to waste any time. Here comes the "but".

"But, this new bunch, they're not like us. They're from Syria, a spawning ground for terrorists. They might seem like regular people, but we don't know what they're really like. Our government has promised to bring in 25,000 of them. For sure, a few of those bad guys will slip in. How do we know if this crowd aren't some of those? They don't even speak English!"

A few people shouted out, "Right!"

I don't like where this is going! Bob stepped up to the mike. Good, Bob will know how to handle this. His dark suit, white shirt and tie give him an air of authority.

He opened with, "Richard, we've known each other for a long time. As your mayor, I'd like to answer your question."

Richard shook his head, but someone in the crowd shouted, "Let's hear what the mayor has to say."

As he motioned Bob to the microphone, Richard's exaggerated bow said it all.

"Thank you." Bob let his eyes slide over the crowd, while he paused for just a few seconds. "Many of you have come tonight because you're concerned. We've all been listening to the news over the last few years. We know there are terrorists killing innocent people in places like France and Germany. Like you, I don't want that to happen here in Catalpa Creek."

He stopped to take a breath. A few people applauded.

Good start Bob, I thought. You're expressing their thoughts.

"Opening our town to a refugee family is a new experience for all of us. So how do we cope, cope with our fear and—welcome the Ahmadi family?"He clasped his hands on the lectern, his eyebrows knitted with concern." Now, folks, many of you have known me for a long time. You know I care about you, and I care about Catalpa Creek."

Bob's a smart politician, I thought. He's going to talk this crowd down. I leaned back in my chair and waited.

"First of all," Bob said. "I need to give you some information. We're talking about a mother and father and three children—a family, just like yours and mine. Khalil Ahmadi is a medical doctor, who practiced in Syria, taking care of people just like our own Doc Campbell, and Doc Siddiqui that we all love and trust. Two days a week, Doctor Ahmadi gave his time free of charge to work among the poorest of the poor in Aleppo. He led delegations to the government demanding decent housing and clean water for those living in garbage dumps at the edge of the city. Does that sound like a terrorist?" He paused and waited. No one spoke.

Ah, he's got their attention.

Bob pointed to Richard's wife. "Helen, Nazira Ahmadi is a nurse, just like you. She cared for political prisoners who had been tortured. Last year, Nazira and Kahlil were labelled political activists by the Syrian government. Khalil was ordered to stop his work among the poor. He didn't. This earned him the label, dangerous traitor. Their oldest daughter was abducted and killed. This couple have been terrorized. Why would they want to hurt us?"

Good question. Great background. Bob knows what he's doing.

Leaning on the lectern as if he was having a conversation with close friends, Bob smiled. "Afraid to travel in their car because cars were stopped regularly, and identity papers checked, Kahlil, Nazira and children hitched rides in the back of farmers' trucks, hiding under tarps. They walked miles to escape. The last two years, they have been in a refugee camp in Turkey. Many of us have heard about the horror, the hunger, the hopelessness of refugee camps crowded with desperate people. Just imagine two years of a living hell."

Someone yelled, "Come on Bob, you know the news media exaggerate everything. It's not that bad in a refugee camp."

How can people be so stubborn? I looked over at Tony. He just shook his head.

Bob zeroed in on the heckler. His voice calm and controlled, he asked, "Fred, do you know David Carp?"

"Yup," Fred replied.

"David returned last week from his mission appointment at a refugee camp in Turkey. He told me there were 10,000 people in that refugee camp. It was equipped to handle 6,000. Each day, one of David's jobs as a foreign aid worker was to choose who would eat. I remember David's exact words: 'You might think I could choose children first. No. I was ordered to choose those who were healthy and strong. We couldn't waste food on the young and the weak who would die anyway. I love my church and want to serve, but I'll never take a mission appointment to a refugee camp again. It was awful, so awful. I'll never be the same.'"

My God…we've got to do better than that, I thought. I'm so glad we're doing something for at least one family.

Another heckler yelled. "C'mon Bob, you're telling us these people are damaged beyond repair. We don't need them here. What use are they to our community?"

"That's your assumption," Bob fired back. "Our Canadian government has brought us Dr. Kahlil Ahmadi. Both he and his family been screened and deemed safe, as safe as you and me."

Bob paused. Once more he scanned the crowd. His voice, strong and determined, "Bottom line, we need another doctor in this town. We need the Ahmadis as much as they need us."

Several people nodded their heads in agreement. I could feel the tension in the room lessen. Bob's bringing them round, I thought.

Bob removed his jacket and loosened his tie. "The Ahmadis are seeking a new home among us. They want only to live in safety. They have much to offer our community. Khalil is the doctor we've needed for three years, ever since Doc Byrne retired and moved. Yes, he'll have to qualify as a doctor here which means studying and testing. When he fulfils those requirements, he will be an answer to our prayers."

Yes, that's it, appeal to their self-interest. No wonder Bob's our mayor.

Dennis Carding stood up, "I've a question for you, Mayor. What good is a doctor who doesn't speak English?"

Heads nodded.

"First of all, Dennis, Dr. Ahmadi and his wife Nazira already speak enough English to make their needs understood. As Dr. Ahmadi works through his qualifying time, his English will improve. Remember, the family also speaks French as well as Arabic. In Syria, children traditionally have learned French in school. The last few years English has been added to the curriculum. The two older Ahmadi children manage some in English. Thuraya is learning. All are willing and able to improve. Having already learned two such disparate languages as Arabic and French, adding English will be a challenge, of course, but should come more quickly."

Richard had been frowning for the last ten minutes. He tapped Bob's arm. "I have a question."

Inwardly, I groaned. C'mon Richard, give it up. I know you're a good guy underneath.

Once again, the mayor nodded.

"Are these people Christian or …" Richard paused to add emphasis to his words, "or are these people Muslim? We don't want Muslims with their treatment of women, and their Sharia Law here." He shook his head. "No burqas here." People nodded and clapped in agreement.

I knew it. Bigotry, like bile, it always comes up.

Bob shook his head. Disappointment registered on his face. "First of all, Richard, we are talking about the Ahmadi family, not 'these people.' Second, yes, they are Muslim, and so, by the way, is our own Dr. Siddiqui. I know you've all heard about fundamentalist Muslims and read the news reports of honour killings. I remind you that Christians are not perfect either. It was Christians that led the slaughter during the crusades in medieval times, and it is Christians who have fought each other in Ireland for years. The Klu Klux Klan down in the States claim to be Christian. Fanaticism corrupts. We have no reason to believe that the Ahmadis are fanatics of any kind. I tell you again, we are talking about a mom and dad, and three children who have been through extremely tough times, tougher than most of us have ever experienced. They are here in Catalpa Creek, strangers in our midst. They are alone and frightened, and they need us."

In my head I yelled, "Yes, yes, yes. Love the stranger in our midst. They could be God's angels."

Bob pulled the microphone from its stand and moved out closer to the crowd. "If you really believe in the hospitality we preach in Catalpa Creek, come out to Don and Dorie's Fundraiser on Saturday night. You'll get a chance to meet this family. I've always been proud of Catalpa Creek. We have a reputation for being warm and welcoming. I'm confident we'll keep that reputation on Saturday evening."

Some of the crowd applauded. Bob handed the microphone back to Richard. Most people shook the hand he offered.

To my mind, Richard didn't look pacified, but on the whole, the crowd was friendly. I stepped over beside Tony. "Looks like we have a temporary truce tonight."

Tony smiled. "I think there are only a few real dissenters. Hopefully, they will crawl back into their holes."

People started to leave. Tom Long pulled Bob aside. It looked like Tom was thanking him. Over in one corner, I saw Richard talking to one of the strangers that had come. I nudged Tony and pointed. "Do you know that guy in the green shirt?"

Tony shook his head.

"I wonder if there aren't people here who have come to town just to stir up trouble." "Think I'll mention it to Tom before we leave."

"Good idea. I'll just say hi to Eleanor while you do that."

"See if Eleanor would like to go for coffee. I'll invite Tom." As I made my way through the crowd, a flash of colour caught my attention. Janice Lawson, wearing a yellow jacket, skin-tight jeans and knee-high boots was speaking animatedly with Dennis Carding, her ponytail bobbing. She swivelled her head and looked in my direction. When I lifted my hand to acknowledge that I'd seen her, she smiled. We locked eyes for a moment.

What are you thinking? Why are you here?

Janice turned back to Dennis and made a comment I couldn't hear. She pushed past him and out of the room.

Half an hour later, I joined Eleanor, Tom, and Lee Ann at Lakey's Restaurant. "Where's Tony?" Eleanor asked as I slipped into their booth beside Lee Ann. "I thought he was coming."

"He got called into work. I dropped him off at home." I turned to Lee Ann. God you're gorgeous, I thought, even in that power suit and hair wound tight in a bun. "I didn't see you at the meeting."

"I arrived late. Had to stand at the back. Eleanor called and told me I needed to be there. She was right. I have responsibility for Mustafa when he's at school. I needed to learn about the community's reaction to the family."

"Well, what did you think of the meeting?" Tom asked, as he loosened his tie.

Eleanor tapped her long red nails showing her agitation. "There shouldn't have been a meeting in the first place. I have no patience with these people who are always looking for trouble."

Lee Ann spoke up, her voice calm and cool as usual.

"Sometimes, it's good to get those kinds of feelings out. Now the Ahmadis are here, what was just an idea has become a reality. Sometimes our fear is hidden even from ourselves. Let me tell you a story."

"That's my line," Eleanor interrupted, "but I'll let you do it just the same."

We all laughed.

Lee Ann smiled. I felt her body settle more deeply into her seat. It brought her just a shade closer to me. I considered moving over. I wanted to feel her thigh touch mine…I remembered Janice in this same situation. Maybe not, I thought.

"When my son, John was fourteen, he had a skiing accident," Lee Ann said. "It resulted in a serious concussion. I remember sitting with him at the hospital all afternoon, waiting for the neurosurgeon. John was in desperate pain. Our family doctor had refused to order any pain medication. He said that John needed his head as clear as possible for the neurosurgeon's examination. It was a long, long time for both John and me. I thought I was going to welcome that special doctor with open arms if he ever finished in surgery.

She paused a moment. I watched her fiddle with her napkin. She's nervous, I thought. That's not like her.

"Finally, a tall man, dressed in green "scrubs" walked into John's hospital room. He must have been 6'6" or more. He had the brown skin, thick black braids and wide forehead that said to me he was native Canadian."

I drew in a deep breath. Prejudice, I hate it.

"That doctor's only words to me were, 'You'll have to leave. I want no distractions for my patient.'"

"There was no hello, how are you, or my name is … I walked out of that room, terrified. My son was in desperate pain. I had to leave him with… a stranger."

Lee Ann had folded that napkin into the tiniest of squares. She squeezed it hard until her thumb and index finger turned white. I could feel the tension building in the four of us.

Lee Ann continued her story. "I leaned against the wall just outside the door of David's room. Tears of fear poured down my cheeks. One of the nurses stopped and asked what was wrong. I remember dumping my life story on her. You see, my parents, who were kind and loving people, were also deeply prejudiced. If you weren't white and Anglo-Saxon in origin you were hardly human. Black and native Canadians in my parents' minds were the cause of all the violence in the world. According to my father, all the crime that ever happened in our small town was committed by the "Indians" on the reservation down the road.

Lee Ann dropped the wadded up Kleenex onto the table and tapped it several times. Like me, Eleanor was watching Lee Ann's hands. Tom was staring straight at Lee Ann. For me, it felt like the world had been reduced to just the four of us sitting there in a vacuum.

"At school, and in the world, I had learned that my parents were wrong," Lee Ann said. "Over the years, I had experienced and made friends with many Canadians—native, black, brown—whatever. I thought I had put all that negative thinking behind. On that day in the hospital, when I was so upset, all of my old lessons from childhood washed over me, and I was afraid."

That nurse touched my arm and asked, "Can I help?"

Lee Ann paused.

Her hands moved up to her face and wiped away her tears. God sends help, always. I sure know that, I thought.

"That nurse helped. She listened and understood. She told me all about Dr. Carmichael, a well-known Canadian neurosurgeon. 'Yes, he doesn't talk much,' she said, 'but he's wonderful. He has just completed a very intricate five-hour operation removing a tumour from the brain of a young child. He doesn't know yet just how much effect his work will have on that child's abilities. He's exhausted, yet he left the operating theatre and came directly here to care for your son.'"

Lee Ann smiled, picked up the Kleenex and slowly began to unfold it. Even with the space between us, I felt her body relax as she finished her story.

"I remember as if it were yesterday, hearing that nurse's words and being ashamed of my fear…My experience tells me that there will be people here in town who will need to get to know the Ahmadi family. They will need to hear their story. Bob Handel gave out some of that knowledge tonight. It was helpful."

"Yes, it was good," Tom responded.

"That's one powerful story," Eleanor said. She reached across the table and squeezed Lee Ann's hand. "Thank you."

I wanted to give Lee Ann a hug, but not in such a public place.

"I'm not sure that all the trouble is over," Tom said, "Mayor Handel did a fine job of putting out the fire tonight, but chances are there will be a few sparks left. Richard and his friends may not give up so easily. We will need to remain vigilant."

Chapter Five

SS Dominion

Friday, September 22

Renée

Dad and I were running late. We barely had time to choke down some cold cereal before rushing out to the car. I was grateful. While he drove, we sat in silence, together and yet not. I didn't want to talk to him about Ms. Hamilton. I was still angry. Why does he have to replace Mom already? He can wait a few years, at least till I'm away at school. I looked over at him, his knuckles white as he gripped the steering wheel. Guess I should break the silence. After all, he's all I've got now.

"How did the meeting go last night?"

His fingers softened. "Could have been worse. A few seemed intent on causing trouble. Mostly they were just our townspeople, trying to adjust to the idea of having someone different among us. All the news media talk about is terror. No wonder they're afraid."

"Isn't there a Bible story about welcoming strangers?"

"Yeah, angels in disguise." His face and body drooped. "I guess most people don't know or care what the Bible says anymore."

We pulled up to the school. Relieved, I hopped out of the car. "See ya tonight."

Susie was waiting just inside the big doors. "Hey, nice T-shirt. Purple's good."

"Thanks, it's from that new store Teen Connection." The bell rang, calling us to class. "Let's read some more of my Nana Sinclair's diary tonight," I said as we rushed down the hall.

"K."

When we met to walk home together, Susie said, "I'll have my homework done by supper time. Be there by seven. I like reading that diary, even if it's sad."

Several cars whooshed by, spraying dirty water from the puddles. We jumped over onto the grass to stay dry.

Susie kept right on talking. "I talked to Mustafa today. Well, sort of. Actually, he has quite a lot of English. We didn't use Google translate hardly at all. Language doesn't matter. I love his hair—so dark and wavy. And those eyes, those gorgeous black eyes."

"You'd better be careful. At lunch today, it looked as if Tracey had claimed him."

"Not yet. He's brand new. He's still fair game."

"I thought Mustafa looked nervous. I was glad Harrar was there, even if he didn't say anything. Harrar would be such a good friend for Mustafa."

"Course, you'd know."

I rolled my eyes.

"Well, I think they're both gorgeous. I'll concentrate on Mustafa. Harrar's yours."

I'm not so sure about that, I thought, but joined in her laughter. Our conversation moved to homework, endless homework. When we reached my place, I ran up the front steps. "See you tonight," I called back.

The door's unlocked. Dad must have come home early. Well, I guess I can't avoid this any longer. I took a deep breath and stepped inside. "Hey, Dad," I called as I slipped off my shoes.

"In my study," came his muffled reply.

I dropped my knapsack as I trudged by the hall table. He looked up when I opened the door and flopped on the couch.

"Be with you in a minute," he said, and returned his eyes to his papers.

Three neat piles of folders lined one side of his desk. The rest of the surface was clear with the exception of the in/out basket on the other side, holding only one item, and the three sheets directly in front of him. Neat. Predictable...That's what he is. That's what's wrong with my life right now. There's gaps in the predictable. Dad and Ms. Hamilton? What will happen? And Harrar? What's going on with him?

Dad gathered up the papers and shoved them in the top file. "Good," he said to no one in particular, as he pushed his chair back from the desk and came over to sit with me. "Now, Renée," he started, "we have to talk about this."

Needing to get past it as quickly as possible, I cut in with, "It's okay. I've thought about it all day. Yes, I'll be uncomfortable. Yes, I wish you didn't have to move on. Go ahead. Bring Ms. Hamilton to the fundraiser. I'll endure it. Just don't give her too much attention, please, and don't look too happy." Dad opened his mouth to say something, but I wasn't finished. I put two fingers over his lips to stop him. "And don't ask me if I'm sure, because I'm not, and that will make me feel worse. Just go ahead and do what you need to do, but don't expect me to be all smiles. I'll do my best." I dropped my head and stared at my toes. Slowly, I flexed them back and forth.

He said nothing. We sat in silence.

Finally, I asked, "When is our next appointment with Dr. Sampler? I need to talk with him." Maybe he can use his psychology to slow Dad down.

Relief flickered across his face. "I'll check my calendar. I think it's next week."

"Good. Can I go now? I have homework to do. Susie's coming over after supper. We're planning to read some more of Nana Sinclair's diary. Is that good with you?"

"Yes, I've finished with John's file and besides, I'm just as caught up in her story as the two of you. I'll finish getting supper so we can get started. I came home early and made leek and potato soup."

"Great." I grinned at him. "Guess it's a good thing you've moved on to cooking." That attempt at humour wiped a few of the lines from his face.

He chuckled. "Thanks, hon. It's a good thing you like soup, since that seems to be my specialty."

I got up to leave. "Susie's not coming 'til seven. You don't have to hurry supper." I paused a few seconds. "I take that back. I'm actually hungry, and the clock over your window says 4:30. I could eat and do homework after."

He smiled. "Me, too."

At 6:45 the doorbell rang. Susie yelled, "Hey, you two, I'm early."

I looked up from my mystery novel. Of course, right in the middle of the big race. I shrugged my shoulders and stuck the bookmark in place. I heard Dad's footsteps going to the door, then his voice.

"You look different. No books. You're usually a pile of books walking."

She giggled. "Must have lost about thirty pounds when I left them behind."

I picked up the diary from the coffee table and joined them in the hall. "I've set up the breakfast nook for us. Chairs aren't as comfy as the couch, but the light's better."

The three of us traipsed into the kitchen and sat down.

Susie's bright green sweater matched Dad's sweatshirt. "Hey, you too, you match," I said.

Dad quipped, “Good taste.”

Susie looked down at her sweater. “I like it too.” She wriggled her wrist, jangling a whole cluster of matching green bangle bracelets. “Found the sweater and the bracelets at the thrift shop last weekend. Great place to shop…I’ve been thinking, Nana’s diary is special. We need some sort of ritual for each time we read it.”

“I’ve an idea. I’ll get Mom’s candle. Then we’ll know Mom is here with us.”

Dad added, “Maybe we could say a little prayer of thanksgiving for the diary after we’ve turned on the candle.”

“Sure,” Susie said. She looked at me and rolled her eyes. I’m glad she’s a church kid like me. She appreciates my Dad for who he is. I shoved back my chair and headed for the stairs.

“Get mine off my shelf, too, please,” he called up the stairs.

Both candles on, he prayed. I opened the diary.

“Wait a minute,” he said, placing his hand on the diary. “Let’s hear about your research.”

I groaned and opened my laptop. “Well here’s what I’ve got so far. Dr. Barnardo opened a home for boys. He gave them job training. Later, he set up cottages for the girls that he called The Village. I’ve focused my research on The Village. The girls were well fed. They had meat twice a week and all the bread they could eat.”

Susie shook her head and frowned, “That doesn’t sound very great to me.”

“It is when you compare it to the workhouse where the staple fare was usually one slice of stale bread and a small bowl of gruel a day.”

“Really.”

“Yup. And at Barnardo’s, each girl even had her own bed with a mattress and sheets that were changed once a week, and her own blanket.

"My brothers complain about having to share a room."

I scrolled down my screen. "Each cottage had a house mother who had complete control over the girls."

"Giving someone that much power over others is a recipe for abuse," Dad said. He ran his hand through his hair and frowned. "A cruel house mother could do a lot of damage, just as cruel teachers did so much damage to our aboriginal children in the residential schools." He leaned back, his chair balancing on two legs.

"We humans can be so mean," Susie said. "I don't like that about us. Why do you think God created us with that mean streak? Animals don't have it."

"Deep question, Susie. Let's ask Reverend Linda on Sunday," he said and tipped his chair back down, as if he was ready to get back to business. "In the meantime, I think Barnardo meant well, but intention and reality are not always the same. He probably didn't even think about the culture shock and loneliness these children would experience. He took them from everything they had ever known and dumped them in pioneer Canada, tough life."

"Whoa, now," I tapped Dad on the arm. "I think Dr. Barnardo expected their gratefulness to overcome all that. There were few jobs in England. If he didn't ship them out, they'd end up educated and still back on the streets."

Susie shook her head and rubbed her eyes. "Why does everything have to be so complicated?"

I closed the lid on my laptop. "I read last night that refugee camps today can be worse than the poorest districts in London at the turn of the century."

Susie jumped up and plugged in the kettle. "This discussion is just plain depressing. I wish I didn't have to grow up and know about these things… Let's get to Nana."

I picked up the diary and began to read:

September 21, 1903
Diary, today we had thick creemy porige for breakfast and reel milk and sugar. It felt so good in my tummy. Doctor Barnardo came. He told us about Canada. He said that in winter the ground is hard and covered with snow. The water gets hard to. Everything freeses. That's scary. He showed us a trunk. It was covered with tin to keep it dry on the boat trip. The tin looked like the skin of an alligator, I saw in a picture book once. He said we would all have one of these trunks as our own when we got to Canada. The trunk was full of cloes. Just two more days and we leeve. That's scary to.

When I paused to turn the page, Susie said, "I'd certainly be scared. What a horrible plight. If she stayed, she might get sent back to the workhouse. If she went to Canada, she'd freeze and heaven knows what else."

I laid the diary down again and reopened my laptop. "Just a minute, I need to make some notes for my project. I'm thinking both Nana and today's refugees come with high expectations and a need to escape, and neither really have a choice. Both face disillusion once they arrive." I tapped in my notes.

"Being a country built on immigration must mean we're mighty strong people," Susie said.

Dad joined in. "We are…at least, we were. We survived in a strange and tough environment but now, we have it mighty soft."

"Let's get back to the diary," Susie said. "I'd like to get them on board the boat tonight. I'll read."

September 22, 1903
Today was hard. They called it prosesing. We had to take off all our clothes even our nickers. We lined up in front of a doctor and nurse. They laughed at us. They told me I was skinny. I felt bad.
We got our trunks today. We had to fold all the cloes carefully and pack them in the trunk. There was a bible. On the first page someone had writen Immigration to Canada, September 23, 1903. My trunk has my name on it. They took our trunks away. I wanted to keep it. Doctor Barnardo promised we wud get them back when we got to Canada.
Tilly can't wait for tomorrow to get started. I'm afraid.

"Sounds like Barnardo tried to make things good for the children," Dad said.

I scrolled down my computer notes. "Listen to this, 'The children's clothes were made in homes of excellence. In fact, Barnardo's children were some of the best dressed emigrants to enter Canada. Besides a trunk, each child carried a personal travel bag, his Barnardo number, destination and landing card. And before they left they received what was called the *Canada Lectures* and they saw agricultural slides telling them of the great future awaiting those who worked hard.'"

"Okay, now, back to the diary," Susie said.

I looked at my watch and then at Dad. "It's just 8:00. We've time."

September 23, 1903

Diary, today we marched down the street to the train. We were a parade. Doctor Barnardo came to the docks to say goodby. A band played and people cheered as we got in the little boat that took us out to the ship. That was fun. Up close, the ship was huge like a mountain. We looked way up its black side to the white part Tilly called the deck. The ship was long, long, long with lots of little round windows along the side. It looked like my birthday cake when we were with mama and papa. That's sad. At the top of the ship was a monster candle that someone had blown out. I could still see the smoke. Tilly says the candle is a chimney for the ship's enjins. When we were tied up beside the ship, a man played a horn. A long line of sailors wached us walk up this long steep bridge thing. Tilly called it a gangplank.

They herded us down into the bottom of the ship. It's crowded and hot and smelly down here. We can only go up on deck when matrin allows. My only space that's mine is my bed and it's so close to the ceiling I can't sit up. There are two beds below me. I'm afraid.

"Not a good beginning," I said.

"Sounds like the ship will be worse than the workhouse."

September 24, 1903

Diary, today the ship steamed out of the harbour. The enjins make a lot of noise. Tilly helped me sneek past matrin and up the stairs to look for little Bill. I climbed the gate onto the deck and found him hiding in a corner behind a pile of ropes. I hugged him close. He was hot, so hot and coffin all the time.

In my mind I saw them, huddled together, squashed against the side of the ship, barely hidden. Little Bill's tiny body jerked with each cough. My throat hurt. "What will they do," I asked. "Nana's too young. She must be frightened. I hope it's just the flu."

Dad rubbed my back and sighed, "Back then, even the flu was dangerous.".

"Hush, you two, I want to know what happened," Susie said. She started reading again.

I half dragged him back to the gate. Tilly was waiting. She helped me get him over it. She told matrin. Matrin was kind. She brot us to the ships doctor. He listened to little Bills breth and then shook his head. "Newmonya" he said. He put little Bill to bed right there in the sick room. He let me stay until bedtime. Little Bill was trying so hard to breeth. They gave him something warm to drink. It made him sleep.

September 25, 1903

Diary, after I ate my grool this morning, matrin took me to little Bill. He's not better. I sat with him all day. He is sicker tonight. I wanted to stay with him but the Doctor sent me to bed. It's much better where little Bill is. Its not hot and stuffy and it doesn't smell of vomit but Tilly is here. It helps to talk with Tilly. I hear others cofin. Tilly says we will all be sick before we get to Canada.

September 26, 1903
Diary, I sat with little Bill all day. Mostly he slept. The nurse was telling me to leeve when he started coffin reel hard. He coffed up blood. He didn't stop. He threw up. I was trying to clean his face when he stoped coffin. He just stoped. Then he stoped breethen. He lay there so still. I wiped his face clean and the sheets. I tried to wake him up. Nurse came over. She put her arm around me. He's ded, she said. I cried. She let me sit there with him. She brought a cleen shirt for him. She helped me put it on him. Then she covered him with a cleen blanket. He looked like he was asleep. I cried. Now, I'm all alone cept for Tilly. And you, Diary. I hope little Bill is with Mama and Papa. Tilly says he's better off than we are. I wanted him to see Canada. Tilly says she will stick with me always. I hope so. I'm so afraid. Can't cry no more.

Susie looked up from the diary.

"Life sure was hard for such a young child," Dad said. "I think children grew up sooner back then. They had to. Still, …."

"Poor little Nana. I'm seventeen. Mom died nearly three years ago, and I still wonder at times if I'll ever learn to cope."

Susie jumped up from her chair. "We need some more tea. Any of Mrs. Logan's treats?" She picked up the cookie tin from the counter and shook it. Her face drooped. "Oh, empty." She grabbed the Kleenex box from the top of the fridge. "Here," she said. "Mop up your faces. That's enough diary for tonight."

Knock, knock, knock.

Dad opened the back door to Mrs. Logan carrying two brightly coloured tins. She slipped off her shoes and handed Dad her jacket.

"I had a lonely day today, so I baked. I've brought you some of my sea of cookies."

"Yay!" we said.

I reached out and hugged our little round neighbour. I love having an older friend. "Thank you, you're a life saver. Susie just shook your last cookie tin and it was silent. We're about to have tea and…*ta-da*…cookies." I opened the tin. "Chocolate dreams, my favourite."

We all cheered.

Meow, meow. Ebony joined in.

"What's this?" Mrs. Logan asked as she picked up Nana Sinclair's diary.

Susie gave her a long explanation.

"My, that sounds interesting. I remember hearing about the Barnardo children. There were thousands of them." She sat down at the table with us and waited for the kettle to boil. "So, your great-great-grandma was one of those, Renée. What started you on this topic?"

I explained about my history project. We munched cookies and sipped tea. Soon enough, Susie's phone chimed. Her Dad was outside waiting for her. Our little impromptu party broke up.

"I'll walk you back through the hedge," Dad said to Mrs. Logan.

Dad was gone just the few minutes it took for me to put our cups in the dishwasher. When he returned, I picked up Mom's candle, and the diary and started up the stairs. "Think I'll crawl into bed early," I said.

"Me too… By the way, just so you know, Lee Ann and I are going to the Fundraiser together Saturday night."

His words felt like a kick in the stomach. "Right," was all I could manage as I ran up the last few steps to my room.

Chapter Six

The Fundraiser

Saturday, September 23

Steve

After Susie's parents picked up Renée, I drove out to Lee Ann's. She opened the door in a flash of color, as I came up the walk. "Great skirt." I said and thought, but it covers up your lovely, long legs.

Lee Ann smiled. "Thank you, I love the bright colours," she said, as she lifted up the gauzy material and made the colours swirl.

I followed her inside and kissed her cheek as I held her cape for her. "Beautiful lady," I said. She blushed a soft pink, just enough to tell me she liked the compliment. As I followed her outside, that skirt floated around her in the breeze like flames. I felt fire rise within me. I caught my breath. When I opened the car door for her, she looked up. It seemed my fire was reflected in her eyes. "You'll look marvellous dancing in that skirt tonight," I said. If I had just stopped there but my tongue kept on flapping, "Serena always said… Oops, sorry. I'm trying not to do that." To hide my embarrassment, I picked up the part of her skirt that was still draped down over the door opening, and carefully tucked it under those fabulous legs.

"It's okay, Steve," was all she said.

I nodded and closed her door. Once seated behind the wheel, I reached out and stroked Lee Ann's soft cheek. Trying to cover my embarrassment said, “You’re not at all like Serena. Serena was tiny, and … I clamped my lips together. “I’m sorry, I’ll shut up.”

Lee Ann laughed. Her whole face seemed to sparkle. “All this because of your compliment. You’re sweet.” She blushed again.

I leaned towards her. Our lips met. I wrapped my arm around her shoulders to draw her closer. She pulled away, her forehead creased. “We’d better get going, I don’t want to miss part of the program.

I sighed and started the car.

“My turn to say, sorry,” she said. “Could we reschedule that kiss for the end of the evening? Oh dear, that sounds…”

“Very much like the vice principal talking.” We both chuckled. “I’m going to take that as a promise and hold you to it.”

“Good,” she replied and grinned.

We drove into town enjoying an easy silence between us. I turned my mind to Renée and her feelings about Lee Ann and me. That thought tamped down the desire that was rising within me.

At the arena, it took a few minutes to find a place to park. We stepped inside the upstairs hall just as Reverend Linda was introducing Mayor Bob Handel. The place was packed, but we managed to squeeze into the back row. Janice Lawson, sitting next to the wall in the row ahead, turned around and stared at us. She raised her eyebrows, frowned and then winked before she turned away.

“Looks like you’ve another admirer,” Lee Ann said, the dimple in her cheek dancing.

“Right,” was all I could manage.

Bob Handel walked onto the stage and raised his hands for silence. Conversation gradually ceased. He invited the Ahmadi family to the stage, welcomed them officially, and gave them each Maple Leaf lapel pins and a bag of gifts that had been donated by local businesses. He introduced each one and told a little about them. He added that David Sims was doing a feature on them that would be in next week's paper.

That's good, I thought. We'll all get the same information.

When the Mayor finished, Doctor Ahmadi stepped forward, his family beside him. He gripped the mike so fiercely his knuckles turned white. "Thank you…for generosity," he said, his accent thick. "We happy in Canada." He looked at Mustafa and gestured.

Mustafa took the mike. He towered over his father, who looked even smaller on the stage than he had at the airport. Mustafa's English, although heavily accented too, flowed more easily. He told us how grateful his family was to feel safe again. "Your country beautiful," he said. "Many lakes and rivers. From airplane, we saw much blue water. Beautiful and good." He stepped back. We all applauded.

Nice young man, he'll probably fit in well. Renée hasn't said much about him.

Bob took over. "We have entertainment for you. First up, two of our young people from Catalpa Creek High School, Susie Tomchuk and Joe Laplante, have collaborated on writing a special song for tonight. Let's all welcome them to the stage.

Susie is so talented, I thought. I'm glad she's Renée's friend. We settled back to listen and enjoy. By the time the show was over, Thuraya Ahmadi had fallen asleep against her mother's shoulder. Bob announced that the Ahmadis were exhausted and going home. People gathered round them to shake their hands.

I took a deep breath and let it out slowly.

"What's that about?" Lee Ann asked.

"I was worried there might be trouble tonight. I'm glad the Ahmadis are living at the Glen Forest apartments with their secure entrance. Now, enough of that. Come on, let's help move chairs so we can dance."

Janice left her seat and stopped directly in front of me. She looked up from beneath her long lashes and smiled. "Hi Steve, this is quite the evening."

I stepped back. "It certainly is."

She looked at Lee Ann, shook her head and returned her eyes to mine. "I don't know many people yet. Can I hang out with you?"

I felt Lee Ann's body stiffen beside me. "Ummm…Sure."

Chaos reigned for about fifteen minutes, while I helped arrange tables and chairs around the outside of the hall. Work done, I found Lee Ann, with Janice at her elbow, out in the kitchen. Lee Ann was making coffee while Janice watched.

"Let's go find a seat," I said.

"Be with you in a minute," Lee Ann replied.

Janice said, "I'm ready for you now, Steve."

Lee Ann rolled her eyes.

Ignoring Janice, I walked over to Lee Ann and asked, "Can I help?"

She pushed the start button. "Too late. All done. Let's go."

I followed her back into the hall with Janice trailing right behind me. "There's Tony and crowd, over by the stage. Let's go sit with them. They've empty seats at their table."

As soon as we got close, Tony called, "Hey, you two, we've saved you seats." Tony noticed Janice and looked confused. "Oh…maybe we can find another chair."

I locked eyes with Eleanor and shrugged my shoulders.

She grinned and jumped up. "Janice, I'm so glad you're here. If we'd only known, we'd have saved a seat for you, too." She enveloped Janice with an overwhelming hug and looked across the room. "There's one empty chair at Mayor Handel's table. I'll just take you over and introduce you. It's time you met the Mayor's wife and Kasun and Rashimi Siddiqui. The town's important people are sitting with them." Eleanor took Janice's arm and steered her away.

When Eleanor returned, I squeezed her hand. "Thank you. You are a true friend."

"Don't mention it. You can return the favour some time. My advice: don't encourage Janice."

"I'm not. She doesn't need any encouragement."

Tony couldn't resist the opportunity to tease. "Don't let the attention of a pretty little woman go to your head, Steve. Just sit down and forget her."

My cheeks blazing hot, I sat down. Lee Ann looked into my eyes and smiled. "The music's started. Let's dance," she said.

"Thank you for being so gracious," I whispered as I drew her close. "You feel good. And smell good, too."

About an hour later, during the band's break time, we heard some lively discussion happening over in one corner. It quickly escalated to raised voices. Two of the town's police constables walked over in that general direction.

"We want rid of those foreigners," someone yelled. It was Richard, and he was looking at Dennis Carding.

The room had gone totally silent.

Dennis, his voice calm but firm, answered, "Now Richard, these Ahmadis are people, good people. You leave them alone."

"Well, you've certainly changed your tune, Mr. Carding," Richard yelled. "Yesterday, you were ready to run them out of town."

"I hadn't met them. I thought they might be terrorists, but they're not. Anybody can see that. And we need another doctor in this town. So, leave them alone."

I looked across the room. Renée was standing with a group of friends, Harrar at her elbow. What's she thinking? Her only experience of Dennis Carding was at the police station two years ago. He was hard and abusive with Russell. I looked around for Russell, but didn't see him.

The police constables walked up to Richard. Tom joined them. I overheard Tom say, "Okay now, Richard, you just sit down here. We need to have a little talk."

The band started up again, and we could no longer hear what went on. No more problems arose, at least in terms of our refugee family. At one point, while Lee Ann and I were dancing, Janice tapped my shoulder and said to Lee Ann, "I'll have a turn now."

Lee Ann just smiled and handed me over. I watched her walk back to our table without looking back. Superb from behind, too, I thought.

"There's more than one fish in the sea, Steve," Janice said, and snuggled in close.

This woman may be cute, but she's pushy. I twirled her out as part of the dance. When she came back, I kept some space between us. The dance over, I thanked her and retreated.

"Another time," Janice said. "You might like a change of diet."

I said nothing but thought, guess there's always that possibility but not with you, my dear. Back at our table, I slid in beside Lee Ann. "Well that duty's done for tonight," I said.

Tony winked.

Lee Ann, her face serious, said, "I hope no one ever feels that way about me."

"Never," I replied. "Absolutely never."

As we pulled into Lee Ann's driveway, she said, "I'm glad the police were there and ready when that argument started. Let's hope Tom was able to talk some sense into Richard. He seems determined to cause trouble."

"Richard's not a bad sort. I think he's easily led. Somebody must be manipulating him. Dennis Carding's reaction surprised me." I shut off the engine.

"People can change, and I'm glad." She turned to look directly at me. "I'm not much of a church person, but somewhere in the Bible it says we're supposed to think on the good things."

"Reverend Linda gave Renée and me a list of scriptures to help us with our grief." I said. "That passage was one of them. I've read it so many times I think I can quote it. Here goes:

> "Whatever is true, whatever is noble, whatever is right, whatever is pure, whatever is lovely, whatever is admirable—if anything is excellent or praiseworthy—think about these things… And the God of peace will be with you."
>
> (Philippians 4:8-9)

"I've shortened it to "search for the good and find peace." It helped me with the grief." I shifted in my seat so I could look straight at her. The moonlight bounced off several curls that had escaped from her French knot. I reached out and tucked one back behind her ear. "Let's look for the goodness in tonight. I'll start with I loved dancing with you. You…"

She interrupted me with, "Tonight was great. Our community has accepted a refugee family. That's goodness, monumental goodness."

I dropped my hand, "Yes, and I loved Susie and Joe's song and the participation from the high school kids."

"The entire program was good," Lee Ann added, her face beaming with delight. "The elementary school's song, 'I'd Like to Teach the World to Sing' was spot on. I love that song and when everyone began to sing it again at the end of the program, I could feel my heart soar."

We both paused a moment. I started up again. "Then there was the change in Dennis Carding and the fact that as a committee we had prepared for trouble by having the police there."

"Yes, and the Ahmadis had left before that happened. That was a good thing too. All in all, it was a great evening. And we raised money for the refugee project as well." After pausing for a moment, she continued, "Thanks, Steve. I enjoyed doing that. Tell me your motto again. It's concise. I want to write it down." She pulled a small notebook from her purse.

She's sure working at keeping this light, I thought. "Search for the good and find peace. Now I remind you, that doesn't mean we close our eyes to the possibility of trouble. There's a difference."

"Don't I know that." She raised those beautiful blue eyes and looked directly into mine. "I'm glad we went together this evening, Steve. You're wise and you're fun. Thank you for asking me."

I felt my desire growing again. Keep calm, Steve. "Thank you for saying, yes."

She sighed. "It's getting late."

I hopped out of the car, came round and opened her door. We walked up the sidewalk, hand in hand. "Time to keep your promise," I said and drew her close. Our kiss was long and deep. I felt the warmth and softness of her body mould to mine. More, my body wanted more. We kissed again. Go slow, Steve, my head reasoned. Slow down. Take a deep breath. This is too important to spoil. I stepped back. "Are we ready for this?"

"I want to be, Steve, but…"

"Let's make this a first step."

"Thank you."

After she unlocked the door, she turned and put her arms around my neck. "One more…please," she said. She placed her soft lips on mine.

"Yesssssss."

She stepped back and smiled, face flushed with desire. "Goodnight, Steve." She waved as she closed the door.

I swallowed hard and walked to the car, scarcely aware that my feet were touching the ground.

By the time I got home, worry had crept into the corners of my mind. I wondered how Renée did, seeing Lee Ann and me together. I wondered what her friends said. As I climbed the stairs, I could see no line of light at the bottom of her bedroom door. *Guess I can't ask her tonight.*

I brushed my teeth. Troublesome Janice marched into my mind. *Well, Serena, who would have guessed this stuffy old accountant would have two women in his life?* I chuckled and crawled into bed. *It feels rather good.*

Chapter Seven

Risky

Sunday, September 24

Renée

My alarm rang at seven the next morning. *Ugggggh*, I groaned. Forgot to change it last night. Without opening my eyes, I reached for my phone on the night table. Swipe. Silence. I snuggled down under my comforter, but sleep eluded me. After about ten minutes, I gave up. Maybe it's warm enough for a bike ride. Think I'll cycle along the creek. I dressed in layers, beginning with my old grey sweats.

The memory of Russell Carding standing under the willow flashed through my mind. I won't see him this time. I won't even see the tree from the path.

I slipped quietly down the stairs, tore a sheet from the kitchen list pad on the fridge and wrote Dad a note. That should satisfy him. My jacket pockets stuffed with nuts, a protein bar, and my camera, I grabbed my bike from the shed. No wind, good. The path along the creek was deserted. Silence reigned except for the birds. Even the distant traffic seemed to have stopped on this beautiful, sunny Sunday morning.

My mind travelled to last night and my frustration with Rachel. She's supposed to be my friend. I could feel my face burn with embarrassment as I remembered her reaction to Dad with Ms. Hamilton. It sounded as if… he'd just come out of the closet. Susie's such a true friend. She rescued me. "Don't be such a jerk.

Of course, Renée knew. Do you think she and her dad don't talk? End of discussion."

My bike tire ran over a rock and I wobbled and almost fell. Guess I'd better pay attention to what I'm doing. For a few more minutes, I rode along, watching the path. A curve in the trail brought me close to the creek again. I braked, left my bike in a thicket and climbed down towards the water searching for Corny the crane. I pulled my camera from my pocket. Maybe I'll get another neat picture.

Just below me, the giant willow appeared, its branches trailing in the creek. Yuck. I would pick this spot to stop. I paused a moment. I don't care. Russell doesn't scare me. Why can't I be here? This isn't his property any more than its mine. Still, I won't go in under the tree. Besides, it's warmer in the sun.

I found a flat rock about twenty feet further along the riverbank and stretched out. *Mmmmm,* lovely. I closed my eyes. As my muscles and nerves relaxed, my mind turned to Mom, as it always did during my still moments. Dad and Ms. Hamilton together make you seem far, far away, Mom. I felt hot tears slip down my cheeks. Dad won't leave me, too, will he? I wiped my tears on my sleeve.

The crack of a stick breaking tore into my thoughts. I opened my eyes. Russell Carding, huge and smiling, stood just a few feet away. Fear clutched at my heart. What do I do? I opened my mouth to scream but no sound came.

"It's okay, Renée. I'm not going to hurt you," Russell said, putting out his hand.

I scrunched up on the rock, my heart beating so fast I felt faint.

He withdrew his hand. "Believe me, I don't want trouble with you or the police. This has been my safe place since I was a little boy. What are you doing here?"

"I…I…I didn't mean to trespass. I just stopped to rest and think."

"Where's your canoe?"

"I didn't bring it."

"You came all this way on foot."

"No. I rode my bike. My Dad knows where I am. If I don't come back, he'll come for me."

Disgust registered on Russell's face. "I told you already, I won't hurt you. I was a jerk. I've grown up. I'll never do that to you or anyone again."

"Okay," I said. I could hear the tremble in my voice. "I'll leave."

"Thank you," he said.

Why thank me, I thought. It's not as if I have a choice. I turned and climbed the embankment. He didn't try to stop me. I pedalled away, hard. By the time, I turned into our driveway, my eyes were stinging from the sweat.

I parked my bike. Don't need to tell Dad. He'll explode. "Hey Dad," I called as I came through the kitchen door and encountered a perfect picture. He stood at the stove, wearing Mom's frilly apron, spatula in hand. I pulled out my camera. "That's one for our photo album," I said. "Love you."

Chapter Eight

Settling In

Monday, September 25

Renée

"Hey Renée," Harrar said, when he stepped in front of me as I hurried down the hallway to the cafeteria for lunch.

Startled, I said, "Where did you come from?"

"Here's your flash drive. I loved the ducks swimming in the mist. I made a copy. I'd like to paint them. Okay?"

"Sure. I love that photo too. They look like Spirits emerging."

"Great composition."

I blushed. "Thanks.

The cafeteria doors opened, and Mustafa strode through, Tracey on one arm, Rachel on the other. He looked at Harrar and said, "Women…nice." His smile said it all. Harrar lowered his head, "Yeah," he muttered. I sighed. Mustafa and friends moved on. Harrar took a step in the opposite direction.

"Just a minute, are we still on for Saturday at the kartway?"

He hesitated. Without looking up, he said, "I'll pick you up at 1:00."

"Super."

"Gotta run," he replied and almost ran away down the hall.

"Wait."

He disappeared round a corner. Didn't even look back. Wish I knew what was wrong. He seemed okay at the fundraiser.

Maybe I'll find out on Saturday. I shrugged my shoulders and stepped into the noise of the cafeteria.

On the way home from school that same day, I announced to Susie, "We're going to Grandma Grenville's for Thanksgiving, It's Grandma's 70th birthday. All of my cousins will be there, even Jade. She and her family are coming all the way from South Africa."

Susie reacted with astonishment, much as I expected. "They're coming from South Africa just for the weekend?"

I grinned with satisfaction. "No, for sure not. Uncle Richard and Aunt Nancy have a conference next week in Boston. Jade graduates this year. They will be checking universities both here and around Boston.

"She must have such an exciting life, living in all those exotic places," Susie said. "I envy her."

"Suppose so…Guess it's all in what you're used to."

"Now it's time for my Big News! Mustafa and I are going to the movies tonight."

"Hey, congratulations. How did you manage that?"

"I didn't. He asked me as we were coming out of Physics class. As if I would say no. He's so gorgeous. Conversation will be easy, too. At the movies, we won't have to talk, and after we'll talk about the movie."

I laughed. "Oh, Susie! You think of everything."

"What about you?" Susie asked.

"Harrar and I are going go-karting on Saturday. I know that's not romantic, but he's a good buddy."

"Do you want him to be more than a buddy?"

"I don't know. It's great having him as a friend. No pressure."

Susie just shook her head. "No fun either."

"In your mind, maybe."

"How's your Nana Sinclair project going?"

"Good. Let's get together tomorrow after supper. I think Dad will be home. Will that work for you?"

"Yes, as long as it isn't Wednesday, any week night is fine."

"I'll check with Dad tonight. We are a team when it comes to Nana's diary."

That night at supper, Dad opened the conversation with, "How is Mustafa doing at school? He tells the committee he's fine, but I wonder if he isn't just saying what's expected."

"He's fine, Dad. He's in two of my classes and is doing very well. Considering he's still struggling with English, I think that's amazing. He's obviously very smart and a hard worker." I paused and thought for a moment. "He's not like Harrar. Mustafa likes to be at the centre. Good thing because all the girls at school have fallen for him…even Susie has snagged him for a date. They're at the movies tonight. She's raved about him ever since she met him at the airport."

Dad finished chewing his mouthful, swallowed. "Good for Susie." The kettle started whistling. He jumped up to lift it off the burner. While he filled the teapot, he continued. "Our committee has been hoping that the Siddiquis and the Ahmadis would be good friends, since both are Muslim. Are Harrar and Mustafa friends at school?"

"No. Just because they're both Muslim doesn't mean they will hit it off as friends. They're very different. Harrar is quiet. He's content to be in the background, happy to just do his best and not make any waves. Mustafa is very much "out there". He doesn't brag exactly but I'm sure he would if his English was better. He likes to show that he knows…It's hard to explain. If they had both been born and raised in Catalpa Creek, I still don't think they'd be friends. What about the parents?"

"Rashimi and Kasun had them over for dinner one night, but that's all. The Siddiquis are so busy, they don't have much time for socializing. Kahlil and Nazira seem to be settling in well without them. Nazira's English is improving. I think working with Eleanor at Lights Out is helping. She's waiting to hear when she can write her nurse's qualifying exam. Kahlil hopes to start a residency at the hospital in six months' time."

"Wow, they're getting right into it." I scraped the last of the gravy off my plate and took a big drink of milk. "By the way, Harrar and I are going go-karting this Saturday afternoon."

"Sounds like fun.

"Yup. Oh, before I forget, are you free tomorrow night? Susie and I would like to do another instalment on Nana Sinclair's diary."

"Can't. Badminton. How about Thursday? When's your project due?"

"End of semester. Don't worry, I'll have it done."

I reached into my pocket for my phone. Empty. "Must have left my phone in my jacket pocket. Be back in a minute. I need to check with Susie about Thursday."

"Remember you're on dish duty tonight."

I groaned.

Chapter Nine

Strong Women

Thursday, September 28

Renée

As I laid Nana's diary on the breakfast nook table, I realized that I hadn't had more than five hurried minutes with Dad each day since suppertime Monday night. Even that was barely a half-hour's conversation about our refugee family. Sometimes I wonder if I'm not just a drag on his life. It's a good thing he's so interested in Nana's diary. Otherwise, we'd spend the whole week just rushing past one another.

The day had been unusually hot and sticky for September. In an effort to keep cool, we all wore shorts. Dad and Susie watched as I spread towels on our chairs so our bare skin wouldn't stick.

"Good idea," Dad said. "You think of everything, just like your mother."

Susie added, "You are a lot like your mom, Renée. It's strange. You don't look like her, but you have her personality. I'm glad you do, because I miss your mom…Oh oh."

I could feel my heart sink, my smile disappear.

"That's okay, Susie," Dad said. "We miss her too. We need our candles."

"I'll get them," I said.

Once both candles were in place and flipped on, I said, "Okay, Dad, you're in charge of the prayer."

"Not necessarily, maybe Susie would like a turn."

I frowned. Sometimes, I could just shake my Dad.

Susie didn't miss a beat. "I'll pass this time," she said.

I grinned at her and made the thumbs-up sign.

After he prayed, Susie said, "I wish I could have seen that ship."

"I found a picture," I said and held it up along with several more sheets of paper. "It must have been awful on board those ships. People in steerage were treated like cattle. When I think what's ahead for Nana on this voyage, I shudder. Let's begin." I reread the last bit of the September 26th entry.

> Now Im all alone sept for Tilly and you, Diary. I hope Little Bill is with Mama and Papa. Tilly says he is better off than we are. I wanted him to see Canada. Tilly says she will stay with me always. I hope so. I am so afraid.

"Poor Nana, can it get any worse than having her brother die?"

Susie being Susie said, "There are lots of days when I would gladly pay someone to take my little brothers away for a while, but I wouldn't want them to die. I'm so glad Nana has Tilly. She's not totally alone. Friends are so important."

"Don't we know it," Dad and I said in unison. We sat in silence just thinking. Dad roused himself first.

"Okay," he said. "Let's get started on this voyage."

I handed him the diary. He moved his hands over the soft leather, obviously enjoying the feel of it. Sometimes, he surprises me. He's not just a nerd with numbers.

September 28, 1903

Dear Diary, yesterday was awful. They dropped my little Bill into the sea. I hope he's not cold. He's gone, reely gone. The matrin gave me an extra rashun of food. She says food always helps. It sort of does.

Dad looked up and winked. "See, I'm not the only one."

September 29, 1903
Dear Diary, today, the sun shone. We were on deck all day. Some people are home sick. Not me. There's no one there but Uncle Bruce. It's all his fault I'm here and little Bill died. Tilly says I have the consteetushun of a horse so I'm not seasick either. She tells me to count my blessings. I thot of 3.

1. I'm not sick.

2. They give us three meals a day and hot grool before bed.

3. When they make us xersize up on deck, the sea air wipes the smell of vomit from my nose.

I try not to think about little Bill. It hurts. Tilly says it won't bring him back.

October 2, 1903
Dear Diary, We had a big storm. We cudn't go on deck for two days. The smell down here was awful. Tilly and me laid together in her bed. We hung onto each other and the bed when the ship rolled from side to side. Everything, even lanterns crashed to the floor. We had no light. I couldn't write in you.

I reached out and touched Dad's hand to stop him. "Imagine what it must have been like down in the bottom of that ship."

"Closed up down there," Susie said. "The floor awash with puke and glass and overflowing potties, the two of them huddled together in that narrow bunk..." Susie's screwed up face mirrored her thoughts. "At Jake's after the movie, I asked Mustafa about the refugee camp. It sounded similar." She rubbed her forehead in concentration. "He said the camp was just mud— all the plants gone, trampled long ago. When it rained, the port-a-potties overflowed. Their muck ran down the footpaths between the tents."

"I've seen pictures of that," Dad said.

Susie continued, "I remember Mustafa's harsh laugh when he said, "Kids here wear something different every day. I wear same pair jeans three months. No wash. Water only for drinking."

A single tear slipped down Susie's cheek. "He said it all in a rush, as if he couldn't get it out fast enough. Then he stopped. He covered his face with his hands. After a moment, he took a deep breath, looked up and clamped his teeth together. 'Enough,' he said, 'It's over. I here now. We begin again.'"

"Sounds like you and Mustafa had a heavy conversation," Dad said.

"Yeah. Don't think we'll go out again. He's cute, but…he's…not really my type."

Dad opened his mouth to ask another question but I nudged him. "Let's get back to the diary," I said.

Dad started reading again.

October 4, 1903

Dear Diary, I saw an iceberg. That's what they called it. It looked like a sea monster. It's freezing on deck. My fingers are stiff. Its hard to push the pencil. There's a coat in my trunk. I know I folded it, but we can't get to our trunks cause they are way down deep in the innards of this ship. The fog makes everything wet. I brought my blanket up on deck and wrapped it around me. Now it's wet to.

October 6, 1903

Dear Diary, Today, Tilly pointed to a grey line where the sea and the sky meet. She said that was land. She said we would be in Canada tomorrow. We will stop in Kebec but have to stay on the ship til we get to Montreall. I don't know how she knows so much but I'm glad she does.

I'm counting my blessings again.

1. We're nearly there.
2. Both matrin and Tilly have watched out for me. They've made sure I had my rashins.
3. Most people are a little afraid of me. They think I might give them the diseeze that killed little Bill. That's a blessing too.

He stopped reading. "Nana sure is resilient."

"Maybe she's just gotten numb to the loneliness and pain. That's sort of what's happened to me. At times, I feel numb. It's like I've closed a door, not on Mom, just on the feelings."

Instead of responding to my feelings, Dad said, "Nana is the start of a line of strong women in our family. I only met your great-grandma, Nana's daughter, once but I remember her ramrod straight back. Her childhood was horrendous, too, but she wasn't defeated. She certainly was a survivor. Your Grandma

Rushton survived being adopted as a toddler, a divorce, and lots more and still she loved life."

I cut in with, "Mom didn't live long enough for us to know if she was strong."

Dad leaned forward and looked right at me. "Oh yes, she did. Your Mom was extremely strong." He reached over and squeezed my hand. "When you were born, she had a rough time. She was sick for months after, but she never complained. She just kept on celebrating you, her wonderful baby girl. Grandma Rushton couldn't get extended leave from her work, so my mom, your Grandma Grenville came to help us. Grandma Grenville said over and over, she didn't know where your mom got her strength. Your mom and I always believed that you have such a special relationship with Grandma Grenville because she lived here with us for nearly four months after you were born." He sighed and looked down at his hands. "I miss your mom, too, Renée, every day. She was my special friend, like…you and Susie are. She was never too tired or too busy. She was always there when anyone needed her, when I needed her. Oh yes, your mom was strong." He reached out and touched my cheek. "And you. You're just amazing. You handled that whole Russell Carding episode with such strength. All you were interested in was making sure he would be okay."

In the magic of the moment, we'd both forgotten that Susie was even there, but as usual she chimed in. "Your dad's right. Remember how determined you were to be part of the trap for Russell Carding. Yup, you're impressive."

Embarrassed, I took a sip of tea. Cold. Yuck. "I've never heard that story about Mom."

"Well, it's time you did," he said.

Breaking the moment, Susie said, "Let's put the diary away. Nana's almost in Canada. That's enough for me, for today."

"Okay." As I closed the diary, I thought, me, strong… or maybe foolish. I still haven't told Dad about seeing Russell again.

Susie's phone chimed as we shut off the candles. "That's my Dad. He's here early. Have to go."

I tucked the diary into its box and gave Susie a quick hug. "See ya tomorrow."

She gave Dad a hug too, and ran, picking up her jacket and sliding on her runners at the door. "See ya," she hollered as the door slammed shut behind her.

Dad looks as tired as me. I think this diary is bringing Mom close for him too. I picked up Nana's box and Mom's candle. "Thanks for the story about Mom. Think I'll do some more research on refugee camps and crawl into bed early."

"Me too. Crawl into bed early, that is." He gave me a quick hug

I walked up the stairs, still feeling the warmth of the story about Mom… and the connection with Dad.

Chapter Ten

Friendship

Saturday, September 30

Renée

Harrar picked me up for our go-karting date shortly after lunch. He sure is cute, I thought, as I watched him drive. He keeps tightening and loosening his fingers on the steering wheel. He must be nervous. That's unusual. Hoping to help him relax I asked, "Have you a painting project on the go?"

He glanced over at me and smiled. "Always. I've been asked to do a painting for family friends—a fall scene. The colours are so vivid right now. I'm enjoying painting a spot down at Jackson's Point. Last week, I saw a beaver building a dam there." He paused and made the turn for Andrew's Rolling Karts. "I made our reservation here for 1:30. We should arrive right on schedule."

We had the kartway all to ourselves. Our time just melted away as we careened around the track, laughing, racing, calling to one another.

When we climbed back into the car, Harrar said, "Let's pick up something at Jake's and go sit by the creek and talk. I'd like to show you that beaver dam. It's a neat spot."

My first thought was, would I see Russell? I must have frowned.

Harrar said, "It's okay, Renée. I'm safe. We're friends. I would never hurt you."

I reached out and touched his arm. "I know that, Harrar. I wasn't worrying about you."

We stopped at Jake's for ice caps and doughnuts. Harrar drove out the creek road past where I had encountered Russell. Good, I thought.

As we passed the old stone bridge, Harrar sighed. "Nearly there," he said.

Within minutes, we were settled on the bench soaking in the sun and listening to the water as it chugged along. A beaver's dam stretched several feet out into the creek. The water rippled as it rushed around it. Above us a maple tree towered, its leaves brilliant reds and yellows. Framing it was a clump of catalpas, their broad leaves still a deep green. I snapped a picture with my cell phone. Harrar's friends will be thrilled with his painting, I thought.

After a bit, Harrar said, "Renée, I want to tell you something." He paused and rubbed his hand across his forehead. "I value our friendship and want to keep it, but I can't…" he stopped again. His frown deepened. He scuffed his feet in the grass under the bench. I waited. I was sure I knew what he was trying to say. Something inside me told me he needed to say it himself. He took a sip of his ice cap. "Okay… I'm gay, Renée. I'm gay. You're a wonderful friend, but that's all you can be. I'm gay." He dropped his head.

I watched his slender, artist's hand trace over a knot in the wooden bench. I let his words sink into my heart. I knew, I thought and yet…I didn't want this. I wanted more. Now, it can't ever be…A robin's song interrupted the silence. He lifted his head and looked directly at me. I saw fear and desperation in his eyes. My friend is afraid. I reached out and touched his arm. "It's okay, Harrar. I knew…well, I wondered. I guess, I just didn't want you to be gay. Yes, I'd like it to be more, but you're my friend. You'll always be my friend."

Relief rushed across his face. We hugged. For what felt like a long time, we just sat there watching the water in the creek flow gently past.

Eventually, Harrar said, "How did you know? What did I do?" His voice was filled with worry. "If you knew, then others will know, too. What will I do?"

"Wait a minute, Harrar. It's not like that. It's not something you did. It's what you didn't do. It was obvious that we liked each other, yet you never even tried to kiss me. At first, I thought it was because you were Muslim and your faith said you couldn't touch a female that wasn't your wife. After a while, I decided that was my stereotype speaking." I picked up a stone and threw it in the creek. "About a year ago, when the bunch of us went to see that movie about a gay man, I can't remember the name, I decided then you were probably gay and that I am blessed to have you for a friend. In fact, it's made our relationship easier for me."

We both laughed. "Now that I've told you, it will make our relationship easier for me, too." He took a big bite of his doughnut. Once it was chewed and swallowed, his face was anxious again. "Have you told anyone what you suspected?"

"No, I didn't figure it was my news to tell. When you were ready, you would. It has been difficult for me at times, with our friends thinking we're a couple. The hardest part is that I'm not getting asked out a lot."

"I'm sorry, Renée." He paused. Before I could respond he said, "I need you to keep this to yourself. It's just that my faith condemns homosexuality. My parents would be expected to cast me out. Maybe my dad would have to stop practicing medicine. It would be awful for our family if they knew."

"Are you sure? I don't know much about your faith. What I do know is that some Christians condemn homosexuality, but my form of Christianity doesn't. My church teaches that God loves variety and has made every person unique, some gay, some straight. Maybe there are those in the Muslim faith that believe the same."

Harrar shook his head. His eyes were filled with tears. "There are liberal Muslims. I've checked that out on the net, but my parents don't fall in that category. Once, we watched a TV show together that talked about homosexuality. You should have heard their reaction. It was as if I was … worse than the worst criminal. My father is a doctor. You would think he would know, but he doesn't. They would cast me out if they knew."

I reached out and took his hand. I wanted so much to help. There was nothing to say. We listened to the creek. A bird sitting in a catalpa tree sang on relentlessly. The sun continued to shine. Finally, Harrar shook himself and said, "That's why I'm avoiding Mustafa. When a group of the guys were making fun of one of the openly gay kids at school, he joined in. I don't trust him. He can't find out. Please promise me you won't tell, Renée."

"Of course, I won't. Will you promise to still be my friend?"

"Oh, yes."

We hugged again. We both wiped away our tears. I drew in a deep breath. "Well, that was mighty heavy," I said.

He smiled and nodded.

"Tell me about your painting. Are there any people in it?"

We talked a bit longer while we finished our treats. Harrar said, "Guess we'd better get back before someone realizes we're gone and accuses us of…" That brought laughter.

We picked up our garbage and climbed back into the car. "Thanks, Renée," Harrar said. "You're the best."

"Thank you, for trusting me with who you are."

Chapter Eleven

Jade's Wisdom

Friday, October 6

Renée

For the next week, life rushed by in a blur. As usual, Dad was preoccupied with work and our refugee family. I forgot about Russell. Concern for Harrar hovered at the edges of my mind. I saw him in class but that was all. When the bunch of us gathered at lunch time, he was conspicuously absent. Tracey always made sure Mustafa was included. I guessed that Harrar just didn't want to join us. I looked around but he wasn't in the cafeteria. I tried texting him but he didn't answer. Thanksgiving weekend, I brought Nana's diary with me to show Grandma Grenville.

When we drove up Grandma's lane, my cousin Jade came running from the house in her sock feet, her long black ponytail flying. Oh, she's grown taller than me and even skinnier, I thought. Don't they feed her in South Africa?

She wrapped her arms around me, "I miss you," she said. I was surprised to see her eyes full of tears.

"Miss you, too. I've lots to share. Let's go for a walk later, just the two of us. I've a question for you as a young woman of the world."

"Mysterious! I can't wait."

Inside, Dad and I hugged everyone all around. I listened to the excited conversation and soaked in the family love. My mind slipped back to coming here right after mom's funeral. Guess

Dad knew that Grandma's love would help. I gave myself a shake and slipped my arm around Jade's shoulders. You may have amazing adventures travelling, I thought, but nothing can replace time with Grandma. No wonder your family returns here at every possible opportunity. We all need a dose of Grandma's love now and then.

I looked over at Grandma, her sprained ankle propped on the coffee table. In the midst of this joy hammered in the thought, *Grandma won't live forever*. I shivered and focused on her, laughing and happy. No she won't, so I'll enjoy her now, soak in her love so it will always be a part of me and I can pass it on to others.

"Hey, Renée," Jade said. "Let's go for a walk up the back lane."

Uncle Richard interjected, "Great idea, we could all…"

"No, Dad," Jade objected. "We'll all go later. Right now, I'd like to visit just with Renée. Besides, if there's any wildlife out there, the noise of a crowd would scare it away."

"Okay, but know that I'm disappointed," he teased.

Grandma added, "Besides, I can't walk that far on this ankle. I don't want everyone to desert me already. Renée and Jade, make sure you have time for a game of crokinole later."

"Of course, Grandma," Jade and I said in unison.

We gave her another big hug, put on our shoes and jackets and left.

We were barely out the door, when Jade said, "Okay, what's the mystery I can help you with? At least, I hope I can help you."

I looked over at my beautiful Chinese cousin. She's almost the same colour as Harrar, I thought. She could be Sri Lankan like him. She's never looked like my idea of Chinese. Stereotypes are such funny things. I wonder if I fit her stereotype of white; probably not. Now Susie would, with her white, white skin and red gold curls.

"I can share this with you," I said, "because you don't live here, so it won't matter."

Jade frowned. "Before you start," she said, "Next year, I'm coming back to Canada for university. I'm hoping to be in Ontario, so I won't be far away and safe with your secret. Do you still want to tell me?"

I thought about that for a moment. "Yes, I trust you, Jade. I've always trusted you. Besides, you're not a talker. You can control your tongue, and I need your help. I have to talk with someone."

"Okay, what is it?"

"I have a friend. He's Sri Lankan, tall and handsome, and lots of fun and he's Muslim."

"Ooooh, sounds yummy. Are you in love?"

"No, it's not like that. He's a good friend, and he'll always be a good friend."

"Why, because he's Muslim and you're Christian?"

"No, that's not it either. Last week, Harrar told me he's gay. And he's terrified. He's afraid someone will find out. He's afraid of his parents' response. He loves them dearly."

Jade nodded.

"And he's afraid of Mustafa , another one of my classmates. Our church and town are sponsoring Mustafa's family. They're Syrian refugees. As Harrar says, 'Everyone expects Mustafa and me to be friends, since we're both Muslim.' Harrar thinks Mustafa will condemn him for being gay."

We walked down the lane past the old climbing tree of our childhood. I looked up into its spreading branches. Bright reds, yellows, and golds glistened in the afternoon sun.

"I'm worried about Harrar, Jade. I know very little about the Muslim faith or about how the world deals with gay people. I do know there are people in Catalpa Creek who would shun Harrar or maybe even harm him, if they thought they could get away with it. People latch onto the weirdest ideas. Right now, there are a few in town who are sure Mustafa and his family are terrorists in disguise. Harrar is my friend. I want to help him." I reached up and pulled on my ponytail to tighten it. "He's naturally quiet, but lately, he's been…totally absent. I don't know how to explain it. I'm worried about him."

"Wow!" Jade responded. "This is serious stuff."

We stopped walking. I wanted to focus on our conversation. "Your boyfriend is Muslim. You must have met scads of people who are Muslim. How do they treat gay people? What would be the best way to help Harrar?"

"Renée, I don't know the answer to your question. Yes, Rami is Muslim, but we don't spend our time talking about his faith. I haven't thought much about homosexuality either. I don't know anyone who is gay. Me and my friends at the international school are really too busy just trying to survive the homework load and relationship problems to worry about who's gay or whatever."

Disappointed, I started walking again. I kept my eyes on the pathway, staring at the ruts and ridges. "I just want to help my friend. He's hardworking, smart, a wonderful artist and good fun. He sounded so sad and lonely, almost desperate when we talked. There are things I don't tell Dad, but I can't imagine being afraid that Dad would find out who I really was and automatically throw me away."

Jade put her arm around my shoulders. "I'm sorry Renée. I don't really know anything about the Muslim faith. I could ask Rami when I get home."

We stepped around a big pothole in the track as Jade continued. "I do know that you can't fix Harrar, no matter how much you want to."

I shook my head. "I don't want to fix him. He's the way God made him, and he's great that way. Mind you, I wish he weren't gay, but that's not my problem. He's afraid, terrified. I don't want him to be afraid. I want to help him with his fear."

Jade shrugged. "Last summer, when my friend Hailey was so badly hurt in that three wheeler accident, I was angry that the accident happened. Why wasn't she more careful? She looked so sad lying there in that hospital bed. The doctors said it would take months of therapy for her to walk again. I was afraid she'd give up. I wanted to give her courage somehow. I wanted to…help her. My stomach hurt every time I thought about her. I talked with Grandma Grenville. She listened and then she said, 'Sometimes, all we can do is love people through their pain.' Maybe, tell Harrar that you'll be his friend no matter what."

I kicked a stone hard. It flew up ahead of us. "I've already done that."

Jade squeezed my shoulders. "Grandma offered to pray for Hailey. I wasn't sure that would help, but that's what Grandma does. You know that my parents don't practice any faith. I'm not sure why, since Grandma does. You're Christian like Grandma. Maybe you can pray for Harrar and his family."

I looked up at Jade and smiled. "Of course, I can pray. I can put Harrar in God's hands. I know from experience God won't fix everything for Harrar, but prayer does help. God helps. Thanks for the reminder, Jade."

We hugged.

"It's helped to talk to you," I said. "I'm so glad you came home right now.

"Me, too."

We started walking again. "Let's talk about something else. Tell me about your school."

"Sure. I've got pictures." She pulled out her phone. "Just a sec."

I looked up ahead. Something moved at the side of the laneway. As I stared, a moose stepped out of the woods and stopped. He stood like a statue in the middle of the laneway and stared straight at us. "Stop," I whispered to Jade, and grabbed her arm.

The moose stared for just a few more seconds, then turned and walked on across the lane and off into the woods, his strides and stature majestic, kingly.

"I got him," Jade said. She flung her arms in the air. "He's on my cell phone. Let's go back and tell the rest."

We ran all the way back to the house. As I ran, I thought, Jade's great. I'm glad she's my cousin. The moose captivated everyone's envy, and of course concern for our safety from Grandma Grenville.

The rest of the cousins arrived Saturday. What a crazy day. We were twenty-five gathered round the table for Thanksgiving dinner. Grandma lit two votive candles—one for Grandpa and one for Mom before she asked us all to join hands for the blessing. Silently, I thanked Grandma for including Mom and Grandpa. I looked from face to shining face. Regardless of what was happening in their individual lives, at that moment everyone of us shared in the joy and love of family.

We kids did all the clean up while the "grown-ups" yakked in the living room. Laughter, foolishness, love abounded in that kitchen. It wasn't work, it was fun.

After a family crokinole tournament, which Grandma easily won, we cousins trekked off to our sleeping bags in the rec room. Eight bodies, end to end on the floor, meant lots of talk and silliness. Last to fall asleep, I surveyed the group—some stretched out flat snoring, some curled into a ball, everyone different and yet the same. I thought about the Ahmadis and Harrar, a whole world away from all their extended family. My last thought before sleep: we are truly blessed to live in safety.

When we left Grandma's on Monday, I gave Jade an extra long hug. "Email me… Let's actually write to each other. I want to know what's happening in your life."

"Maybe we'll end up at the same university. Wouldn't that be great?"

"Yup. Thanks again for your wisdom," I said.

"Come on, Jade," Aunt Nancy called from the car. "We have a plane to catch."

"As always," Jade said to me. She answered her mom, "Coming."

Chapter Twelve

Woman Trouble

Saturday, October 14

Steve

Our Thanksgiving weekend away left me behind at work. At Tuesday night badminton, Lee Ann and I trounced Eleanor and Tony. I've improved my game over the last two years. In fact, I'm almost as good as Lee Ann. Janice Lawson played at the far end of the gym. We didn't hear much laughter coming from her area.

I spent Wednesday and Thursday evenings helping the Ahmadis fill out government forms using Google translate and my high school French.

"I do," he kept saying, as he lifted the pen from my fingers.

But he would get bogged down trying to understand the questions and turn back to me frustrated. I tried to remember to let him work on each question first. Thursday afternoon, I picked up a French copy of the forms. When I handed them to him on Thursday evening, his face relaxed. "Thank you," he said and sat right down to start. The process went much faster. He still struggled with some questions. I explained that many Canadians needed help with government forms. Once finished, Kahlil clapped his hands. "Done," he said, his smile reflecting his delight.

I grinned at him, happy to share his relief.

The rest of the week flew by. Renée and I were reduced to a few sentences at breakfast and on the way to school. I knew she wanted more, but I'm only one person doing my best. By Friday night, I was exhausted. Still, I would have spent time with her. Problem was, she had planned a movie with her friends and a sleepover at Susie's.

Saturday morning, I slept in. Once up and dressed I decided to try the buffet brunch at the new restaurant by the creek. Who can I call for company? Lee Ann will have had her breakfast hours ago. I'll call Janice Lawson. She lives in town and is so willing. Maybe it will placate Renée. She keeps telling me I need to date someone other than Lee Ann. I'll explain to Lee Ann tonight. She'll understand.

Janice answered on the first ring.

"Well, hi Steve," she said.

Just three words and already I knew I'd made a mistake. Still, I soldiered on. "Hi, Janice. Have you eaten as yet? I'm going out for brunch at Donatelli's by the creek. Want to come?"

I heard her draw in her breath. "Certainly, Steve," she said, satisfaction dripping from her tone.

"Okay, see you there in half an hour," I said. "Bye." My forehead was wet with sweat. What is it about that women that makes me so anxious? Oh well, it's a public place. I'm probably just borrowing trouble. I slipped my phone into my shirt pocket.

When I returned home at three o'clock, I slammed the door. That felt good. Women, I'll never understand them. Think I'll tell Renée about brunch. It might help her accept Lee Ann. If nothing else, maybe she will laugh.

"Renée," I shouted up the stairs. "You working up there?"

"Yeah."

"Want a cup of tea?"

"Sure."

By the time I had the kettle on, Renée had come downstairs. "What's up?" she said. "You slammed the door mighty hard when you came in."

"Women!"

"Want to tell me about it?"

"I'm not sure you want to hear."

"Is it about Ms Hamilton?"

"NO!"

"So tell me."

"Like I said, it's about a woman."

"Your tone of voice tells me I don't have to worry about this woman."

"For sure." I felt us both relax. "It's actually rather funny now that I think about it. I met Janice Lawson for lunch at Donatelli's."

"Not smart," Renée said.

"Don't look so smug. I went early so I was already settled in a booth expecting her to sit across from me. When she came in, she marched right over and slid in beside me. Right beside me."

Renée wrinkled her nose. "You left yourself open for that."

"Anyway, Eleanor came in with several friends. She took one look at me and said, 'Why don't you two join us at this nice big table? It's always more fun when we're a bunch.' Good old Eleanor. I almost had to shove Janice out of the booth to get her to move." By this time in my story, we were both laughing. "Guess I'm pretty naive, eh, Renée? Janice sure helps me appreciate Lee Ann."

I watched Renée's laughter disappear. Stupid comment. When will I learn? Enough of that. Better move on. "Let's talk about your project." That sullen look had settled onto her face. She didn't answer. What do I do now? My phone rescued me. I pulled it out of my pocket and swiped. Eunice Logan's name appeared. "Hi Eunice, what's up."

"Would you and Renée like to come for supper? I'd like some company tonight."

"I'm already out this evening. Just a minute and I'll see what Renée's doing." I turned to my unhappy daughter and said, "Eunice is inviting us for supper. I can't make it. Would you like to go?" I watched her visibly bury her anger. She reached for my phone.

"Hi, Mrs. Logan," she said. "Supper? Sure. What time? Shepherd's pie's my favourite. Thanks. See ya at six."

She clicked off and handed the phone back. Her sullenness returned. "Where are you going tonight?"

Great, I thought. This will just be fuel for the fire. Better to plunge in headfirst. Besides there's only the truth. "I'm having dinner at Lee Ann's."

With her eyes flashing daggers, Renée said, "Well, at least she's an improvement on Janice."

Renée

Just before six, I switched off the computer and piled up the books. Time to go. I picked up Ebony. "You might as well come, too, and have a visit with your sister, Shadow. I'm sure you don't want to be here alone." I carried him downstairs and stopped at Dad's study. "Ebony and I are going to Mrs. Logan's now. What time do you plan on coming home tonight?"

He ignored the ice in my voice and said, "No later than 1:00 a.m.You don't have to wait up for me."

"Thank you." I turned away. Mom's voice in my head said, "Easy Renée. Just let it go."

I pulled on my old jacket that hung by the back door and ran through the rain to Mrs. Logan's house on the other side of the hedge.

As usual, I knocked and walked in. With her hearing loss, I didn't expect her to hear my knock.

"Shadow and I are in the kitchen, Hon," she called. "I saw you coming through the window."

I slipped off my shoes, hung my jacket in the hall closet, pasted a smile on my face and walked through to her kitchen. Ebony wiggled out of my arms and dropped to on the floor beside Shadow. "Okay, you two. Have a grand time together," I said, as I watched Mrs. Logan pull a steaming shepherd's pie out of the oven. "Smells good."

"I hope it'll taste good, too," she said, as she placed it on the waiting pie cradle. She untied her flowered apron, gave me a hug and carried the pie to the dining room table. "I thought we'd eat in here. I love using my pretty things. Sometimes, I get them out when I'm here by myself."

I looked at the dishes. "These are very old… I mean these are beautiful antiques. What a delicate pattern. What do you call it?"

"Royal Albert."

"I'll be careful with it."

"Don't worry about it. Cliff and I bought these to use for Sunday dinner and any other special occasion." She pointed to a crystal dish full of layers of whipped cream, strawberries, and other yummy stuff.trifle. "Now this is old. My grandmother used to serve trifle in it when I was a little girl. I remember her telling me that it was a wedding gift to her grandmother. It holds a lot so I hope you're hungry."

I felt my body relax as she talked. I love Mrs. Logan.

"Let's have a little dish of trifle, as an appetizer," she said. "I've always wanted to eat dessert first."

"Sure, why not?"

Her eyes twinkled like two blue stars as she picked up the crystal fruit bowls and put a healthy helping in each one. "Your dad is missing out," she said. "You know, I'm kind of glad he's not here. It means I can concentrate on you."

"I'm kinda glad too. I've some stuff I need to talk over with you."

"That sounds ominous."

"Well, it's serious stuff, and I need some advice, or at least a sounding board. It always helps to talk with you."

"Thanks, Renée. That's a wonderful compliment. Would you like to give thanks for our supper?"

"Sure, that will be easy, because I am grateful." We joined hands and bowed our heads. "Thank you, God, for Mrs. Logan. She's a good friend and neighbour. Thank you for this trifle and the shepherd's pie and whatever else we're eating tonight. Thank you that we're having dessert first, that we don't always have to do everything exactly right. Amen"

"The trifle is wonderful," I said between mouthfuls. "I'm glad we're eating in the dining room. When I was little, as a special treat, Mom used to do this kind of thing at lunchtime. She'd set it all up in the dining room with the good dishes. We even had our milk in wine glasses. But she never let me eat dessert first. This is new and very special."

"Since she's with us in Spirit, do you think she approves?"

"Yes. If she'd thought of it, I'm sure she'd have done it, too."

During supper we talked of Mrs. Logan's work at the women's shelter. Her face glowed as she described teaching the residents how to make pastry.

"My Sunday morning Bible study is a great hit, too" she said, "even if it does make me late for church."

I grinned. "It's a great reason for being late."

The meal finished, she said, "Let's just stack the dishes on the counter. I've lots of time to do them tomorrow. Come and sit here on the couch and tell me what's bothering you."

Our cats appeared as soon as we sat down. They jumped up on the couch between us and settled down together, their bodies entwined.

"These two certainly understand the togetherness of family," she said.

I took a deep breath. "Think I'll start with Dad. He's becoming more than friends with Ms. Hamilton. Don't get me wrong, I like her, but I don't want him to get serious, not yet. She's the only woman he's dated since Mom died. Well, almost." I laughed.

"What's so funny?"

"Oh, Mrs. Logan, I wish we both could have been flies on the wall at Donatelli's today." I told her about Dad's adventure with Janice Lawson.

Mrs. Logan chuckled. "Great story and good affirmation of your dad's ability to figure out stuff. He's really a wonderful man."

Needing a moment, I reached up and rewound the elastic in my ponytail. "Okay," I said, "It's just…I'm worried about Dad. He's vulnerable right now. I've done some reading on men and grief and love. Men are much more likely to get serious again right away. They don't always make good choices. Besides, there's so many more women than men in his age range. Maybe it would be good for him to try out a few."

She smiled, "Sort of like window shopping or maybe, fishing? Do you want him to keep catching nice women and throwing them back?"

A picture of Dad, fishing rod in hand danced before my eyes. I felt my tenseness lessen. "Well, no."

"Are you sure you're not just worried about him replacing your mom?"

I nodded. I could feel tears flood my eyes.

Mrs. Logan patted my hand. She looked right into my eyes and said, "Renée, when the time comes for your dad to forge a new relationship with another woman, she'll be his wife, but not your mother. I'd like her to be your friend, and for the two of you to have a loving relationship, but she won't be your mother. She can't be Serena."

I wiped my eyes. "Thank you, Mrs. Logan, I needed to hear that."

We just sat there. There was nothing more to say.

The grandfather clock chimed the hour.

We both sighed.

Mrs. Logan patted my hand again. "Now, is there anything else you need to talk about?"

"I don't think so. Oh, I sort of gave Dad a curfew."

Mrs. Logan laughed again, "Renée, you're neat. What did he say?"

"He told me I didn't have to wait up for him. I asked when he'd be home. He answered 1:00 a.m. at the latest."

"Your dad loves you very much. Never forget that. Now if our serious work is done, would you like to play a game of crib or crokinole?"

"Crokinole? You have a crokinole board? Grandma Grenville has one. She loves to play it with us. Yes, I'd like to play."

"Are you sure? I used to be pretty good. I was the Senior Women's Champion a few years ago."

Steve

I waited until Renée had left before getting ready for my own dinner date with Lee Ann. As I drove to her house, I thought, for two years, we've seen each other every Tuesday night at badminton. We've enjoyed a few movie dates. I want this to be more than just friendship. Why isn't it happening?

Headlights on high beam came round a corner fast. Felt like they were coming directly at me. I took my foot off the gas as I turned the wheel to put my car on the shoulder. At the last moment, the oncoming car swerved to the right missing me by inches.

I stopped on the gravel, my heart pounding, my hands shaking. "What was that?" I said out loud. I punched in 911. When the operator answered, I gave my name and told her what had happened. She took my location. I had been blinded by the headlights. Disappointed with the lack of identifying information, she promised to alert the police officers in my area. I touched "End," pocketed my phone and pulled back onto the road. Not a good beginning to the evening.

By the time I turned into Lee Ann's, I had begun to relax. She lives in a very secluded area, I thought, as I drove through the dark tunnel created by the trees that lined her driveway. I hope that idiot in the car wasn't coming from here.

I pulled up in front of Lee Ann's garage. My heart raced. Get a grip Steve, I told myself.

At the front step, Pachelbel's *Canon in D* wafted on the air. I listened for a moment. Lee Ann opened the door before I could ring the bell.

"You may come in," she said, a smile dimpling in her cheek.

"I was enjoying Pachelbel. Guess I got lost in the music."

Her eyes glowed. I tried a hug as a greeting. When I opened my arms, she slid into them as if she belonged there. Her silky green shirt felt smooth to my fingers, her body soft and pliable as she leaned into me.

Much too quickly, she stepped back. "Supper's ready and waiting." She took my jacket. As I slipped out of my shoes, she asked, "Would you like a glass of wine before dinner?"

"Right…yes," I said, as I drew in a deep breath. She started down the hall—heels, legs, shirt rippling over those hips, swaying like tall grass in a soft breeze… I slapped my forehead with my palm. The flowers, I thought. "With you in a minute. Left something in the car."

Back inside, I handed her the flowers hidden in their wrapping.

"Oh…lovely…Thank you."

"Serena trained me to bring a hostess gift…" I clamped my mouth shut for a few seconds. "I'm sorry," I said. "That just came out."

"It's okay, Steve," Lee Ann said. "Come to the kitchen and talk to me while I put these in water."

She's so gracious, I thought, and … keep a lid on it, Steve. I followed her to the kitchen. She ripped open the package. "Fuschia! They're gorgeous."

"I asked the florist for Fireweed. I remembered seeing that painting of fireweed in your office. The florist didn't have any, of course. I looked around. These were the same colour and looked a little the same."

"How sweet, Steve. You are very romantic for a man…" It was her turn to blush. "Now I've put my foot in it. Let me begin again. Steve, I'm touched. Thank you."

She set the flowers on the counter and reached out to give me a hug. She lifted her lips to mine. Yes, I thought. I've missed this so much.

Suddenly, she jerked, as if someone had hit her. She pulled away. "Sorry, Steve," she said, "I'm not good at this."

I let my arms fall to my sides. We both stared at the flowers. A vase, I thought, and raised my eyes to scan the kitchen. A row of them lined the top of the cupboards. "Let me get one of those vases for you. I'm a little taller. Which one?"

She pointed to the tall, green vase at the end of the row. I handed it to her and watched her trim and arrange the flowers, greenery and baby's breath. When finished, the arrangement was beautiful. "You're good at that."

"Thanks," she replied. "As a kid, I worked in a florist shop. You bring the wine and I'll carry the flowers. Let's sit and sip in front of the fire for a few minutes before we eat."

We sat together on the couch although our bodies weren't actually touching. We clinked glasses and I said, "To us and friendship." We watched the fire.

"I owe you an explanation for what happened in the kitchen. Can it wait 'til after dinner?" she said.

"It can wait for as long as you need it to wait. This isn't easy for either of us."

"Thank you."

There didn't seem to be anything to say, so I kept quiet. I remembered my mother telling me, "There are times, Steve, when words are unnecessary. When you find someone you can just be with, enjoy it and keep quiet." This was one of those times.

The music shifted from classical strings to *Unchained Melody*. "Time to eat," Lee Ann said. "Come. Help me bring in the food."

The meal was superb. "You're beautiful and you're an excellent cook. Believe me, I've come to appreciate good cooks over the last two years. I'm slowly becoming good at soup. That's a start." We kept our conversation light. With Jade's picture on my phone to illustrate, I told her Renée's story about seeing the moose. That led to my giving her a description of my childhood on the farm.

Lee Ann talked about her kids. They were all home for Thanksgiving. They helped her get the property ready for winter. "The kids insisted on putting up the outside Christmas lights. Now, all I need to do is plug them in when it's closer to Christmas. I told them no one will see them back here but they argued. 'They're on a timer. They'll greet you every night when you come home from school. Surely, you'll do some entertaining.

You want your friends to enjoy your place, not think it's dark and forbidding.'"

After dinner, we stacked all but the pots and pans in the dishwasher. "I'll do the rest in the morning," she said. "Let's take our coffee into the living room." Once again, we sat together on the couch. This time she settled a little closer, our thighs touching.

"I promised to explain," she said, "I hope you'll still want to spend time with me after you hear my story."

I reached for her hand.

"Here goes. I married my childhood sweetheart when I was 19. He was quarterback of our high school football team, and a star hockey player. In fact, he was good enough to play Junior A."

She shifted her weight so she was leaning against me. Yes! I thought.

"I don't know what happened to Matt. I do know we were too young when we got married. All three of our children were born in the first four years."

I looked up at a picture above the fireplace. Three little children smiled down at us from their formal studio portrait. The oldest looked to be about six.

She sighed and continued. "Matt had to give up hockey. He had to have a job. My parents helped and his, too, but three in four years is a lot. With three wee tots, I needed to be at home with them. Besides, I couldn't make enough teaching to cover the cost of child care." She looked at me as if she expected me to affirm her.

I wanted to. I searched for the right words. Before I could respond, she started talking again.

"Matt was depressed, and I probably was, too. Somebody offered him some 'happy' drugs. That's what he called them. He wanted me to do them, too, but I just couldn't. I couldn't lose control, or I wouldn't be able to care for the kids."

"I can understand that."

"Matt liked his "happy" drugs; they made his life brighter, well, at least while they were coursing through his system. Problem was they left him flat, down—depressed even more. Very quickly, his free supply dried up. 'You have to pay,' his so-called friend demanded.'" She drew in a breath.

If you're gonna play you gotta pay, I thought.

"If I had known what I know now, I think we might have gone to the police for help, or at least told our parents. Instead, we limped along. Matt spent most of his pay on drugs. I didn't know he was also selling. Addiction drove him hard. He lost his job. When the high wore off, he was angry, angry at the kids, angry with me, angry at the world. Everything became my fault."

She shifted again, leaving several inches between us and pulling her hand away.

Wanting to comfort her, I said, "You don't…"

She interrupted. "I need to tell you this, all of it." Staring down at her feet, she started up again. "You have to understand. I was crazy in love with Matt. When he was high, he was fun and loving. But it never lasted. One night he totally lost it. I don't know what had happened, except he had no 'happy' drugs. He screamed and yelled. He called me horrible names."

By this time, tears were pouring down her cheeks. I reached out to hug her, but she pushed my arms away.

"The baby, John, he was only two, woke up and began to cry. 'Shut that kid up,' Matt demanded."

He didn't hurt the baby, I thought, horrified.

"I rushed to the crib and picked up my beautiful little one. Matt followed me to the bedroom. I found John's soother and settled him. Matt watched. He had a strange smile on his face. Carefully, I tucked John back into his crib and beckoned to Matt to follow me from the room. Afterwards, I gave thanks to God that he did. We went to the kitchen. 'I'll make you a cup of coffee,' I said. For some reason that set him off. 'Coffee? You think coffee will fix this. I don't want coffee. I want…you, you'll have to do.' He grabbed my arm…"

I knew what was coming. Her sobs were uncontrolled. Fear radiated from her being. I didn't want to hear this. I wanted her to stop. Desperately, I wanted her to stop. I reached out to her.

"Don't touch me," she said, her voice a whisper.

I knew she had returned to that awful moment.

"He ranted and raved. He slammed me against the wall. I heard my arm crack. He grabbed the butcher knife from its block beside the fridge. I screamed, 'Matt, don't do this, please, don't do this.'"

"Oh, my God," I gasped.

"Something touched a chord of sanity in his being. He froze, towering over me, staring at his hand as if it belonged to someone else. I lay there, terrified, expecting…His eyes flicked to mine. He turned and slammed that knife deep into the table and stomped out the door. Sobbing, I staggered to the phone. It took all my strength to punch in the police number. By the time the police arrived, my oldest, Andrew, who was just five, had crept out of his bed and come to sit with me. I remember him crying, 'Mommy, Mommy, I love you…'

"I never saw Matt again. He disappeared that night. The police found his body in the river, several days later."

I let out a long deep breath. He's out of his misery, I thought.

"You're the first male friend I've had in over twenty years. I'm afraid, Steve, afraid—terrified of a relationship with a man." She stopped talking and crying and just sat there. She lifted her blotched and swollen face and her eyes found mine. "You're a good man, Steve. My Matt was a good man, too. He was sweet and kind. It was the drugs that turned him into a monster. I'm afraid of a relationship with anyone."

I wanted only to hold her, to tell her she was safe with me. Hell, I don't even take vitamin pills. I dragged myself through Serena's death and all that grief without taking so much as an aspirin. I hate drugs. I knew now wasn't the time for that. Now was the time for silence and prayer. *Help me God. Tell me what to say, what to do.*

I held out my hand to her. That was all. A silent invitation for comfort. She stared at me for a long time. Finally, she reached out and placed hers in mine. I let it lay there. This was her choice. She reached up and touched my cheek. Once again, her tears began to flow.

"Can I have just a hug?" she whispered, "Just a hug…nothing more."

"Oh, yes," I said, as gently I enfolded her into my arms. Time passed. Finally, she stirred.

"Thank you, Steve. Thank you."

I looked into those tear-stained eyes that spoke of so much pain. "You're safe with me, Lee Ann. No matter what, you'll always be safe."

A Beethoven sonata filled the air around us. *Thank you, God*, I prayed silently. *Thank you for Lee Ann. Help me to care for her as she heals, for I know you have begun healing in her. Thank you for the privilege of being here tonight. Lee Ann is your precious child.*

The clock struck midnight. I felt like Cinderella. It was time to go. I knew that Renée would be waiting up for me.

Lee Ann spoke, "I'm exhausted, Steve. That was hard, hard work."

"Yes, it was," I agreed. "And it's time for me to go home. Thank you for dinner. And Lee Ann, thank you for confiding in me. I'm very touched." I got up from the couch. She followed me to the door. I wiped some stray tears from her cheek. “Goodnight,” I said, “I’ll call tomorrow.” She nodded.

When the door closed behind me, I heard the lock click. I thought, that’s an evening I’ll never forget, and I don’t want to either. Whatever happens between Lee Ann and me, tonight I’ve been blessed. Thank you, God.

Chapter Thirteen

New Life Begins

Sunday morning, October 15

Steve

Great sleep last night. Probably my relief that Renée hadn't waited up for me. Eunice must have been helpful. It's already seven-thirty. I stretched, dragged myself out of bed and opened my blackout curtains to the rising sun. Wonder how Lee Ann is today? Maybe she slept too. Maybe telling her story helped. I hope so.

I pulled on track pants and plaid flannel shirt. Feels good to be comfy. Think I'll make pancakes. They're Renée's favourite, and they're easy

I had a healthy stack on the warming tray when Ebony appeared, arching his back and stretching out his long, sleek, black body. "Good morning, my friend. Would you like some breakfast?" He ran over and wrapped himself around my leg.

Renée stepped into the kitchen yawning and sleepy-eyed as I set Ebony's breakfast on the floor.

"Pancakes, my favourite. Thanks."

We consumed three each before conversation began. Renée opened with, "Tell me about our refugee family. How are they doing?

"Think they're fine. Eleanor and Nazira are good friends.

"Friends? Really?

"Yes. They spend nearly every day together, shopping, running errands, practicing Nazira's English. Eleanor says Nazira is a big help at the store. She's taken over the endless job of dusting the stock."

Renée took a big gulp of milk. "They're friends? Eleanor is so wildly outgoing. Nazira's an introvert."

"Maybe that's why they get along. Nazira can just enjoy Eleanor without making a big effort. I know sometimes I'm relieved to have Eleanor around. I can just sit back and relax and let Eleanor carry the conversation. In some ways, she's … restful for me."

Renée's fork, loaded with pancake, paused on its journey to her mouth. "Well, I never would have thought of Eleanor, with her wild clothes and giant personality, as restful."

As I tipped my mug for another swallow of coffee, the kitchen clock came into view. "It's already 9:30. We better get moving or we'll miss church."

"Can't miss this morning. Susie and I are talking with Reverend Linda during coffee hour about helping with Children's Time. Let's leave this mess till later."

"Gladly."

"Susie's coming over after lunch. Are you available to read some more of Nana's diary this afternoon?"

"Think so. Just a minute." I brought my calendar up on my phone. "All clear."

We left our plates in the sink. At 9:58, we slipped into a pew with Susie and her parents. Right behind us was the Ahmadi family. Surprised, I turned around to welcome them, just as the choir started down the aisle singing "Joyful, Joyful, We Adore Thee." Khalil gripped my hand in friendship. Nazira smiled. All three kids were so busy staring at the choir they didn't even see me. Reverend Linda started the announcements with a welcome to the Ahmadis. She invited Khalil to come forward. He smiled and strode up to the pulpit looking confident.

In stilted English, he said, "Thank you…We grateful. In Qur'an, Jesus good prophet, teacher. Mohammed, peace be upon him, our great prophet. Mohammed teach us to live in peace, to care for poor, to love." Kahlil stopped and looked to Reverend Linda for direction.

She nodded. "Thank you," she said. "We are pleased you have joined us this morning. She shook his hand again and then motioned for him to return to his seat.

Kahlil smiled and sat back down with his family.

I looked around the sanctuary. Almost everyone was smiling. Sponsoring the Ahmadis is good for our congregation, I thought. Now if we can just control the dissenters.

On the way home from church, we met Tom Long at the grocery store where we stopped for milk. "Hey, Detective Long, you on duty?" Renée asked.

Tom took the teasing with ease. "Any copper who can't get personal business done on company time, just isn't organized."

"Have you had any leads about our Catalpa Creek bank robber?" I asked.

"Possibly. There was another robbery yesterday just down the highway in Rodman. Same M.O. Disappeared into thin air again. There'll be more details in paper, Monday.

"Another one?" Renée responded.

Tom shrugged. "Same game, different rink."

I changed the topic. "The Ahmadis came to our church this morning to thank us and to check us out. They were well received. Have you heard of any more possible trouble brewing?"

"No, but that doesn't mean it's not happening. It could have just gone underground. Being out in the open wasn't successful, but often people who are motivated by fear or hatred aren't that easily deterred. We're keeping our eyes and ears open. If you hear of anything, either of you, let us know right away."

"We will."

"How was your Thanksgiving trip?" Tom asked.

"Great," Renée answered immediately. "My cousin was here from South Africa. She and I went for a walk and surprised a moose on the path to the beaver pond. I've got a picture on my phone."

"You took a picture?"

"Not me. Jade. She's used to seeing all kinds of wild animals: lions, elephants, hyenas, you name it. She was calm, cool and collected."

Renée found the picture and showed it to Tom.

"Looks like you two were too close for comfort," Tom said.

"Yes, I don't need to do that again."

"Good. How's your mom, Steve?"

"Same as ever. She had fallen two weeks before and sprained her ankle, but it didn't slow her down any." I glanced at my watch. "We'd better get going, Renée. We've got to be home by 1:00. Besides my stomach's growling. I don't know what it is about church, but I always come home hungry."

Renée raised an eyebrow. "What about the three brownies you consumed at coffee hour?"

"All sugar. That disappears in minutes."

"I need to get my stuff and get home, too," Tom said.

We paid for our milk and left.

"I like Detective Long," Renée said as we climbed into the car. "I'm glad he's paired up with Eleanor."

"Yes, they both need a companion," I said, trying hard to keep a straight face.

"Okay, Dad, I get your point."

Susie arrived shortly after one carrying a cookie can filled with brownies.

"Leftovers from church this morning," she announced. "That's the advantage of being on coffee duty."

I grinned and scooped a couple, ignoring Renée's frown.

Our Serena candles waited on the breakfast nook table. Tea made, and brownies set out on a plate, we sat down, turned on the candles and prayed.

I picked up Nana's diary and turned to October 7th.

October 7, 1903

Dear Diary, Our trunks were on deck this morning. Matrin told us to undress, wash and put on a clean one from our trunk. Some of the older girls made a circle around us so the sailors cud not see us. The water was cold. My teeth are still chattering. I'm glad we're nearly there.

I like my new dress and coat. There are lots of clothes in my trunk. They are plain, but they're clean, and they're mine. We had to leave our trunks on the deck.

We landed today at a place called Kebec. They speek different. Tilly says its French. They made us undress again. Tilly said they were checking to see if we were helthy and strong. If not they wud send us back. A man in a white coat, called a medical inspector, rolled back our eyelids. The nurse said he checked for trakoma - whatever that is. It was mighty painful. Tilly and I passed it all. They stamped our Barnardos cards. A strange old man signed a paper and gave it to me. He said I was now officially admitted to Canada. The matrin in charge of us told me that this paper was very important. I folded it and slid it into the ripped lining of you diary. It will be safe there.

"Whoa, stop," Susie said. "Let's look for the form."

Renée took the diary and carefully examined both front and back covers. "Just a minute," she said, "I think I found it. I'll get a table knife so I can slide it out. We don't want to crack the binding on the book."

It took some careful jiggling but eventually Renée eased a yellowed paper from behind the leather. "There's another one in here."

"Don't take it out yet," Susie said. "Let's wait till your Nana mentions it. Let's keep it a mystery at least for a bit."

I said nothing. After all, who is to say that this is the landing document. Maybe the other one is.

Renée eased open the fragile document. The print was still quite clear. I guess being tucked into the lining had kept the sunlight from fading it.

The Dominion of Canada
Admission Form

October 7, 1903

"I do solemnly declare that the 200 children named in the following are brought out to Canada for the purpose of settling therein, that they have not been inmates of workhouses, and that they have passed a satisfactory medical inspection at the point of departure; and I make this solemn declaration, conscientiously believing it to be true and knowing that it is of the same force and effect as if made under oath and by virtue of the Canada Evidence Act 1893.

Signed A.B. Owen
Declared before the Justice of the Peace.

"But they were inmates of the workhouse," Susie said.

"Well no, not exactly," Renée said. "They were actually living in Barnardo homes when they left. Whatever! Let's get back to the diary." She picked it up and began reading:

October 8, 1903 Thursday
We got on a train and waited. Train left after dark so we couldn't see out. Long night. Hard to sleep on rattly old train. When the sun came up, I saw only fields, water and trees. Matrin said it was beautiful. To me it looked lonely. Where were the roads, the buildings, the people? I was frightened. The train stopped. Tilly and I watched them carry crate after crate of eggs onto the train. What will they do with all those eggs.

October 9, 1903 Friday
Dear Diary, Last night on the train, we each had two boiled eggs and a slab of bread. First food since we left the ship. The train stopped in a place called, "Port Hope. Tilly said, Maybe this place is a sign we'll find a good home. At Port Hope, the train divided. The cars with the boys went to a city, Matrin called Toronto. Our part of the train went North to Peterboro. For breakfast the porters brot porige in huge tubs. I never seen so much porige in one place. It was still morning when we got to Peterboro. I'm scared.

Susie grinned. “At least Nana’s in Canada. That will help.”

“That’s not guaranteed,” Renée answered. “The Canadians feared that these slum children would contaminate the country. They called them refuse and street Arabs. The labels stuck.”

“It seems to me that things haven’t changed much over the years,” I said and leaned forward. “Today, we’re bringing in refugees, good people like the Ahmadis. Many of our citizens call refugees terrorists or believe they will steal our jobs.” I looked at Renée and Susie, their faces so fresh and innocent.

“We have so much; why can’t we share?” Renée said.

I sighed, “Okay, that’s enough talk. Let’s get back to the diary.” This time I read.

October 11, 1903 Sunday
Dear Diary, When we got off the train in Peterboro, Matrin lined us up and marched us down the street and over a bridge to a big old house with a huge lawn. Tilly pointed out the sign, "Hazelbrae". An extra part has been added to this house for sleeping. Our beds are lined up against the wall, kind of like in the boat but its clean and there's lots of room. There's lots to eat too. My bed is right beside Tilly's. I like it here.

October 17, 1903 Saturday
Dear Diary, I'm being sent to a farm near a village called Turner's Station. I'm frightened. I don't want to leave Tilly. I'll be all alone.

I glanced at Renée. I could feel her distress. I'm not so sure this diary is a good thing for her to be reading. I'm glad we're doing it together.

"Let me read," she said. "It feels easier when I'm reading."

October 19, 1903

Dear Diary, The farmer came for me yesterday. He just grunted when the matrin told him my name. He carried my trunk out to a wagon pulled by horses. Climb in, he ordered. He didn't talk to me. He's old, grumpy and dirty. I don't like him. There are big holes in the road. One bump was so big, I fell backward into the wagon. The farmer laughed and stopped the horses till I had climbed back onto the seat. Better hang on, he said.

I have my own little room up high in the attic. I wish Tilly was here. My trunk is in the corner. It's mine, all mine. It's locked and I have the only key. It has my name on it. They can't take it away from me. It smells like the sea. I'm keeping the key under my mattress.

Supper was good. Plenty of food. I eat in the kitchen by myself. She told me I was to call her Mam and him Farmer John. She said tomorrow I would be helping with cooking and cleaning and gardening. Tonight was an easy night, she said. I only had to do the dishes and wash the kitchen floor. I'm afraid. I miss Tilly.

Renée let the diary drop down onto the table. She drained her tea cup.

Susie's back stiffened. "How could they be so cold?" She shook her head back and forth. "She's just a little kid."

"Nana must have been…so frightened that first night," Renée said. I know she's survived the workhouse but at least Tilly was there."

"Nana doesn't write much, but I imagine lots," Renée said. "Wish I could turn my imagination off."

"Me, too," Susie added.

"Have we had enough for today?" I asked.

"No," Susie said. "It's like a mystery story. We know Nana will survive. If she didn't, Renée wouldn't be sitting here. We just have to get through the tough stuff." Susie looked over at Renée and stopped. "Oh…guess it's different for you, Renée, Nana's family for you."

"It's okay," Renée said, and managed a weak smile. "I'm from a long line of strong women, remember?" She picked up the diary.

October 20, 1903

Dear Diary, I'm tired but not so tired I didn't open my trunk before bed. I wanted to be sure that all my things were still there. They were, everything on the list, down to the last stocking. I put the list of things in your lining, diary.

"Oh good," Susie said, "We're going to get to see the second paper today."

Once again Renée ran her finger along the edge of the diary until she found the opening. She picked up the kitchen knife and slid it under the lining. This much smaller paper slipped out easily.

Barnardo Girls Canadian Outfit

1898

new box	*2 pr. hoses (thick)*
trunk	*2 pr. hoses (thin)*
label	*2 flannelette petticoats*
key	*1 winter petticoat*
stationery	*1 summer petticoat*
brush and comb	*2 coarse aprons*
haberdashery	*2 holland aprons*
handkerchief	*2 muslin aprons*
Bible	
hymn book	
2 stuffed dresses (blk/gold)	*ulster*
2 print dresses	*tam o'shanter*
2 flanelette n'dresses	*hat*
2 cotton n'dresses	*1 pr boots*
garters	*1 pr oxfords*
shoe and boot laces	*1 pr slippers*
toothbrush	*1 pr plimsoles*
8 small towels in a bag	*1 pr gloves*

Courtesy – F. Rightmeyer

"Let's look up some of these things," Susie suggested. "I'm sure haberdashery is hats, gloves, accessories, stuff like that. What's an ulster?"

Renée booted up the laptop. "An ulster is a man's long, loose overcoat made of rough cloth with a belt at the back. I'm guessing both the hat and the coat would be for a child, and probably a little big so the child could grow. Let's hope so."

"Three kinds of aprons—they sure expected the kids to work," Susie said. "At least there are two rather nice ones made of fine muslin. Maybe that's because the Barnardo people expected the girls to be servants in a rich household. And tam o' shanter, look that up Renée. I think it's one of those funny looking flat Scottish hats."

"I think you're right," I said.

"Here's a picture of a tam o' shanter worn by a man wearing a kilt." Renée turned the computer screen a bit so I could see too. "At least she had lots of clothes.

"What about underwear? Where's the underwear?"

"Oh Susie," Renée answered, "must have been an unmentionable or maybe part of haberdashery or …I'm sure they gave them underwear."

I looked at my watch. "Let's stop now," I said. "I have a refugee committee meeting tonight, and we still have to have supper."

Susie frowned, but Renée nodded. "Okay, Dad. I have homework to do and more research. I'd like to find a picture of Hazelbrae. What about you, Susie? Is your homework done?"

Susie slumped in her chair. "No," she said, "I guess I need to work on mine, too."

With that, Renée closed the diary.

They both looked glum. "Reading a true account about someone we know is tough," I said. "It takes energy. I don't feel great either. Let's go for a walk along the creek. Maybe we'll see your duck family, Renée." I looked at my watch. "There's a meat pie in the freezer. We can walk while it cooks. The fresh air will be good for us."

Renée jumped up. "Come on, I'll take my camera. The light this time of day creates wonderful pictures." She took Susie's arm and pulled her up.

"Oh, alright," Susie said, as she dragged herself to her coat and shoes.

I wrapped my arms around both of them. "Okay, my girls, it's the three of us against the world. Are you ready for an adventure? Let's go."

They gave me grudging smiles as we headed out the door.

Chapter Fourteen

Taking Risks

Saturday, October 28

Renée

Saturday morning. It was still dark when I woke up. I checked my clock—seven a.m. No need to get up. I pulled the covers up to my chin, closed my eyes and waited. Nope. Sleep was done. I got up and flipped over my daily calendar. Two weeks had flown by since we had gathered round the table with Nana's diary. I walked to the window and watched as night slipped into dawn.

Thoughts of last night with my friends rolled through my head. It was good even without Harrar. What's going on with him? At school he hardly speaks to me or the rest of the kids. He's quiet but this is ridiculous. A crow screeched as it flew into our catalpa tree. I frowned. Even the birds sound unhappy. The sun began to peek over the horizon. I decided a walk would help.

Dressed in my sweats, baggy hoodie and warm socks, I slipped quietly down the stairs. I wrote the required note, pulled on my hiking boots and my fall jacket that was hanging by the back door. I texted Harrar. *What's going on? I miss you.* My phone in my pocket and camera round my neck I stepped out into the new day.

Look at that fabulous sky. It's on fire. *Click.* I stood and waited, taking a picture every three minutes. The fire spread, then darkened as it melted into the clouds and the flaming sun rose.

Catalpa Creek gurgled along offering sound effects to God's amazing display. The show over, I struck out along the bicycle trail.

As I walked, I opened my mind to Mom. "Hey, Mom, are you there? Is God with you?" A couple of squirrels chattered from a nearby bush. "Are the two of you chattering like those squirrels? What can I do to help Harrar?" I checked my phone. No answering text from him. "If you were here, Mom, you'd know what I needed to do to help him. I miss you." I walked and listened, hoping for an answer from Mom or Harrar.

After a moment, I thought, I can ask him to help me lay out my Nana Sinclair project. He'll know how to make the slides look special. It might help him feel not quite so alone and give us some quiet time together…Thanks, Mom. You, too, God. I knew I could count on both of you. All I need to do is ask and listen.

I was thinking about turning around when down by the creek I spied the big willow tree, among the catalpas. Should I go down there? Why not? He doesn't own this spot. I picked my way through the brush to a big flat boulder. Close enough.

I sensed his presence before I felt his hand touch the middle of my back. I yelped in surprise.

"Just can't stay away, can you…?" Russell stepped around into my view.

"Why didn't you call out to me, or make a noise or something to warn me? Did you want to frighten me?"

"Why were you spying on me?"

"I wasn't spying. I didn't think you were in town."

"It's dangerous for you to come here alone. It could have been the bank robber that just touched you."

His words felt deliberately intended to frighten me. My eyes filled with tears. Dear God, help. I took a deep breath and focused on his face. Russell's eyes are blue like Dad's. Actually, when he stands up straight, he's built a lot like Dad. "You're not wearing a coat. Aren't you cold?"

This time, Russell laughed. "Are you worried about me?" He unzipped a few inches of his coveralls. "This suit is fully lined for winter. I'm warm as toast. I was going to make some hot chocolate when I heard your footsteps. Would you like to join me?"

I looked at my watch. "I left Dad a note that I'd be back in an hour. I've already been gone forty-five minutes, so I need to get going."

"Wait while I throw some sand on my fire. I'll walk back with you, at least part of the way. When we get close to town, I'll leave you. After all, the law says I can't come near you."

"Okay."

Back out on the path, I searched for something to say. "Have you plans for college?" He surprised me with his answer. It was so…normal.

"Thinking about being an airplane mechanic. I work after school in a garage close to my Mom's. I've discovered I'm actually pretty good with motors. I thought maybe working on airplanes rather than cars, I might get to travel. What about you?"

This could be one of my friends from school. This isn't the tormented kid from two years ago. "I'm not sure. I'm working on an independent research project at school. I'm totally enjoying that. Historical research is sort of like solving a mystery."

Russell frowned. "A mystery?"

"Well, yes."

"For you, maybe. I'm not sure about all that reading." We walked in silence for a while. "I think it's time I disappeared," Russell said. "Thanks for the company."

He turned back north and started running. I watched him until he disappeared around a corner. I glanced at my watch and groaned. I'm late.

As I jogged toward home, I thought about what I would tell Dad. Think this is one of those adventures I'd better abbreviate.

"Dad, hey Dad!" I shouted as I opened the kitchen door.

"In my study, coming," came his muffled reply.

I hung up my jacket and unlaced my boots. "Sorry, I've been gone so long," I shouted. Dad appeared in the kitchen doorway, coffee in hand.

I lowered my voice. "It's such a beautiful morning, I forgot about the time. You should have seen the sunrise. It was magnificent. The whole sky was on fire. Reds, oranges, yellows of every shade, purples and even blues. I took lots of pictures."

"Good," he said, and dumped the last of his coffee in the sink. "I got your note. Thank you."

"I did some thinking while I walked. I'm going to ask Harrar to help with the artwork on my project. I've found heaps of pictures, and he could help me use them effectively."

"Sounds good," he said. "Speaking of Harrar, are you two becoming an item?"

The look on Dad's face told me he was teasing, but his words gave me a jolt.

"No Dad. You sound like the kids at school. We're friends, just friends and I like it that way. I'll let you know when I'm getting serious about someone."

Dad obviously got the message. He frowned then his face cleared. He smiled. "Okay, okay, I'll do the same."

I grimaced. Dad changed the subject.

"Eleanor called a few moments ago looking for you," Dad said. "She'd like you to do some English-as-a-second-language tutoring. Thuraya has some learning problems. She's struggling with her relationships with the other children as well. What do you think about tutoring her?"

Visions of homework, the Christmas pageant at church and more tore through my head. "She should ask Susie. She's the one who's good with kids."

Dad looked concerned.

"Don't worry, Dad, I'll call Eleanor right now and talk with her. I'll make sure Thuraya has a tutor."

"Okay, I'll leave it with you."

I called Eleanor and said I would talk with both Susie and some of my other friends. Eleanor suggested I speak with Thuraya's teacher, Miss Grainger, on Monday.

Next, I called Susie. Her immediate reaction was "Oh what a wonderful idea. When do we start?" Rachel, reacted the same way when I talked to her.

Over lunch I reported to Dad on my phone calls. Between bites, I added, "Susie and I plan to take in a movie tonight with a few friends. What are you doing?"

"I'm going out. I'm not sure you want the details."

I groaned.

"There'll be four of us. I know about safety in numbers. Tom and Eleanor, Lee Ann and I are going to the movies. We'll probably see you at the theatre, but it won't be the same movie, I'm sure."

"Right. Well…I'll cope."

He took his plate to the sink and poured himself a fresh coffee.

"Think I'll have tea," I said and flipped the button on the kettle.

"One other thing," Dad said as I settled back at the island.

I frowned.

"You'll be away at university next year. I'm thinking you need to get your driver's license. I know you haven't really needed it here in Catalpa Creek, but you will, and now is the best time for lessons. We need to get that organized."

I grit my teeth and shook my head. “Driving…it’s just that…Mom.”

“Renée, you can’t…” Dad stopped mid-sentence “Let me rephrase that. What can I do to help you get past your fear?”

I took a deep breath. “I know it makes no sense. I ride with you, and with the other kids. It’s just that…”

“I’m thinking that we better add driving to your list of topics for Dr. Sampler. Now, we’re only seeing him once a month. We have a long list.”

I’m not sure why, but the mention of the list triggered a crazy vision in my head. “Can’t you just see the two of us, Dad? Marching into Dr. Sampler’s office and handing the little round doctor our long lists that trail down the hall and out the door behind us?

“Oh, yes,” Dad said. We both laughed.

Chapter Fifteen

Trouble Erupts

Saturday Evening, October 28

Steve

Susie, Rachel and Tracey came by early for Renée. They were going shopping before meeting the boys at the theatre. Tom and Eleanor came for me shortly after 7:00. Our movie didn't start until 8:00, but we still had to drive out to pick up Lee Ann.

"I'll get her," I said to the other two as we drove down her laneway. I hopped out of the car, almost before it stopped. When I rang the bell, she answered immediately. "Gorgeous," I said. "That red cape and hat remind me of little red riding hood. I see mischief in your eyes tonight."

She blushed like a young teen. "Thanks, Steve. I'm looking forward to this movie. Did you read the letter to the editor about it?"

"Yes, no better advertisement for a movie than a bad review."

Her door locked, she took my arm and we walked to the car. I opened the rear passenger door with as much flourish as possible. "For the beauty queen," I whispered. She blushed again. I walked round to the other side of the car.

"Hi, Lee Ann," Eleanor greeted her. "Fantastic cape, and you wear it with style."

"Thank you. I didn't think it was cold enough for my parka. Winter's not quite here yet."

"Supposed to have a few flurries tonight," Tom said. "Have you got your snow tires on your car yet?"

"I drop it off at Patterson's on Monday."

"Good girl," Tom responded.

"Wise woman," I said quietly. Lee Ann smiled.

The movie was excellent. It ended at the same time as Renée's. We all walked out together. "Quite a bunch," I said to Renée, and nodded towards the other seven kids.

"Safety in numbers," she responded. Her eyes flicked to Lee Ann, then back at me.

We both heard Rachel say, "Looks like Renée's dad has a permanent girlfriend."

My eyes met Renée's. She frowned and shrugged. Susie stepped into the silence.

"Did you like your movie? I sure enjoyed ours."

"Yes, it was good." I said and turned to Renée, "See you at home. We're going to Lakey's."

"We're going to Jake's, home by 12:00."

The kids wheeled off to the left towards the school.

"The wind's dropped. It's really a beautiful evening," Lee Ann said. "Let's leave the car and walk to Lakey's.

Following behind Eleanor and Tom gave us a few moments of private conversation. Lee Ann asked, "How's Renée doing, Steve? I mean in terms of us."

"She's coping. I think the hardest part is dealing with her friends. Otherwise, she tries to ignore our relationship."

"Speaking of our relationship, would you like to come for dinner again on Friday?"

"Are you sure?"

"Yes, I'd like to try again."

"Me, too."

The music of Tom's cell phone and the scream of a siren, interrupted our conversation. Tom pulled his phone from his pocket and barked, "Detective Long here." He listened, nodded, and said, "I'm on it." As he pocketed his phone, he looked directly at Eleanor.

"Sorry. Emergency. Gotta go. I'll call when I'm finished if it's not too late." He turned and walked swiftly back towards his car. In less than two minutes, his car streaked by us.

Eleanor climbed up onto the bench in front of Lakey's window. "Looks like he's stopping on the other side of the river, near the Glen Forest Apartments. Oh, I hope it's not trouble at the Ahmadis'."

"I hope not," Lee Ann added.

"Let's walk over and check with them, just to make sure they're all right," Eleanor suggested. "It's not that far."

"I'll call first. If it's not their place, we're better to stay out of the way," I said. "No answer. I'm game to check it out. We can call a cab to take us home after. Lee Ann, I'll drive you from my place." We started walking. "I'd better call Renée and let her know what I'm doing."

We had very little conversation as we hurried down the street. By the time we reached the bridge, we could see two police cars and a fire truck in front of the Ahmadis' building.

"They don't need this, whatever it is," Lee Ann said.

There were lots of people gathered out front when we arrived. The Ahmadis were in a cluster, talking with Tom.

"Oh dear," Eleanor said, "They have no peace, even here."

"What happened?" I asked Bob Handel, who was standing next to the police tape.

"We're not sure, yet," the mayor responded.

Richard Wallace, who was standing next to the mayor, butted in. "See, I told you. These people are trouble."

"Settle down, Richard," the mayor commanded. "Thought you'd changed your tune about the Ahmadis."

Richard grimaced but said nothing.

A few moments later, Don Lakey joined us. "Heard someone threw a fire bomb through the living room window. Drapes and sofa were burning when Khalil woke up. He called 911. Firemen were here in minutes. Most of the damage is in the living room."

"Who would do that?" Eleanor interrupted.

Don replied, "Someone said they saw some guy dressed like a clown lurking around the building.

"A clown," Eleanor interrupted again.

"Yeah, he was small and round and his face was painted white."

At that point, Tom walked away from the Ahmadis. Eleanor was at their side almost immediately. Nazira and Thuraya both reached out for a hug. We joined them. All but Mustafa had tears streaming down their faces. He just looked grim.

"The terror has followed us," Khalil said.

"This is not part of a terrorist network," I said. I put a hand on his shoulder. He was shaking. "This will be a bigoted soul from right here in Catalpa Creek. Someone who doesn't understand and is living in fear themselves. The police will find him or her."

Eleanor added, "You can stay with me tonight. I have room. We'll ask Tom if you can get in to your apartment for the things you'll need."

Nazira reached out for another hug from Eleanor.

"You're going to be okay. You're not alone here, my friend," Eleanor said, as she drew her close.

I called Renée again to let her know what was happening.

It was nearly two a.m. before the Ahmadis were ready to leave. The police drove them all to Eleanor's place. Lee Ann and I called a cab to my house where we transferred to my car.

As I drove towards her place, Lee Ann reached out and placed her hand on my arm. "Thank you, Steve for caring enough to be on the refugee committee. Most of all, thank you for being you."

I smiled and patted her hand. We rode in silence. At the house, I hopped out to open her car door. Before going inside, she turned and reached out for a hug. I folded her supple body into my arms. She tilted her head to look into my eyes, her lips parted, ready. "Are you sure?" I asked.

She smiled and nodded.

One kiss, that's all we had before she let her arms slip down from around my neck. Her eyes were shining with tears. Gently she pushed away. "Thank you for being safe, Steve." She glanced back as she stepped inside and closed the door. I heard the lock click into place.

When I reached the car, I realized I was still holding my breath. Relax, Steve. You can take a cold shower when you get home. I started the car. Think about someone else, I told myself. My mind returned to the Ahmadis. No one was hurt, thank God. Glad they're with Eleanor. Better focus on driving. There may be another idiot on the road.

Renée was asleep on the couch when I got home. I touched her arm. She groaned and rolled over but didn't surface. Pulling the afghan from the back of the couch, I covered her. I wrote a note and propped it on the coffee table beside her.

You were sound asleep when I got home. I'll tell you all about everything in the morning. I'm exhausted. Sweet dreams.

Love
Dad

Chapter Fifteen

We Respond

Monday, October 30

Renée

Monday after school, Susie and I walked to Catalpa Creek Elementary School. Susie said, “I hope Thuraya is at school today. Maybe her parents kept her home. Their fear must be over the top.”

“Miss Grainger would have called to cancel. Any ideas about who did it?”

“He’s a jerk, whoever he is. I hope the police get him.... Don’t you think Tracey’s amazing. This morning, we were all wringing our hands, wanting to do something. Thanks to Tracey we’re already in gear and running with her idea.”

“It’s a good thing the Ahmadis have lots of courage. I’m not sure I’d be willing to speak at a high school assembly, especially in another language.”

Susie pulled open the big glass doors at the school. “Helping Thuraya will be fun. I brought along my CD of children’s songs and wrote a poem about Thuraya. I’m hoping those two things will help make it fun for her.”

“Neat idea. You think of everything. Miss Grainger said her room was the second door on the left.” Our running shoes made small *thud*, *thud* sounds as we trudged down the hall. Thuraya was waiting just inside the door of her classroom. She reached out with a hug for both of us and took our hands to lead us to the front seats. Miss. Grainger brought over the ESL materials.

"I thought you might start at this introductory level. It has games to play and exercises to do."

Rachel opened the classroom door. "May I come in, too?"

I introduced Rachel to Miss Grainger and Thuraya.

The three of us had worked with Thuraya for almost three-quarters of an hour when her dad arrived to take her home.

"Thanks you so much," Dr. Ahmadi said.

"We had fun," Susie answered. "Thank you, Miss Grainger, for letting us help."

She smiled. "Will you be back tomorrow?"

"Yes," Rachel and Susie spoke together.

"I'm not sure I can," I said.

"That's fine," Susie said. "I have riding on Wednesdays. As long as there are two of us, we'll have enough for the games."

We said goodbye to Thuraya and Dr. Ahmadi. Rachel walked with us for a couple of blocks.

"I've been thinking about Tracey's assembly," Rachel said. "I think we should invite the whole community."

"Did you tell Tracey that?" I asked.

"No, I just thought of it while we were playing with Thuraya."

"I'll tell my dad. He's on the refugee committee," I said.

Rachel peeled off for her place, and Susie left me at our house. I ran up the sidewalk. The door was unlocked. "Dad, Dad," I called.

As usual, he replied, "In my study."

I bounced in and flopped down on the sofa. "Tracey's organizing this special assembly at school in support of the Ahmadis. She's hoping to show them how much we care and how glad we are they are living here. She's also hoping they will tell the story of their journey. On the way home, Rachel came up with the idea that we should invite the entire community. I'm sure everyone wants to hear their story."

"Whoa, slow down a minute." Dad said as he looked up from his papers.

"Sorry. It's just that it's such a good idea. We're all horrified over what happened Saturday night."

"All?" He frowned.

"Well, everyone I know."

He stood up "Our committee is already planning a storytelling event. You might suggest to Tracey that she call Eleanor and they plan something together. We don't want to overwhelm the Ahmadis."

"Will do." I pulled off my sweater. "There, that's better. We had a great time working with Thuraya today. All three of us were there. We won't all be there every day, but we're going to try to make sure that two of us are. I feel good being able to do something to help."

"Good." He joined me on the couch. "What about Mustafa? How's he doing?"

"Most of the kids try to be nice to him, but it's easy to see that they are getting fed up with his attitude."

"Maybe hearing the family's story will help you kids understand him a little. We all have different ways of coping with stress. Some of us withdraw, and some of us try to take over and get control."

"Well, he's certainly trying to take control…I'm hungry, and I have hours of homework. Can we order in pizza?"

"I'm ahead of you on that." Dad looked at his watch. "The delivery man should be here any moment." On cue the doorbell played its Westminster Chimes. "I'll get the pizza. You set out paper towels and glasses."

After supper, I went upstairs to do homework and call Tracey. Turned out, she'd already talked to Eleanor. They had everything worked out. Tracey would talk with the student council and Ms. Hamilton about the kids' presentation. Eleanor would organize the hall, emcee and guest list. She asked me to talk to Reverend Linda about a presentation or greetings or something from the churches in town. Tom Long had promised a healthy police presence. I called Reverend Linda. She agreed to do her part.

My responsibilities finished, I called Harrar. He answered this time. We talked for nearly half an hour. He made excuses for not being part of the group at lunch time but didn't actually tell me what he had been doing. I asked him to help with the layout for my Nana Sinclair project. He just put me off. I told him about our movie night and invited him along to the next one.

"Sorry, Renée. Don't think so," he said. "I'm working a lot of extra hours right now."

I kept at it him until he gave in. "Okay," he said, sounding defeated. Then added, "I've gotta go now." He clicked off even before I said goodbye.

Oh Harrar, what's going on? Why are you avoiding us? What's changed? I said a quick prayer for him and started on homework.

At 10 p.m. I powered down the computer and switched on Mom's candle. Setting it on the window sill, I settled down on the floor to talk with Mom. "Well Mom, bet you're proud of us kids. This storytelling evening is such a good idea. I sure hope there's no more trouble but…I'm afraid there will be. Wish you were here. I miss talking with you. Dad's doing his best but…he's not you. Oh Mom, why is life so complicated?" I sat cross-legged on the floor and just let my mind roll until my back started to complain. My legs were stiff when I finally shut down the candle and stood up. "Goodnight, Mom." I yawned and called downstairs to Ebony. He came bounding up and wrapped his body around my legs. "Bedtime, my friend."

In fifteen minutes, I'd completed my nightly routine and crawled into bed. I closed my eyes and a vision of a firebomb coming through my window appeared. I shook my head to clear the image.

Don't be silly, I told myself. They're not after us. I tossed and turned, my mind slipping from the Ahmadis to Mustafa to Harrar, to Ms Hamilton. Finally, sleep closed in.

Chapter Sixteen

Joy & Tragedy

Friday, November 3

Renée

I finished my novel for English and slammed it shut. Done. Hurray! I crossed over to the window. It's already dark and it's just five o'clock. My stomach growled. Need a snack. I was at the bottom of the stairs when I heard a car door slam. That'll be Dad. He won't be home long. Another dinner with Lee Ann. No time for me but lots of time for her.

He opened the door into the kitchen as the big garage door rumbled shut. "How's my girl?" he said and reached out for a hug. "Hey, that hug barely happened. What's up?"

"Do I have to lay it out for you?"

He peeled out of his coat and dropped it on the table. "Okay, you're upset about my having dinner with Lee Ann tonight."

I shrugged. "Surprise. Surprise."

"She's my friend and I enjoy her company."

"And you don't enjoy mine."

His frown deepened. "Renée—."

"Leave it. Just leave it."

He reached out towards me. I backed away. "A hug won't fix it, Dad."

He dropped his hands. "I can fix supper for you before I go."

"You don't have time. I'll have a protein shake." His shoulders slumped. He looked pitiful. Trying to smooth things a bit, I said, "How about going for a hike along the creek tomorrow morning, just you and me. We could pack a lunch. I'll get up early.

Dad's face relaxed a little. "Sure, hon, I'd like that. But what about tonight? I thought you had plans for tonight too, don't you?"

"Yes, but it's just that..."

"I'm spending more time with Lee Ann than with you."

"Well yes, you are. Dad. I feel like…I'm losing you, like you've forgotten about Mom."

"Oh Renée, Honey. You aren't ever going to lose me. I'll never forget your mom. It's just that Lee Ann is a good friend. She's fun to be with. I need that kind of friendship."

He reached out again and this time I wanted his hug.

I stepped back. "Now, go have your shower." I watched him run up the stairs. I love you, I thought. What would I do without you? Please don't leave me for Ms. Hamilton. Out of nowhere came the thought, *Of course he won't leave you. He'll always love you.* It felt just as if Mom had stood beside me and spoken. "Thanks Mom," I said out loud. "I needed that."

I made my smoothie and headed upstairs for a bubbly soak in the tub. By the time the tub was full, Dad was ready to leave. "Have fun with your friends," he called as he ran out the door. I heard the door open again.

"Renée," Dad called up the stairs, "Please come down and lock the door before you get into the tub."

"Right," I yelled back. "Coming down now."

He waited at the bottom step. "It's snowing outside. You kids be careful on the road."

"We're just going to a movie in town. Tracey's driving. You be careful. The country road might be slippery." I gave him a hug, shoved him out the door and clicked the lock.

Steve

With flowers in one hand and a bottle of wine in the other, I used my elbow to ring Lee Ann's doorbell. Remember, Steve, I told myself as I waited, you're not eighteen. You have control of your hormones. Lee Ann is a good friend. You don't want to ruin that.

Her voice came out of nowhere. "Hi, Steve, I'll be there in a minute." I searched until I spied the camera and small speaker partially concealed in the overhead light. A few seconds later, she opened the door looking elegant as always, in black silky pants and a bright blue shirt that hung loose and touched in all the right places. "Wow," was all I managed as I handed her the flowers.

She blushed. "Thank you, Steve," she said. "Sorry to keep you waiting. I was in the kitchen. Come in. I've set a fire in the fireplace. We will be cozy tonight."

I followed her into the kitchen. "*Mmmm*, smells wonderful."

"Irish stew—it's my mother's favourite recipe."

"That, too," I said.

She looked at me. A smile appeared. "Would you please open the wine? The glasses are on the dining room table. I'll just arrange these flowers and meet you at the fireplace."

"Yes, Ma'am," I said and saluted. We both laughed.

I poured the wine. Settled on the sofa in front of the dancing fire, I enjoyed her every movement as she placed the flowers on the mantel. I stood and handed her a glass.

We clinked. "To us, to our friendship and … whatever," she said, her eyes revealing a mischievous glint.

"Our friendship," I said, grinned and echoed "and whatever." We sipped. I reached out to touch her cheek. This time she didn't flinch. "Soft as velvet," I said, and leaned in for a long slow kiss… I took a deep breath and leaned back determined to let her set the pace. "Maybe we should sample some of that stew."

She smiled and sat back too…Let's eat. It's all ready."

Eating brought its usual comfort. My nervousness subsided. The stew was delicious. We talked about the Ahmadis and the upcoming storytelling at St. Dominic's Church. Finished with that topic, I said, "I never noticed your security system before. Is that new?"

"Yes. After the trouble at the Ahmadis' and the robbery at the bank, I decided my neighbours are too far away. I needed to take some precautions."

"Good idea. The camera is much better than a peephole in the door, although if someone is determined …" I cut myself short.

Too late. Lee Ann knew where I was going and responded with, "The system is tied into a main depot downtown. If the camera gets obstructed or someone tampers with the system, an automatic call goes into the police station."

"Smart lady, and beautiful, and caring."

"Let's move to the living room and the fireplace for our coffee and dessert," she said.

"Sounds good, but could we put off dessert for a little while? I shouldn't have had that second helping."

"Certainly."

We carried our coffee into the living room and settled onto the couch in front of the fire. I looked around the room. A crokinole board hung on the wall back in one corner. It had obviously been handmade. The craftsman had used a variety of woods to create a beautiful inlaid pattern of stars and moons. I got up and walked over to examine it more closely. "I didn't notice this last time I was here. What a wonderful piece of art," I said.

"Dad made that for me when I was a little girl. He was an artist with wood. I treasure it. I've had many happy hours using it. Would you like to play a game? I have to warn you though, I'm pretty good."

I grinned. "I'll take on your challenge. Actually, I like to play games." This time, I managed to leave out, Serena and I used to play all kinds of board games. Instead, I said, "Board games are a Grenville family tradition. We had crokinole competitions when I was a kid."

"This should be interesting, then." She lifted the playing discs from a drawer in a tall pub table under the board. "We'll use this high table. Crokinole for two is best played standing up."

We pulled the table out from the wall so there was room all around it. Lee Ann opened out the gate-leg and covered the tabletop with a felt cloth. Carefully, I lifted the board down from its hanger. I ran my hand over the glossy surface. "Elegant," I said, "just like you." I stepped up close to her. The musky fragrance she wore invited me closer. I reached out, and she slipped into my arms as if she belonged there. Our lips met.

Her cell phone rang. She drew back. "Sorry, Steve. It might be one of my kids." The phone lay on the mantel. When she picked it up, her forehead filled with worry lines. She swiped it and said, "Hello." She listened. "Yes, that's my name…Yes, he's here. Just a minute." She handed the phone to me. "It's for you. It's the police."

I drew in my breath and took the phone. "This is Steve Grenville."

The female voice said, "Officer Fullbright, Catalpa Creek Police. Is your daughter Renée Grenville?"

"Yes. Is she …"

"She's okay. She's had a traumatic experience, but she's not hurt physically. She's at Dr. Siddiqui's home, and she needs you. Can you come?"

"Thank God. Yes, I'll come immediately. I'm about twenty minutes away." I clicked off and turned to Lee Ann. She was already holding my coat, her eyes full of concern. "The officer said Renée's okay, a traumatic experience, whatever that means. She's at Dr. Siddiqui's. I have to go. I'll call when I know what's going on."

"Of course."

I ran out the door.

Thankfully the skiff of snow had melted. I made the trip to Siddiqui's house in under fifteen minutes. It felt like an hour. I parked on the road behind Tony's car. Police cruisers filled the driveway. As I approached the house a police officer fell in beside me. I rolled it down.

"Your name, please, Sir?"

"Steve Grenville. My daughter…"

"Yes, we've been waiting for you. Follow me."

He led me past the house and around behind the garage. The house is in darkness. Where are we going? As we approached a lighted building, I remembered, Harrar's art studio. What…? When we stepped inside, I was nearly blinded by the light. Renée, her eyes swollen, face white, came running and collapsed into my arms. I held her tight and stroked her hair. Over and over I whispered, "I'm here sweetheart. I love you." I scanned the room. Police seemed to be everywhere. Over by the window, stood Susie, her face white, her body motionless, hanging onto her mom's hand. Beside them were Angelique and Tony, hovering over Antonio. Tracey leaned against her dad, her face glistening with tears, staring, just staring. What was she seeing? Tony left Antonio and stepped over to us.

"The kids came to pick up Harrar for the movie tonight," he said. I nodded. "They found Harrar hanging…" He pointed at a beam running across the ceiling. "Ambulance has already taken him to hospital. Rashimi and Kasun were out. They're meeting the ambulance at the hospital." Tony shook his head. His voice trailed away. Tears ran freely down his cheeks.

"Oh, my God. No." I pulled Renée closer. Her entire body shook with her sobs.

One of the police officers touched my arm. "You're Steve Grenville, Renée's dad?" she said.

I nodded.

"Detective Stromberg will be with you in a minute."

We just stood there, huddled in the corner of the room. No one spoke. My heart ached for Renée, the other kids, the Siddiquis, Harrar. Why? Why? Such a fine and talented young man. Why?

Renée sobbed more quietly as time passed. Detective Stromberg joined us. "We will need statements but that can wait until morning. Take your kids home. They're already showing signs of shock. Keep them warm. Best call your doctor. Either myself or Detective Long will contact you first thing in the morning so you can bring the kids in to headquarters."

Wearily, we returned to our cars.

We were silent on the drive home. Once in the house, Renée and I sank onto the couch. "Can you tell me what happened?"

She looked up at me, her face riddled with pain. "You didn't answer your phone. I didn't know Lee Ann's number. It wasn't listed. Dad, I needed you so much. You took such a long time coming. It was awful, so awful."

Silently, I kicked myself for leaving my phone in the car, for not making sure Renée had Lee Ann's number, for doing everything wrong. I wanted to make excuses, but at least I knew enough to shut up and just let her talk. "I'm sorry I took so long. I'm sorry." I couldn't keep the tears from running down my cheeks.

"It was awful, Dad. Just so awful. His feet. They dangled just above the floor. I can still see his feet. Six inches, that was all. They were so close to life. I'll see his feet dangling forever."

Her trembling increased. Sobs consumed her entire body. I held her tightly, crying with her.

When she could finally draw a breath she said, "It's my fault. It's my fault. I should have known." She looked up at me, the pain in her eyes so deep, I was sure it was crushing her soul.

"Whoa, now," I said. "Blaming isn't going to help. First tell me what happened."

"Oh, Dad, the bunch of us had such a good time together at the movies last week. I felt bad that Harrar had missed out. When we decided to do it again, and Mustafa couldn't come, I called Harrar. He's been sort of out of the loop lately. I wanted to include him. It took some convincing, but he finally agreed to come. Tracey picked me up as planned, then Susie and Antonio. We were slated to pick up Harrar last."

She lifted her head. Tenderly, I pushed her wet hair from her eyes. She took a deep breath.

"When we got to the Siddiqui's, the family car was gone. Antonio pounded on the door. No one answered. When he came back to the car, I suggested we try Harrar's studio, at the back of the garage. That's where he paints. I thought maybe he had gotten lost in his work."

She was sobbing again. I rubbed her back and waited. After a few moments, she started again. "We all tramped around the side of the garage, because we wanted to see what he was working on. I'm so glad we all came. What if…"

She shook her head, back and forth as if trying to wipe it all away. "There was a light on in his studio. I tried the door. It wasn't locked. I pushed it open." Her words tumbled out between sobs. She was gasping for air, like she was drowning. "Oh, Dad… It was so horrible. I'll never forget…He was hanging from the big beam in the ceiling. His feet were dangling…just dangling, so close to the floor. He'd jumped off a chair." She buried her head in my chest. "It was awful, just awful. After a few minutes, she lifted her head. "Susie just stood there, staring, shaking her head, saying, "No, no, over and over again."

Renée rubbed her eyes as if she was trying to obliterate the scene from her memory. "Antonio jumped up on the chair and lifted up on Harrar to take the pressure off his neck. I called 911. He handed Tracey his jack knife. She found a ladder in the garage. It took forever for her to cut him down.

She was sobbing so hard she had to stop talking. Eventually, she regained enough control to carry on.

"We were trying CPR when the emergency team arrived. One of the officers started lecturing us about tampering with things, but the policewoman grabbed his arm and told him to lay off. Dad, we couldn't just leave him hanging there. What if he was still alive and died while we waited for the ambulance. Oh, Dad, I'll have nightmares forever."

Finally, after what felt like a year, her tears slowed. She lifted her head, "I love you." She touched the front of my coat, "Oh, I've—your coat"

She was shaking so hard. I held her tight and kissed her on the forehead. "Forget my coat."

"I'm f-f-f-freezing."

I wrapped her in Serena's afghan from the back of the sofa. "I'll just call the doctor," I said. I picked up her phone from the coffee table. "I need to know if there's anything more to do but keep you warm and give you hot tea."

The phone rang and rang. Finally Doc Boyd answered. I barely started talking when he interrupted me. "I know, Steve. The police called me. I'm at Susie Tomchuk's now. Wrap Renée in blankets. Give her a hot drink. I'll be at your place within half an hour."

"Thanks, Doc."

I clicked off and turned to Renée. "He'll be here shortly. I'll just go make you some tea."

"No, Dad, no! Don't leave me. I thought you'd never come." She clung to my arms and started sobbing again..

I rubbed her back and her hands. "Come to the kitchen with me. We'll work together to fix the tea. The doctor said to give you a hot drink." At that point the doorbell rang. Eleanor Weebs poked her head in.

"I heard what happened. I had to come over. I thought you might need a friend, a woman, something…"

"Eleanor, we're glad you're here. Renée's suffering some shock. She needs a warm drink. Doc Boyd will be here shortly."

"I'll fix the tea and yell if I need instructions on finding things."

Renée and I settled back down on the couch.

"It's my fault, Dad. It's my fault."

I held her close wanting to give her the warmth of my body. "Suicide is never anyone's fault, Renée. Be assured of that. It's never anyone's fault."

"But Dad, he told me…he told me…I knew he was troubled. I didn't do anything. When I was a mess after Mom died, Susie went to Reverend Linda about Russell… I didn't tell anyone. I kept Harrar's secret. Oh Dad, I should have…"

"Renée, listen to me. It's not your fault. Suicide comes when people have no hope. It's not logical. We cannot live without hope. I don't know what happened to Harrar's hope, but it wasn't your fault."

Eleanor appeared with three steaming mugs of tea.

"Thank you, Eleanor," I said. "You're a lifesaver, literally." Renée's whole body was trembling so hard she couldn't pick up the cup. I held it for her while she managed a few sips. The doorbell rang.

Eleanor answered it. Dr. Boyd came through the archway into the living room.

Setting his black bag on the coffee table, he said, "Now, Miss Renée, you've had a rough experience. I'll just take your pulse and listen to your heart. Steve, give her some more of that tea."

The doorbell rang again. This time Eleanor led in Lee Ann.

The two of them stood in the archway and talked quietly while Dr. Boyd finished with Renée. He gave her something to help her relax and sleep.

As he was leaving, he turned to me and said, "Keep her warm. Give her more tea and maybe some toast and jam." He touched Renée's arm. "Eating just a little and drinking some will help that pill to work better. I'll call in the morning to see how you're doing."

"Thanks," I said. Eleanor walked him to the door. Lee Ann sat down on the other side of Renée. She reached out and took her hand. "Renée, I'm here tonight as your vice principal. I've already been to see Susie and Antonio. Harrar was a wonderful young man and your good friend and classmate. Suicide confuses us. It's not a rational act. Because we don't understand we look for someone to blame and that person is often ourselves. We think if only I'd known, if only I'd done, if only… Reality is there are no *if onlys*. Yes, Harrar was distressed. I talked with him last week. He did reach out for help and he received it. I don't know what sent him over the edge tonight. We'll probably never know. What we do know is that it wasn't your fault or your friends' or his parents'. For whatever reason, Harrar lost hope. The world looked so black that suicide felt like the only option."

She's offering Renée wisdom from her own deepest, darkest experience, I thought. Please, God, help Renée to listen to her.

Renée just stared straight ahead.

Lee Ann patted Renée's shoulder. "We'll talk again in a few days. Just remember, my prayers are with you. I'll help in any way I can." She looked at me. "I'll call in the morning."

"Yes, please." I answered.

She rejoined Eleanor in the archway. "Think I'll go, too," Eleanor said.

I nodded. "Thanks for your help."

"I'll lock the door on my way out."

Even with the medication, it was long past midnight before Renée was finally asleep. Wearily, I sat down on the window seat in my bedroom. The sky had cleared, and the moon revealed Catalpa Creek, winding its way through the pristine snow blanket that covered the landscape. Feeling lost and alone, I reached for my Serena candle. No, I don't need it, I thought. I think I'll talk to God.

"Where do I begin? My heart aches. I'm so worried about Renée. She and Harrar were such good friends. I don't understand her guilt, but I'm sure you do. How I wish I hadn't left my phone in the car. I can't change that any more than I can change Harrar's death into life. It feels like a tragic waste of a wonderful young man. Rashimi. Kasun. Oh my God, if Renée… I give them to you, God. I send them my caring... and the kids, Susie, Tracey, Antonio, Renée, they all need your peace. I ask for your wisdom in my loving for Renée…for her friends…for Harrar's family…for us all."

I ran out of words, even for God.

I looked out the window. This snow won't last, but tonight, it's beautiful in the moonlight. A deer, a big buck, stepped out of the shadows and walked regally to the centre of the yard. He stopped and turned his head to stare straight up at me. I felt my heartbeat and my breathing slow. Mesmerized, I kept absolutely still. Gradually, peace crept into my heart. It was only a moment, yet that deer brought me the gift I needed. Several does and a fawn stepped away from the dark shelter of the creek bank, their forms outlined in the snow. The buck shifted his attention to his family for a moment. Again, his head swivelled in my direction. He stood so still. Somewhere in my head I heard, "Peace. Be still. All will be well. All will be well." When the voice ceased, the buck bounded off, his family with him. "Thank you, God," I prayed. "Thank you."

I undressed and crawled into bed, hoping for sleep.

Chapter Seventeen

A Very Long Day

Saturday, November 4

Steve

At six a.m., Renée shuffled into my bedroom, her hair awry, her tear-reddened eyes looking enormous in her white face. "I'm sorry. I couldn't sleep." She sat down on the bed… "I keep seeing his feet, dangling just above the floor. Why? Why did he do it? Why didn't I tell someone? I could have stopped him." She started crying again. I put my arms around her and held her until her tears slowed.

"You're shivering," I said. "Let's get our housecoats and go downstairs for hot chocolate." She clung to me as we navigated the stairs. I settled her in the breakfast nook while I made some toast and our drinks. "We both need to eat something," I said, as I slid the plate and mug toward her.

She pushed the plate aside and wrapped her hands around the mug, her knuckles whitened with the pressure. "I want to turn back the clock," she said. "I need a second chance." Her voice quivered. "Help me, Dad. Make it all go away. Even Mom couldn't have fixed this. It won't fix."

The sobs returned.

"I was relaxing in a bubble bath with a book, while he was hanging there…I know I could have stopped him—." she whispered.

"Renée, you can't—"

"I woke yesterday morning so full of sadness. Was he trying to connect with me? Why didn't I do something, tell someone? Why didn't I go over there rather than try to drag him out to a movie. Maybe if I'd … We could have worked on laying out the pictures for my project…"

I scooted my chair closer so I could wrap my arm around her. "I'll call Reverend Linda and Dr. Sampler, too. They'll help. You're not alone in this, Renée. You're surrounded with love and …God is with us."

"But God doesn't fix things. I learned that with Mom." She brought her fist down hard on the counter. "I put Harrar in God's hands. I asked God to help him find peace. This wasn't the way I wanted it to happen. I need God to fix this. I need this fixed. It can't be."

I rubbed her back. A prayer filled my mind. Dear God, Help us. We need you. You sent the deer family to me last night. Give Renée a sign of hope, Lord, a sign of your love, your presence with us.

Renée blew her nose, swallowed, and said. "I'm so glad we have each other. I just feel so powerless, so helpless and so guilty."

"How about a bite of toast?" I coaxed and moved the plate back in front of her.

She shook her head but took a small bite.

"I need to tell you what I saw last night. After everyone left, and you had finally fallen asleep, I stood looking out my bedroom window. A huge buck stood in our yard near the bird feeder. He had a full rack of antlers. He turned his head and stared right at me. I don't know how to tell you this, but as he stared up at me, I felt this… feeling of peace come over me. It was strange and beautiful. After a few moments, three does and a fawn walked up from the creek and joined him. Then they all ran off. You're going to think I've lost my mind, but I believe God sent that buck to give me strength."

Renée sighed. "No, I don't think you've lost your mind. I felt that way about Bella and the kittens. I believe God sent me Ebony and his family to help me cope with losing Mom."

I remembered how much I didn't want that cat family. I remembered Renée's reaction when I suggested we get rid of them. "Forgive me, Renée. I didn't understand." She leaned into me, hanging on tight. Ebony wandered into the kitchen and headed straight to his empty dish. Finding nothing, he came to Renée, winding himself around her feet.

"Can we go for a walk in the snow? I need to do something normal."

"Sure," I said. "Please try another bite while I feed Ebony."

As we picked our way along the creek bank, the rising sun painted the snow purplish pink. We breathed deep of the cold, crisp weather.

Renée stopped and pointed. Up ahead, a fox stood motionless, staring across the creek. He turned his head toward us. With a flash of red, he was gone.

We stood in silence. A blue jay squawked in the distance. The creek rushed by us. "It's beautiful, Dad. The world is beautiful, even now."

A few minutes later, Renée said, "Let's go back, I'm getting cold."

As we walked in the door at home, Reverend Linda called.

"Hi Steve, I've been talking with Eleanor. She told me about Harrar. I'm concerned about you and Renée.

"We're hanging in there. I'm pressing speaker so Renée can hear too." We sat down at the island.

"I'm so sorry about your friend, Renée." She paused. "There are no words." She paused again. Renée nodded. "We've activated the prayer team to pray for the Siddiquis and for you and your friends."

This time Renée spoke, her voice barely loud enough for Reverend Linda to hear. "Thank you."

"I talked with the Imam. Funeral prayers for Harrar will take place at the mosque in Wainwright, today at two."

Renée's tears began to flow again. "Why so soon?" she asked.

"Embalming isn't part of the Muslim tradition. Burial takes place as quickly as possible. The Imam said that friends would be welcome."

Renée shook her head no.

"I'd like to talk with the two of you. How about later this afternoon after the service?"

I looked at Renée. This time she nodded in agreement.

"Okay, give us a call when you get back," I said. "We may not go to the service. Renée may not be up to it."

"Of course. God's peace be with both of you."

"Thank you. Goodbye."

I put my phone back in my pocket.

"Think I'll try lying down with some music on my headphones," Renée said. "I want to go to the service. I don't want to fail Harrar again."

"We don't have to go. It won't be a failure."

Slowly she climbed the stairs to her room, shaking her head.

About an hour later, my phone rang. I glanced at the display before answering. "Hi Tom."

"Steve, I need a statement from Renée. Can you bring her down to the station this morning?"

"Does it have to be now? She's resting."

"I'm sorry Steve. Yes, now is necessary. We want to get this investigation wrapped up quickly."

I checked the time. "It's nine o'clock. We'll be there within the hour."

Sounds good. See you when you get here."

The phone clicked off.

Wearily, I climbed the stairs. Renée had left her bedroom door open. I stepped in. She lay on her bed staring at the ceiling. When she saw me, she pushed the off button on her iPad.

"Tom Long called. We have to go to the police station."

She sighed. "Okay. I'll be ready in a few minutes."

She came downstairs looking a little brighter. She'd pulled on her favourite blue sweatshirt. Her hair was wound into a knot. She'd washed the tears from her face. "Lookin' better," I said.

She sort of smiled. "Let's go get this over with."

When we returned from the police station, Renée was shaking from the ordeal of reliving finding Harrar. "I'll make us a sandwich," I said.

"No. I'm not hungry."

"You need to try to eat a little, if you want to go to the service this afternoon." She shook her head no but sat down at the island. "Dad, tell me again about seeing that big buck in the yard last night."

I repeated the story while I cooked us grilled cheese sandwiches. I put a dill pickle with it, hoping to entice her to eat.

When I placed it in front of her, she actually smiled. "Thank you," she said, and took a bite. "My mouth is dry. It's hard to taste anything."

"Try the dill pickle. Maybe it will get the juices flowing."

She groaned but tried a bite. She screwed up her nose.

"How about setting a date with Susie to work on the diary. The distraction will help."

She sighed. "Sure, I'll talk with her at the funeral."

Her sandwich half eaten, she pushed it away." I'm going upstairs to lie down until it's time to leave.

I cleared up the dishes. Too tired for anything, I set an alarm on my phone and laid down on the couch in the living room.

Just before the alarm was to ring, Renée appeared dressed in a long black skirt and black turtleneck sweater. "I'm ready to go," she said.

"I can be ready in ten minutes." I took the stairs two at a time.

At the mosque, the coffin was laid out on a platform outside the main worship area. We removed our shoes. Renée was given a beautiful filmy scarf to cover her hair. We stood off to one side with a large group of Catalpa Creek families, Susie, Antonio and Tracy and their parents among them. Just before two, the Imam invited us to take our seats. Men and women in separate areas. Reverend Linda sat with Renée.

After the service was completed first the men lined up and then the women to file past the coffin and speak with Harrar's parents. Rashimi wept uncontrollably. Kasun stood like a statue, his face frozen. They accepted our silent handshakes. We had no words. I remembered being in line at Serena's funeral, as our friends and acquaintances came with silent hugs and handshakes. We needed their presence. We needed to know they cared. I hoped this would help the Sidiquis.

Outside the mosque, Reverend Linda gathered our four families into a circle for prayer. "I'd be glad to meet with all of you this evening, if you'd like."

We nodded.

"You can come to the church, or…"

"Come to our house," Renée interrupted, her voice sounding brittle.

Reverend Linda looked at me for affirmation. "Of course," I said. Why not? Anything that will help, I thought.

On our drive back to Catalpa Creek and Reverend Linda's office, Renée sat white faced and silent.

Oh Lord, I prayed, we need you.

Reverend Linda greeted us at the church door, still wearing her coat and scarf. She laid our coats with hers on one of the Sunday School tables and preceded us into her office.

"Please sit down," she said. "I'll just make us some tea. A warm drink will be good for all of us."

With that, she scurried off. Renée and I collapsed on the loveseat. Within a few moments, she returned carrying a tray.

"I found some cookies in the fridge, left over from Sunday. They need to be eaten. Otherwise they'll grow green fuzz."

I glanced at the cookies and had to smile. "I think Eleanor Weebs made these. They look a little like Eleanor with their purple and orange icing, don't you think?"

Reverend Linda chuckled. Renée just stared straight ahead.

After setting the tray on the coffee table, Reverend Linda eased her large bulk into a chair. She leaned towards Renée and waited.

I opened my mouth to talk, Reverend Linda shook her head.

I felt Renée stir beside me. Reverend Linda…Harrar's death…It's…it's…it's my fault." She couldn't control the tears. I reached out to her. She grabbed my hand and squeezed.

"Okay Renée, I hear you," Reverend Linda said. "Can you help me understand why you feel this way?"

Renée took a deep breath, lifted her head, squeezed my hand even harder and began. In a trembling but determined voice she said, "Reverend Linda I'm going to break a confidence I should have broken before. I'm so sorry, just so sorry, I did it all wrong."

Reverend Linda frowned, but stayed silent.

"Harrar and I are—were good friends. Many of the kids at school thought we were dating, but we weren't. We couldn't be any more than friends because Harrar was gay." She stopped and stared at me as if she expected me to object or something. I just stayed silent. Mostly, I was surprised. I didn't know, or even suspect.

"He was terrified, terrified someone would find out. He believed his parents would be ashamed of him; their reputations, their lives ruined if people found out. He told me Islam condemned homosexuals. He believed that even his parents would be found guilty, be ostracized in their faith community. He thought his Dad would no longer be able to practice medicine. He asked me to promise not to tell anyone."

My mind rolled. The poor kid. Did he learn that on Google? I'm sure Rashimi and Kasun would have helped him.

"Harrar was carrying a mighty heavy load." Reverend Linda said. "I can tell you that Harrar may have been mistaken about his faith and his parents' response, but that wouldn't change anything, would it?"

Renée nodded in agreement. "I was sure he was mistaken. But it isn't what I think or believe that matters. What mattered is that Harrar believed being gay was a totally unforgiveable sin. Harrar, who tried so hard to do all the right things; Harrar, who wanted only to be accepted."

With each word of praise, I heard Renée's voice become louder, stronger and more desperate.

"And that's not all. Harrar was terrified that Mustafa would find out. He was sure Mustafa would figure it out and tell..."

My mind lurched. Mustafa! Why Mustafa? Wouldn't they support one another?

"I asked him to help with the layout for my history project. He's a wonderful artist and I thought if would give us time together, time to talk. He put me off. Maybe if we'd been working on the project rather than going to the movies, he wouldn't have…

She reached out toward Reverend Linda. With tears streaming down her face and said, "If I'd only done it differently.

If only I'd told Dad, or you…I tried to deal with him myself." She clenched her fists. "Harrar told me he was afraid, and I did nothing. He might as well have told a stone wall." She slumped into a heap. "I failed him. He was my friend. I loved him. I failed him. If I'd done it differently, he'd still be alive."

The finality of those last words made me shiver. I wanted to shake her, to make her realize that it wasn't her fault. I turned helplessly to Reverend Linda.

She kept her silence. Renée sobbed and sobbed. Reverend Linda waited, waited until the storm of tears had passed. Finally, she reached out and took Renée's hands. "Listen," she said. "Harrar was your friend. He trusted you to keep his secret. You carried out his wishes. He wouldn't want you to carry the blame for his actions."

Yes, I thought. Thank you, Reverend Linda.

She paused. Renée lifted her head. Reverend Linda looked into her eyes and repeated in a slow, firm voice. "Harrar was your friend. He wouldn't want you to carry the guilt of his actions. Can you hear that?"

After what seemed like an eternity, Renée nodded.

"Let's pray," Reverend Linda said, reaching out one hand to me and motioning for me to take Renée's free hand. "Dear God, You love each one of your children totally and unconditionally. I believe you are crying with Renée, with Harrar's parents, with all of us today. We don't know what trigger brought Harrar to total hopelessness. We know that Renée loved him as a friend and wanted desperately to care for him. We ask for your peace for Renée now and always. Enable her to let go of what might have been. We cannot rewrite the past. Help her to step forward, to learn and to grow through this. May she always cherish her friendship with Harrar, as you cherish the two of them. I pray in Jesus' name. Amen."

Silently, I added, thank you God for Reverend Linda, Renée, and our faith. I pray that Kasun and Rashimi can receive comfort from theirs.

Reverend Linda lit a candle. “For Harrar,” she said, “A symbol of his goodness that will always be with us.”

After a few moments, Reverend Linda said, “Thank you, Renée for helping me to understand your feelings. Life is so complicated. We’ll never understand what Harrar has done. Suicide is not a logical, not a rational act.

I agree with you, I thought.

Reverend Linda continued, “I’m not sure there was anything that anyone could have done to prevent this tragedy. When someone decides that they need to leave this world, there’s usually nothing any of us can do to stop them. We can watch them carefully. We can talk and talk to them, reason with them, make contracts with them, even put them in the locked part of the hospital for patients at risk. The problem is that once they’re free and can get access to the means, too often they commit suicide anyway.”

I didn’t know that, I thought.

Renée sighed. “I need a sign,” Renée pleaded. “Something to wipe away the sight of his feet dangling so close to the floor. He hung so close to life...” Her tears returned. She took a deep breath, wiped her eyes and continued. “I need God to give me a sign so that I can believe Harrar forgives me. A sign like the one God sent to Dad last night.” She looked over at me.

I told the story of the deer in our backyard and the peace I received.

“God sent me Bella and the kittens when Mom died. I need something now.” Her voice had dropped to a whisper.

Reverend Linda nodded. “I believe God offers us the help we need, Renée. I’m sure God offered Harrar help too. We aren’t always able to recognize or receive it. God will send something to you. Keep your eyes and heart open."

We sat a while longer, no one speaking. We heard the church furnace click on and sing its reassuring roar. I stood up and stretched. "Okay, Renée, it's time we went home. Don't forget everyone's coming to our place after supper."

Renée nodded.

As she hugged Renée goodbye, Reverend Linda said, "Thank you for trusting me. I won't betray your confidence."

"Thank you," we said together.

Saturday evening, November 4

Renée

Reverend Linda arrived first, with Susie's parents pulling into the driveway behind her. They had barely removed their jackets and boots when Tracey's parents rang the doorbell. Tony, Angelique, Antonio and Gino arrived last. We gathered around the dining room table.

After we were settled in our chairs, Dad asked Reverend Linda to begin with prayer. That done, I said, "When Mom died, I started lighting a candle in her memory. It helped me remember that her spirit was with me." I pointed to the candle in a burgundy holder that sat in the centre of the table. "Tonight, I'm going to light this one in memory of my friend, Harrar."

Reverend Linda said, "Let's begin with our memories of Harrar."

Dad started with the facts. "Harrar and his family are loved and respected here in Catalpa Creek. His parents were born in Sri Lanka and emigrated to Canada as children. They've done well here. I know Harrar was a hard worker. After school he stocked shelves at the Independent. He's…he was well-liked and respected there."

"He was such an accomplished artist," Susie's mom added. "And I certainly enjoyed his artwork whenever I was at the school."

Everyone took a turn. My friends described him as a quiet member of our school crowd. They all said they liked him because he was thoughtful and kind. They all admired his ability to get good grades even though he worked after school. But none of them really knew him, knew why he was quiet, why he asked no one out but me. They never really knew him as a whole person. Now they'll never have the chance. Is that sad, I wondered. Or just the way it needs to be.

Tracey said, "I wish I had known him better. I felt as if…" She turned to me. "You were closest to him, Renée. You tell us about him."

I glanced over at Dad and he nodded at me. I prayed silently. Help me God. I locked eyes with Reverend Linda looking for strength. Susie grabbed my hand under the table. "Harrar was my good friend. I loved his gentleness. He could see the beauty in the world. Yes, he was quiet and yet he was a passionate artist. I always felt good, valuable, when I was with him. And he was fun. He liked to laugh. I miss him already." My eyes filled with tears. I just let them come.

Reverend Linda took over again. "We're here tonight to share our sorrow at Harrar's death and to answer some of our questions. For such a wonderful young man, to have so totally lost hope that he took his own life, is impossible to understand.

Like everyone else, I nodded. Susie passed me the tissues and patted my hand.

Reverend Linda let her eyes move around the circle. She spoke again. "I need to begin by saying suicide is not a rational act. It cannot be explained. It makes no sense. And there is nothing that any one of you could have done to prevent this. And there's nothing any one of you did that caused this."

I wish I could believe that. I want to believe that. I wiped my cheeks.

She paused to give her statement emphasis. “I’m sure the school will have therapists there on Monday. I recommend that each one of the four of you, Tracey, Renée, Susie, Antonio make sure you spend time with that therapist. If you can, it would be helpful for you to talk with a counsellor of your family’s choosing as well. I’m not a therapist.”

Thank God for Dr. Sampler, I thought. I already know he’ll help.

Reverend Linda continued. “What I can do tonight is try to help with your faith questions. That’s my training. For those questions I can’t answer, I will seek out information from others. Now, let’s open this up for questions.”

Susie, wonderful, irrepressible Susie, jumped in first. “How do we care for Harrar’s family?”

“Good question, Susie. First of all, I’m not an authority on the Muslim customs. Already, you came to the funeral prayers in Wainwright. I’m sure that was helpful. I’ll check to find out if there is anything expected in terms of their traditions. I talked with Imam Salim al-Akhbari for a few moments this morning. He said he would have time for a longer conversation next week. He plans to come to the school.”

Everyone nodded. Glad I dragged myself to the funeral, I thought. It helped me, too.

Antonio asked, “Do you know the Muslim attitude to suicide?”

She responded, “I have a little information, not nearly enough. I know that life is sacred for Muslims as it is for us as Christians. To take a life, even your own, is against the teaching of Mohammed.

I frowned. Antonio expressed my confusion. “Why then are there Muslim suicide bombers?”

Reverend Linda grimaced. "I don't know. There are many brands of Muslim faith just as there are of Christianity. You'll need to save that question for the Imam. I can say, that death often brings a crisis of faith. Harrar's parents are not only grieving the loss of their wonderful son, they are struggling with how he died and what that means for their faith."

My heart ached for Harrar's mom and dad.

"What does the Christian faith think about suicide?" Susie asked. "Is it a sin? Would Harrar be cast out from our congregation for killing himself?"

Reverend Linda sighed. "No. We believe that God cries with us when we are hurting. Harrar must have been hurting, hurting terribly. We believe that God loved and still loves Harrar, even though he thought suicide was his only choice."

Once again, guilt engulfed me. If I had only done something, said something. Dad rubbed my back, silently telling me it wasn't my fault.

Reverend Linda looked over at me. Her eyes sent the same message. She continued, "As United Church people, we believe Harrar was, and still is God's precious child. God doesn't abandon anyone. We believe God has received Harrar into this next life with love. Whatever was troubling him is over, finished. He's with God. His new life is full of joy and love."

"Yes!" said Tony.

He's thinking about his daughter, Angelica, I thought. It must have been awful for their family when she died so young.

"Reverend Linda," Antonio said, "At the beginning tonight, you told us we weren't to blame for Harrar's death. I understand that in theory, but in my heart, I feel guilty. I haven't worked very hard at being Harrar's friend. We didn't seem to have anything in common, even though visual art is my thing, too. We could have been friends if I'd tried harder." He paused, "I didn't know he was that desperate."

I swallowed hard and thought, he was my friend and I didn't help him, either.

Reverend Linda's eyes glistened. "Antonio, how do I say this? Of course, you're struggling with guilt. Suicide often leaves behind a trail of guilt. We never know why a person chooses to take their own life. Hindsight gives us 20/20 vision. Remember, we can only do our best with what we know at the time. That's all God asks of us. All we can do is learn from this experience for life in the future."

Mom's death wasn't suicide, I thought. I still have guilt feelings about her, too. I wish life wasn't so hard.

Tracey's Dad spoke up, "Mostly I'm feeling angry, very angry. Why did Harrar pick last night when he knew the kids were coming for him? That was totally cruel. And his parents, how could he do that to his parents?"

Reverend Linda nodded. "Of course, you're angry. Tracey did nothing to deserve this horrific experience. None of you kids did. Anger, like guilt, is another emotion that comes with suicide. I can only repeat that suicide is not rational. I'm sure Harrar wasn't thinking about the effect his action was going to have. He gave up. He could see no other choice."

Susie's mom broke in, "I'm angry too but not with Harrar. I'm angry that God didn't step in and help Harrar. Why doesn't God keep these terrible things from happening?"

Tears slipped unheeded down my cheeks. I want Harrar back, just like I wanted God to give me Mom back. I need a second chance. It's just not fair.

"I wish I had an easy answer to your question," Reverend Linda said. "I've asked it over and over again throughout my lifetime. I'm sure Steve and Renée asked it when Serena was killed in that accident. I sure did, and I'm asking it again now. I don't have an answer."

She looked around the room, her eyes resting on each one of us. “I believe God sends us help in these situations, but sometimes we’re just not able to receive that help. I believe God felt Harrar’s pain, felt his hopelessness, and when Harrar set up that rope and jumped from that chair, God was with him, still loving him. That’s not an answer to the why question, but it is an answer to the what question. What does God do? As our Creator, as our parent, there are times when God cannot make the choice for us. In those times, God suffers with us every step of the way.”

The room was silent. All of us in tears. I’ll hang onto that thought. God was with him.

Reverend Linda sighed and broke the silence with, “I don’t know about you, but I’m

exhausted. I’ve had enough for tonight. I’m going to pray, and then maybe we could have some of those snacks Steve promised at the funeral this afternoon.”

Dad chimed in, “Food always helps.”

We rewarded his attempt at breaking the tension with weak smiles. After Reverend Linda prayed, she assured us that she would be willing to meet with the eight of us another time.

Tracey’s dad stood up. “Thank you, Reverend Linda. Tonight has been helpful. Thank you for drawing us to our faith. I needed it.”

At that moment, Ebony hopped up onto my knee and onto the table. He stalked all the way around it, looking at each one of us. He checked out the cups and paused at the cream pitcher. Before I could stop him, he was lapping away, his little tongue moving like lightning. Dad started the laughter, and the rest of us joined in. The tension was broken.

Chapter Eighteen

Nana's First Job

Sunday, November 5

Renée

At church I invited Susie over to work on the diary. Both Dad and I desperately needed the distraction. She arrived shortly after one o'clock wearing bright pink sweats. She took one look at our faces and said, "I dug these out of the back of my closet. I needed the boost and they're comfortable."

"They are pretty awful," I responded.

"Mom totally missed the mark when she bought these. She meant well, though."

"Let's spend an hour or so with the diary and break for a snack," Dad suggested.

"Oh, Dad, you think food fixes absolutely everything," I said and paused a moment. "You know what? You're sort of right. It usually helps."

"That's because when we're feeling bad, our sugar count drops," Susie added. "And eating works like a soother. It's comforting in your mouth. I read that in a book on grief. Actually, I remembered it because I liked having another excuse to eat."

The three of us laughed. "Thanks, Susie," I said. "That's just what we needed. I'll go get the diary. Where are we going to settle?"

"I vote for the living room," Dad said. "The couch is softer than the kitchen chairs."

"Me, too," said Susie.

"Okay, you two pull the sofa over to a place where my laptop will be close to a plug. I'll run upstairs to get the diary and the candles."

When I returned, Susie had retrieved Harrar's candle from the kitchen. We lined his up with both of Mom's on the coffee table. I needed the candle-lighting and Dad's prayer today. I opened the diary.

November 8, 1903 Sunday

Dear diary, I'm busy all the time. At least there's lots of good food and time flies. As long as I work hard, these people are happy. She decided she didn't like me calling her ma'm. So I call her Agnes. Agnes is expecting a baby. That's why they got me. Old enough to work, but not to be sassy, is how they describe me to visitors. It could be worse. Two days ago, when I was in town with Agnes, I saw Ester. She's three years older than me. I met her on the train. Ester belongs to the people at the store. I don't think they're very good to her. She looked frightened. I could see bruises on her arms. I'll work hard and stay here if I can. They told us at Hazelbrae it's good to stay in one place. There's no reason for me to run away. There's nowhere to go anyway. I sure do miss little Bill and Tilly. I think maybe he's better off where he is. Ester said life is harder for the boys. I'm glad I get to go to school. I'm learning lots. Teacher said my spelling is improving.

The baby is due at Christmas. I'm afraid school will stop when the baby comes. We have a cow named Bessie. I never seen a real live cow before. Farmer John took me out to meet Bessie. He gave me a lesson on milking. Bessie ain't no trouble, he said. She just stands there and waits. I think Bessie likes to be milked.

I talk to Bessie while I'm milking, and I get to sit down on this funny little three-legged stool. Milking's fine even if it is early in the morning. Milk's good, warm from old Bessie. Yes, being here is much better than the workhouse. It's getting colder every day.

Agnes says I'm going to need some warmer clothes, warmer even than the coat in my trunk. She brought a heavy coat and leggings from the neighbor. Her girl outgrowed them. We'll wash em Agnes said. Never know'd what was livin in em. Agnes sure is clean. I'm scrubbing and cleaning every thing 2 and 3 times a week. I didn't think things could be so clean. I'm going to bed now. Good night diary.

"Winter here in this country can be scary," I said. "It would be foolish to run away, even if the people you were staying with were mean. Why, you'd freeze to death before you got to the next homestead."

December 20,1903 Sunday

Dear Diary, It's been a while. I'm freezing in this awful country. It's cold, soooooooo cold. Our baby came last week. She's just beautiful and I get to take care of her. Agnes is feeling better. The birthing was a terrible time. The midwife kept me busy boiling water and washing sheets and cloths. Agnes screamed and hollered. I thought she was dying. Don't think I'll ever have a baby even if little Sara is sweet.

Agnes says there'll be no more schooling for me. She needs me at home. Besides I can read and write. What more do I need to learn? Guess she's right. It's a long walk to school through snow sometimes as deep as my hips. I don't know how anything can look so pretty and be so cold. Feels like I'm trudging through sludge. Yup, I don't mind being at home with Sara. I kept my speller so I can look up words. I want to learn to spell well. Maybe someday I'll be a writer.

"Even in the midst of hardship, Nana has hope," Susie said. "What keeps her hope up?"

"I think some of us inherit resilience," Dad answered.

"For sure," I added. "In the books I read, there were Barnardo kids who ran away and froze to death, and kids who committed suicide. Guess Nana was a truly strong woman."

Dr. Barnardo's supervisor, Miss Ward came by this week. She's nice. She says I have a good place. I'm to mind my p's and q's whatever that means. Anyway I'm doing my best. Seems like I'm always washing diapers. Miss Ward says that money is being deposited in a bank account for me. When I'm 21 I'll get it. Right now it's $2 a month. It'll be more when I get older. She says I'll be rich when I'm 21.

Susie interrupted the reading. "$2.00 a month, why that's slavery. "

"Don't forget," Dad said, "Nana Sinclair was in a workhouse in Britain with no pay. At least here she has her own room, and enough food and clothes to wear. She's much better off even if the work is hard and pay so low. I'm glad she has a decent place."

"We need that today."

December 25, 1903 Friday

Dear Diary, I got presents today. First time since...no point thinking about the past. New boots, stockings and a warm sweater. We went to church in the morning. After church, I peeled a huge pot of potatos and cleaned enough carrots to feed an army. I had to make the stuffing for the turkey. Agnes showed me how to make the cranburry sauce yesterday. Today she sat in the kitchen with Sara in her arms and gave me orders all day. It was my job to serve the dinner once it was ready. There was a whole crowd to feed. Neighbours (looked that word up in my speller) and family. Made me think about home and England and little Bill. Oh how I wish...Nope, I've got it good. I'm fine. There was lots of food left over for me and for tomorrow. It's a good thing

Sara is such a good baby. I'd never have gotten it all done.

May 22,,1904 Sunday
Agnes is pregnant again and she's not feelin well. I've got the care of Sara as well as all the housework. Today was my first day off in a long time. Farmer John, Agnes and Sara went to the next farm for the day. I'm just going to sit here with my feet up on the footstool and rest.

"She's sure not writing very often now," Dad said.

"I think Nana is just amazing," I replied. "She sure is a survivor. Let's read this entry."

September 9, 1906. Sunday
Dear Diary,
I'm back at Hazelbrae. I guess it was too good to last. My leg is beginning to heal. Falling down those steps was not my fault. That horrible Mr. Ramsbottom caught me alone in the kitchen and grabbed at me. He ripped my dress. He held his hand over my mouth so I wouldn't scream. Guess he thought I was just a weak kid. It's a good thing I've worked so hard. I got him good before he pushed me down the stairs. I kicked him hard where it hurts the most and bit his arm so deep I drew blood. He'll think twice before he attacks another girl.

Dad shifted in his chair, “I’d…”

Susie gasped. “Serves him right. How dare he!”

“What a creep.” I said. My eyes scanned ahead on the next page, “Oh, no.”

“What, what?” Susie asked.

“She’s broken her leg. Wait, here’s what she says.”

I broke my leg falling down those stairs. Farmer John felt bad. Old Ramsbottom is there neighbour. Agnes felt bad about sending me back to Hazelbrae, but they just couldn’t keep me. Agnes is pregnant again, they need someone to care for Sara and baby Wilbur. Doctor says my leg will heal even though it’s a bit crooked because the bone didn’t set right and because of the infection. But its going to take time. I’m getting good care now at Hazelbrae. At least Agnes gave me a good letter of reference.

“I guess she would,” Dad said.

“It’s so unfair. Her leg is damaged now, probably for life,” I said.

“And he got away scot-free,” added Susie.

“Keep reading, please,” Dad said. “I don’t want to dwell on the dark stuff today. We’ve had enough of that.”

I like it here at Hazelbrae. There is a long lane lined with big trees. Behind the house is a wide meadow and a hill. When my leg has completely mended I want to roll down that hill like the other children do.

Already, I've been to a tea party out on the lawn. Everyone had to have a bath and wash their hair. They found a new dress for me. Well not quite new. One of the older girls had outgrown it. I don't mind. It has no holes and it's clean. Some of the older girls carried me out to a chair under a tree so I could watch. Important people came and the girls served tea and sandwiches. It was all very la-dee-da. The ladies who came wore silk and satin and smelled of flowers. There was a silver tea pot and pretty cups and saucers. It made me think of Mama and Papa, and home in England before their accident. Mama always smelled of roses. She looked pretty and wore soft dresses. When they went out, she would dress up like these ladies and look like a princess. I miss Mama and Papa. I hate my uncle. Why couldn't he have kept us. We wouldn't have been any trouble. I miss little Bill.

November 24, 1906 Sunday

Tilly came to see me. She's seventeen. She says she's going to get her own place next year. Tilly is a seamstress now. She lives with a widow lady who taught her how to sew beautiful dresses. She thinks she can make a living with her sewing. I sure hope so. I don't think I'd leave a good place if I didn't have to. You never know what's coming next. Tilly laughed at me when I told her that. "I'll be fine," she said.

My leg's much better now. It's shorter than the other one and I have a limp. Worst part is that it is a funny color, kind of purple. It pains at times but at least I still have it. I saw a little girl the other day who has only one leg. She said she had infection in her foot that ran up her leg. The doctor cut it off just above the knee. I'm sure glad that didn't happen to me.

December 16, 1906 Sunday
Dear Diary, Doctor says my leg is as good as it will ever be. I was afraid they'd send me back out to work. Matron said they are leaving me at Hazelbrae until spring. There's not as much work on a farm in the winter. I could have told her there was lots of work at Farmer John's and Agnes' but I kept quiet. I wanted to stay here. There are other girls to talk to. I go to school. Teacher says I write good stories. I like that.
May 19, 1907. Sunday
Dear Diary, I'm 12. Nearly grown up. They've found another place for me. I'll be leaving next week. I'm sad and afraid. At Hazelbrae the girls tell terrible stories about the places they've been. The inspectors for Barnardo's that come around to check on us, don't know the half of what happens. They just keep telling us to be good and work hard and stay where we are. I'm not staying with somebody like old Ramsbottom. I'll run away. Tilly says, "never worry trouble until

trouble worries you." That's easy to say, but sure hard to do. Specially when I'm going off to be a slave for strangers. That's what we are, mostly, slaves.

The nice people here at Hazelbrae gave me a new dress, two new pencils and a pad of paper to take with me. I wish I could stay here. It's safe. That's all I want, just to be safe.

Susie said, "I don't understand it. Why aren't the farm families nice to these children? That's all they are, is children. Nana Sinclair is only twelve. My little brother Josh is twelve. Sure, he's a pain in the neck a lot of the time, but he's still just a kid. Why did they make them into slaves?" She slammed her fist down on the table.

I rubbed my eyes trying to erase the scene of Nana falling down the stairs. "It was wrong to send those kids over here. Today we know it's wrong. Some of the pioneer families thought the Barnardo kids were street trash, little criminals, hardly human, certainly not to be trusted. It was okay to abuse them."

Dad picked up from me. "Things haven't changed much today." He shifted in his chair. "Catalpa Creek is trying to welcome the Ahmadis. Yet some of us are afraid a terrorist is hiding among them. And if they're not terrorists, then they will steal our precious jobs. So, it's okay to frighten them and mistreat them."

I picked up Harrar's candle and stared into the flame. "I don't understand that kind of thinking. The Ahmadis are just people like us, looking for a safe place to live and raise their children."

Susie lifted up the diary. "Nana was no different. She wanted to be accepted and loved."

I could feel tears of frustration gathering in my eyes. In my heart, I heard Harrar speak of hating himself. We judge homosexuals too, I thought. Why… Harrar, I'm so sorry. I set his candle back down and sighed. "We're all just people wanting to live our lives and be safe."

Dad tipped his chair back from the table. "Now there's lots of thoughts for your essay. Let's read some more."

"I think this is a good place to stop," Susie said. "I don't want to know what this next place will be like. Maybe it'll be terrible. Ugh! I couldn't face that right now."

"Okay," I said.

"What's the frown?" Susie asked.

"Just thinking about my deadline for this project. Maybe we should set another diary date."

Dad nodded. "Let's do that, girls, while we snack on crackers and cheese."

Chapter Nineteen

Connecting

Monday, November 6

Renée

Monday morning, I went to school as usual. I needed to be with my friends and find some semblance of order in my life. Dad was glad to go to work, too. School turned out to be a huge ordeal. That's the only way to describe it. All the kids could talk about was Harrar. They kept asking over and over, "Why did he do it?" It felt like all of their questions were centered on the four of us who found him, particularly me, his friend. Some kids actually asked for all the gory details.

At home room that morning, the four of us decided to give no details. Our stock answer was, "I just can't talk about it. Please don't ask me to." That worked for the most part. Mustafa was conspicuously absent. I was glad. I don't think I could have faced him.

By Friday, most of the school buzz around Harrar's death had subsided. The Remembrance Day ceremony helped. We were gradually settling down to our regular lives. Every time guilt started to build in my heart, I repeated over and over the wisdom I'd received.

Suicide isn't logical.

I did my best for my friend.

It's not my fault.

Lots of deep breaths and lots of repetition would eventually drive my guilt back to a manageable level, but no matter what I did, or read, or heard, it just would not totally go away.

Dad and I met with Dr. Sampler, and I joined my friends with the grief counsellor who came to the school. It all helped to chip away at the pain.

The meeting with Imam Salim al-Akhbari helped too. We gained a little understanding. I was still trying to digest his information when I literally ran into Mustafa in the school hallway. He came flying around a corner and crashed into Susie and me as we were walking to English class. Three sets of books scattered in all directions.

"I am so sorry," he said, as together we gathered up our books.

When I handed him his math book, he caught my eyes with his. I could see pain. Maybe he's hurting just like the rest of us, I thought.

"You okay, Mustafa?" I asked.

His answer was automatic. "Fine." Then he added "Thank you."

Susie and I walked on down the hall. Mustafa hurried off in the opposite direction.

"What was that look all about? I thought you didn't like Mustafa."

"I don't know. When I handed him his stuff, our eyes met and I saw pain, real pain.

"Really?"

"Yes. He doesn't seem to have any real friends."

"Well no wonder. He may be gorgeous but…he's not real. He acts like he's got it all together. Even with his language difficulties he still gives the impression that he knows far more than the rest of us."

"Dad says that some people who feel nervous, use that superior attitude to compensate.

"Your dad may be right but I still don't like him."

At the end of the school day, Susie and Rachel went to Catalpa Creek Elementary to help Thuraya. I had a date with Eleanor and Tracey at Lights Out, to finalize the plans for Sunday night's community storytelling evening. I felt like crawling into a hole and pulling the lid down, but that wasn't possible. Life goes on. I had responsibilities. Just like after Mom's death, I knew I had to keep going.

Two blocks from the candle shop Mustafa stepped out of a store and joined me.

"Renée, please, I talk with you."

Surprised, I just nodded.

"You friends with Harrar."

My stomach lurched. The darkness I had kept at bay all day, descended with a jolt.

"I want friends with him. I try. He afraid me…not like me." His forehead wrinkled up into a frown, not angry but sad, very sad. "Most kids nice but…not like me." Sadness oozed from him. "Maybe tomorrow night…my story help."

I wanted to shout at him. It's all your fault. Harrar was afraid of you. Why do you judge others, think yourself so much better? I clamped my mouth shut. I stared at him. He must be lonely. My mind returned to our first meeting at the airport. He was so sweet with Thuraya. *Easy Renée. He's just a kid like you. Harrar's death isn't his fault either.* I took a deep breath. "Well, Mustafa, you come on too strong. You're…too out there."

He frowned. "Don't understand 'come on too strong… out there.'"

I stopped walking and turned toward him. "You're trying too hard to be our friend. Just be you, the real you."

He ran his hand through his hair and frowned. "I do not know…Real me?"

I tried again. "Do you want to be my friend?"

He smiled. "Yes."

"Why?"

He thought for a moment. "You…I see sad in eyes, like me."

I reached up and touched the little gold cross I always wore. "I'm not Muslim."

"I know. If friends must be Muslim…no friends in Catalpa Creek."

His half-smile was kind of sweet. I smiled back. "Right, but there's lots of kids who claim to have no religion. Wouldn't it be easier for you to connect with them?"

He frowned. I was sure he hadn't really understood what I had said.

He answered. "I like you. You friendly. You Harrar's friend. You could be my friend."

I smiled at him. "That's it, Mustafa, that's what I mean by being real. You spoke honestly, from your heart."

"Kids not like me, maybe not like heart."

"Pretending to be what you think we want is turning us all off. You have to trust that most of us will like you, just because you're you, and you have to let the rest go."

He looked at me, hopeful. "You be my friend?"

I thought about Harrar. We all need friends. "Okay."

"Peace," he said, holding up two fingers in the peace sign.

"Peace." I offered the same sign.

His entire face smiled. So did mine.

"I have to go. I'm late," I said. "Okay?"

"Okay. Thank you."

I turned and ran toward Lights Out.

"See you later," he called after me.

"Yup," I shouted back and turned the corner.

As I jogged along, I thought, well Harrar, I'll see if I can't help Mustafa gain some new ideas about being gay. I sure hope I can.

Friday evening

Steve

St. Dominic's Roman Catholic Church offered its worship space for our storytelling evening, because it's the biggest venue in Catalpa Creek. Our planning committee accepted their kindness, even though we wondered if all the Christian icons, sculptures of Jesus and Mary and many more, would be uncomfortable for the Ahmadis. Our answer was to ask Father McGarrity to give the Ahmadis and our committee a tour of the building ahead of time. Eleanor arranged it for after work.

Father McGarrity led us all through the sanctuary, stopping at each icon and explaining its significance. We listened carefully. We had much to learn. I wasn't sure how much the Ahmadis understood.

When Father McGarrity finished the tour, Dr. Ahmadi asked, "Is okay we are Muslim and speak here?"

Father McGarrity smiled. "We want to be friends. Both our faiths call us to respect and care for each other."

Dr. Ahmadi's frown cleared. He reached out his hand to Father McGarrity. The priest clasped it and opened his arms for a hug. The men embraced. Relief flooded into my heart.

Dr. Ahmadi spoke. "Thank you, Father McGarrity. We, my family grateful."

Chapter Twenty

Nana Sinclair – A Life of Terror?

Saturday, November 11

Renée

"There you are, our little Muslim lover," he whispered as he grabbed my hair with both his hands and pulled me from my bed.

I opened my mouth and screamed, "Dad…Dad…"

Behind me, I heard laughter, a woman's laughter. "Dad…Dad…," I screamed again. The stranger's hands wrapped around my neck, closing tighter…tighter.

"Renée…Renée…wake up," Dad said, his voice gentle as he wrapped me in his arms.

"Dad, oh Dad," was all I could say. Tears streamed down my face. I was cold, so cold, yet wet with the sweat that seeped from my body.

Dad kept repeating, "It was a nightmare, hon. You're safe. You were dreaming—a nightmare."

Slowly, the fear receded. "Oh Dad, it was awful. They broke into the house while I was sleeping. I knew they were coming for me. I heard them, but I couldn't get up. I was frozen. I had to lie there and wait for them. It took a long time. He was … I was choking, like Harrar." I pulled Dad closer."I've never been so frightened. I can still feel his hands on my throat."

"Take some deep breaths. Look out the window. See the multitude of pinks in the sky. It looks like that scarf your mom gave you, her last Christmas with us. God has given us something beautiful to help wipe away your fear."

We sat there cuddled together until my breathing and my heart slowed. "What time is it?" I asked as I straightened up.

Dad looked at his watch. "Nearly 7:30. The days are getting short. Let's go downstairs, I'll heat up yesterday's porridge. It will be warm and comforting."

Good old Dad and his food.

Once settled with our tea, my fright seemed far away. I wished the nightmare of Harrar's death would recede as quickly. I watched Dad pull the bowl of leftover porridge from the fridge. My mind searched for something to distract me. "I need another Nana Sinclair day. I think I've researched enough. I need to finish the diary, so I can start writing."

"What about this afternoon or tomorrow?"

"I'll call Susie and see when she's free. This morning I'll make some lemon squares for our snack. Keeping busy helps." The minute minder on the stove chimed. Dad got up to stir the porridge. He added more milk.

"Think it's ready," he said.

As we ate, the security of Dad's love and our home brought peace at least for now.

When I opened the door to Susie that afternoon, she reached up and dropped a handful of snow on my head.

She laughed, "Oh Renée, the look on your face..." She turned and made a huge sweeping motion with her arms. "Just look! Isn't it beautiful?"

I stood shivering in the doorway, wet snow dripped down my face. Better than tears, I thought. A skiff of snow had clothed the evergreens, the grass, even the garage roof, in a brilliant white wedding dress that sparkled with sequins in the noonday sun. "Yes, it's beautiful," I said. "C'mon inside, I'm freezing."

I knocked on Dad's study door. "Susie's here. It's time to start." I said.

We gathered in the breakfast nook, lemon squares, teapot and cups ready. "We've three hours. I hope we finish the diary today."

We lit the candles. Susie asked, "May I pray today?" I must have looked startled because she explained, "I keep thinking about Harrar. I want to pray for him."

"Sure," Dad said. I nodded.

When she had finished, Susie volunteered to read first.

May 26, 1907 Sunday

Dear Diary, The Renwick's came for me today. She's miserable. I can tell from the permanent scowl on her face. She pulled away at my dress as if the hem was crooked. Why should that matter? All I'm going to do is cook, clean and skulk in the kitchen when they have company. That's what a slave does. She doesn't like me, I can feel it.

Mr. Thomas Renwick looked pious like the men at the church when he talked to the matron at Hazelbrae. As soon as he got me into the back of the wagon, his face changed. He leered at me and scowled at Mrs. Renwick. No wonder she looks cranky. Living here is going to be hell. Hopefully, I can keep out of his way, and do some things to please her. Maybe the two of us can gang up on him. That would be great, but I doubt it's gonna happen.

My room is small, but clean. There are dresses hanging in my closet. Mrs. Renwick kept saying what a big girl I am. If these dresses are for me, it's a good thing I'm big. They look as if they would fit her. When we got here, I had to carry my trunk up the thirty-five stairs to my attic room. Thirty-five, that's right, twenty to the second floor, and fifteen steeper ones to the attic. My poor leg, but at least it will be quiet way up here. I have a little window that's covered in dirt and spider webs, but it's better than nothing. Besides I can clean it.

"This place sucks right from the beginning. These people are nasty. A room in the attic. Yuck!" Susie said.

"Poor Nana." I turned the page.

July 12, 1907 Friday

Dear Diary,

Finally, I have a moment to write. These two keep me working from dawn til dusk. At night I'm so tired all I can do is collapse in my bed. They don't much like me but they're putting up with me. Old Renwick told the Barnardo inspector, Mrs. Shaw I was stupid. The Missus just calls me careless and untidy. No matter how hard I try, I can't please her. They promised Mrs. Shaw that I would be sent to school this fall. It's three miles, a long walk with my bad leg, but at least it will be a change. Maybe I can please my teacher. Teachers usually like my stories.

"No wonder she's kept this diary. She's a writer," I said.

"I think writing runs in the family," Dad said. "Your Grandma Rushton wrote eleven books over her lifetime. Your Mom wrote short stories, even had a few published."

"Hey," Susie said, "That's it. You've been wondering about what to study at university. Maybe you should think about journalism. You've really got into the research about your Nana."

I shrugged. "Maybe… right now getting this project finished is feeling heavy."

"Life is heavy right now," Susie replied. "You could choose happy topics if you were freelance."

"Let's get back to Nana." I said. "We didn't finish her July 12th entry."

Old Renwick and sourpuss have gone off to some Orangemen's celebration for the day. I don't know what that's about, nor do I care. She gave me a list of things to do but I'm not going to do them. It's just washing the floor, and cupboards inside and out. She won't be satisfied anyway, so why bother. I'm just going to sit down by the pond and watch the ducks and butterflies. A lovely day to rest. Thank you to the Orangemen. I wonder if they really are orange.

August 15, 1907 Thursday
Mrs. Shaw returned today and signed an agreement with the Renwicks. Guess they are planning on keeping me. While they were having tea in the garden, I sneaked a peek at that agreement. It says, that year one I am to receive my room and board, clothes and schooling and $3.00 per month, year two wages of $4.00 per month and year three wages of $5.00 per month. Since I came here in May that means I'll get a pay increase starting May of next year. Sounds good. Will it happen?

February 16, 1908 Sunday
Dear Diary, I'm surviving here. They are still sending me to school. Old Renwick leaves me alone. I think mostly because she keeps a close eye on him whenever I'm around. I'm glad she keeps me dressed in these huge baggy dresses.

June 18, 1908 Thursday
Dear Diary
Mrs. Shaw came today to do the yearly inspection. I heard them tell her they were going to send me back to Hazelbrae in September. Yay. I'm sure it's because they don't want to keep paying $4.00 per month. Sourpuss is back to finding fault with absolutely everything I do. She told Mrs. Shaw that I was careless in doing my work and very untidy. He said I was stupid.

Sept. 13, 1908 Sunday
Dear Diary,
Yup, I'm back at Hazelbrae and I'm glad. Being at Renwicks could have been worse. At least she kept the old man under control.

"Nana sure is resilient," Dad said. "She can find a positive in anything."

"Yeah, her broken leg got her back to Hazelbrae," Susie added.

I stared at the two of them. “She wouldn’t find anything positive in Harrar’s death!”

Silence.

“Sorry…Let’s get back to the diary. Dad, your turn to read.”

March 28, 1909 Sunday
Dear Diary, This past winter at Hazelbrae has been good. Today, I go to live with the MacDougalls at Greenboro, another farmer. I'm waiting for them to come and pick me up. I sure hope this place is better than the Renwicks.

March 29, 1909 Monday
God how could you have put me here. This place is terrible. It's my first day and already I hate it. I do have a nice room. It has pretty curtains and a lovely quilt on the bed. I wish there was a lock for the door. Something tells me I won't be safe in here.
They said they were going to give me an easy day today, till I get settled in. It wasn't easy. At dawn, she hollered "Get up. Be down here in ten minutes." I scrambled down as quickly as I could. I didn't take time to wash, just threw on my clothes. It wasn't good enough. She wanted breakfast on the table - porridge, toast, coffee - in five minutes. She was angry that I hadn't gotten up and done all that before she got up. He slouched in the corner on a rocking chair and watched my every move. I'm sure he's going to be trouble. They kept me on the run the whole day. I'm exhausted.

"Oh, no," Susie said. "I so wanted her to have a lovely place. I'm not sure I want to hear this."

"Me either, I'm glad you're doing the reading, Dad."

May 10, 1909 Sunday
Dear Diary, My days are all the same. Work all day and collapse into bed at night. He hasn't tried to touch me yet. I haven't had time to wash myself much. She complains about me being dirty. That's good. It seems to keep him from wanting to be around me. I never thought of dirt as keeping me safe.

Dec. 23, 1909
Dear Diary, They've gone to their daughters for Christmas. Praise God, not that I think about you much God. What good are you? You've left me in this awful place. My room looks nice but it's freezing cold. Today I'm sitting by the fire downstairs in the parlour. I don't really mind being alone for Christmas. At least there's no one to tell me what to do and there is food in the cupboard and wood for the fire. I'm going to have a whole week of peace. My leg aches continually now. The purple colour makes it look permanently bruised. Maybe if I rest it while they are gone the pain will ease. Best part of this place is the pencils. They have a whole jar of pencils. And there's paper too. I will write stories this week. It's my only escape.
I'd like to run away but I'm afraid. It's so cold outside and the snow is deep. I'd have to stay on the road. If

anyone saw me, they'd just bring me back. That would give them an excuse to beat me. They may be telling me every day that I'm stupid and worthless but I'm not so stupid as to get lost in the dead of winter. I don't want to freeze to death. I hate being cold. Besides I have a whole week to rest.

Dad paused. "She's one strong teenager."
I could feel tears gathering in my eyes.

December 25, 1909
Dear Diary, I'm having a lovely time. When they see how much food is gone, I will get a beating for eating so much but it will be worth it. It feels so good to be full and rested. I'm lonely though. It's Christmas day. I remember Christmas with Mama and Papa. I can picture the tree. It towered far above me. Mama had so many pretty things to hang on it. She used to let me hang some down where I could reach. I remember dropping one. It splintered into a million glittering pieces. I cried so hard. Mama just hugged me and asked Nanny Kelly to sweep up the mess. She said, "It was an accident." No accidents ever happen here. Anything that's broken is blamed on me and I get the switch on my bare legs.
I won't think about that now. This is my week of good things. I'll think only good things.

"Christmas memories are supposed to be good," Susie said. "Poor Nana, even her good memories hurt."

"I can understand that," I said. "It's hurts to think of Christmas without Mom.

Dad added, "The last two years we've almost ignored Christmas. That's not good for us…"

I let his words sink in for a moment. I didn't want to think about Christmas without Mom. Guess we can't keep ignoring Christmas forever. Oh mom, why didn't you stay home that night? I gave myself a shake. "Let's get back to the diary." I said. "I'll read."

December 29, 1909

Dear Diary,

They're coming home tomorrow. I spent today rushing around trying to do all the stuff they had ordered me to do while they were away. It's snowing real hard outside. I've brought in the wood, scrubbed the floors and dusted everything. I'm tired and my leg has started to ache. Tomorrow it all starts again.

May 8, 1910 Sunday

Dear Diary,

I read over my Christmas week entries again. Oh Diary, it's horrible here. They never stop with the orders and the criticism. I'm stupid. I'm careless. I'm untidy. I won't keep myself clean. I feel like yelling at the missus. "Of course, I'm dirty. It's my only protection from your old man. Maybe you like him focused on me so he leaves you alone."

May 22, 1910 Sunday

Dear Diary, The Barnardo inspection was last Thursday. She must have known the inspector was coming. Right after breakfast she ordered me to heat water and take a bath. She had an almost new dress and undergarments ready for me afterwards. She even gave me a comb for my hair. "There now," she said. "You look quite presentable." The inspector didn't talk to me, only to them. He just looked me over and said, "Well you're strong and healthy looking. This must be a good spot for you." I didn't say anything. I didn't dare. After he left, I could see old man MacDougall staring at me. When the missus went out to the privy, he sidled up to me and put his hand on my shoulder. "You look pretty good now you're cleaned up," and then he laughed, a horrible laugh. I jerked away from him and ran up here to my room. I've pulled my bed in front of the door. I'll go back down once she's inside again. I didn't think things could get worse but ...

"Why didn't that inspector talk to her without the MacDougalls? Wouldn't he know she couldn't talk with them there?"

"He probably had such a huge workload, and didn't want to know," said Steve.

"Or just didn't care," said Susie.

"Maybe a little bit of both. We have to remember these kids were refuse and expendable. And besides, dealing the kids who were visibly battered would be enough trouble for him."

"There are no excuses for him doing nothing…Oh…"

Guilty. Guilty. How dare you accuse someone else?

My heart pounded. My stomach churned. We never know what someone is really thinking. I shivered. Can't think like this. I took a deep breath, "Come on, Dad, keep reading."

August 6, 1911 Sunday

Dear Diary, They've gone away for the day. Thank you, God. I've had all I can take. I'm so tired. My leg aches. The pain never stops. I'm hungry all the time. Saw this green powder in the pantry. Missus called it Paris Green. When I asked her what it was for, she said, "You leave that alone girl. It's for killing rats. It'll kill you too." Those were the best words I've heard in a long time. I have to get away from the old man. He grabs, pinches, squeezes, at every opportunity. Yesterday when I went to the garden for carrots, he grabbed my arm and twisted it behind my back. He slapped his filthy hand over my mouth and whispered in my ear. "I'll have you. You just wait. I want you to be good and ready - that means mighty frightened. You'll bend. You'll see." The missus yelled from the window, "Maggie, what's takin so long. Get in here with that water." He dropped my arm and walked away laughing. I hate him and her too. Good bye diary.

"Oh no! She can't … like Harrar. Oh…"

Susie started to cry.

"Hang on, you two," Dad said. "We know Nana didn't die.

August 15, 1911 Thursday

Dear Diary, It didn't work. Just made me terrible sick. Guess I couldn't force down enough of it. Besides I just want out of here. I don't really want to die. They took me to hospital. Now I'm back here again. Missus is mad but they've let up on me a little and he's keeping his distance. It won't last I'm sure."

"It's warm out now. Why doesn't Nana just run away?" Susie asked.

"It's not that simple," I said. "I remember how I felt after Mom died. I was so depressed. I didn't think logically. I just wanted Mom back. I felt frozen."

Dad added, "Nana's been physically abused and called stupid, useless. She wouldn't have the emotional strength to try to escape. Let's keep reading. The next entry is only one week later.

August 24, 1911 Thursday
Dear Diary, A new Barnardo inspector, Miss Kennedy, came today. Old lady MacDougall reported to her that I was a strong healthy girl, even though not very tidy. She said I refused to go to Church or Sunday School which wasn't true. Why would I refuse an opportunity to tell someone what's going on here? As always, the old man said I was stubborn, unreliable and careless about my work. Miss Kennedy looked at me. I could tell she wanted to talk to me but knew she wouldn't have a chance. She told the MacDougalls that she was taking me to a new place. She must have been contacted by the hospital and knew my story.

August 31, 1911 Sunday
Finally, I'm free. Miss Kennedy came today and brought me back to Hazelbrae. I get to rest here for a while before they send me out again. I will do my best to

please everyone here. Maybe they will decide to keep me. There are strict rules, and plenty of work, but nothing like being at MacDougalls. I share a room with ten other girls. It's wonderful to have company. Tilly came by to see me tonight. She's independent now. She works with another seamstress sewing fine dresses. She's totally free. She has a room above their shop. She sounded so happy. Just a few more years and I will be free too.

"Time for tea and lemon squares," Dad said. "Let's celebrate Nana's return to Hazelbrae."

Susie brightened up. "Yummy. I love lemon squares."

I pushed my guilt into the background and suggested, "Think I'll call Mrs. Logan and see if she wants to join us for tea. She's given us so many cookies and squares. It would be good to serve some to her."

She was home and happily accepted our invitation.

Time slipped by. When Mrs. Logan left, it was 4:30. "Tomorrow we get to hear the Ahmadis' story," I said.

"Great," Susie replied, "although it's going to be sad too."

Chapter Twenty-One

Storytelling

Sunday, November 12

Steve

Sunday dawned cold and clear. Renée and I had a good day together. We went to church as usual. Afterward, she worked on homework. I caught up on some of my paperwork. Mid-afternoon, we made Serena's chocolate sauce for the storytelling evening. We used that stirring time to talk.

"Would you like to hear another instalment in the soap opera of my life?"

Renée laughed, "What now, Dad?"

"Last Wednesday, I took a break from work and went for a walk in the park. Since Harrar's death, I have been feeling…a heaviness. The sun was shining. I thought it might lighten me up to be out in it. Besides, I love these crisp, clear fall days. Anyway, I was marching along at quite a good pace." I left out that I was picturing Lee Ann, in her black pants and clinging blue shirt…"I wasn't paying attention to my surroundings much."

"Suddenly, this female voice penetrated my thoughts with, 'Hey, stuck up. Aren't you even going to say, hi?'I stopped dead. A person stepped right on my heel. I turned around. Lying in a heap in the middle of the path was Janice. Yes, the Janice Lawson. My reaction was, 'What the…Oh, it's you Janice. Are you hurt?' I was tempted to run but thought better of it. For sure, she'd accuse me of leaving the scene of an accident."

Renée laughed.

"Oh, it gets better. I bent down to help her up. She stumbled. She couldn't step on her right foot. I guessed she had sprained her ankle. What could I do? I couldn't just leave her there. When I picked her up, she wrapped her arms around my neck. 'Oh, Steve, my white knight to the rescue,' she said and snuggled her head against my shoulder. I groaned. I'd only taken about two steps when a runner appeared in the distance. I recognized Lee Ann's blue track suit immediately."

By this time, Renée was laughing out loud. It felt so good to make her laugh.

"What did you do, Dad?"

"I felt like dropping Janice but …"

Renée shook her head, "Of course, you couldn't do that, could you?"

"No… I trudged resolutely to the nearest bench and set Janice down as gently as possible, unwinding her arms from around my neck. About two seconds later, Lee Ann appeared at my elbow. I'm sure my face was beet red, and not from the cold. My breath was coming in short gasps. Janice may be small like your mother, but she sure is heavy."

By now, Renée was laughing so hard she struggled to speak.

"Oh Dad, I can just imagine what Ms. Hamilton thought."

"Janice looked up at Lee Ann with a very satisfied grin and said, 'Oh dear, caught in the act.' Renée, you know I'm not great with women. I'm sure Tony would have a flip remark to offer. I just offered excuses, stumbling over my words."

Renée had to sit down; she was laughing so hard. It was funny. At least it was funny as I retold it. I joined in with Renée's laughter. It felt so good, a release or something. The timer went for the chocolate sauce. I moved it to a cold burner and flopped into a chair across from Renée.

Her laughter had shifted to a self-satisfied grin. "And Ms. Hamilton's reaction?"

"She just smiled and waited, saying nothing at all. I had the greatest urge to pick up Janice and shake her. Once again, Eleanor came to my rescue. She was supposed to be running with Lee Ann, but she had fallen behind a bit. By this time, she'd caught up. Her eyes shifted from Janice to Lee Ann. 'What happened, Janice?' she asked. 'I fell and sprained my ankle,' Janice replied. 'Really?' Eleanor said, disbelief colouring her voice. 'It's a long walk home on a sprained ankle. Guess you'll have to call 911.' 'Oh no,' Janice said, 'Steve can carry me.'"

Tears of laughter dripped down Renée's cheeks. Her eyes were sparkling. "Oh Dad, what did you say?"

"I just gasped. Eleanor stepped in with, 'I don't think so. We wouldn't want Steve to have a heart attack…'She looked at me, her eyes full of merriment. 'What actually did happen, Steve?'

"Happy to have a chance to defend myself, I said. "I was just walking along, when I heard someone call my name. I stopped and Janice walked right into me. I didn't even know she was there. 'Okay, Janice,' Eleanor said. 'Come on now, stand up. I'm sure you can walk. It's not fair to pick on someone as defenceless as poor Steve.' She grabbed Janice by the hand, yanked her up off the bench and the two of them walked away. Janice didn't even limp."

Renée wiped her eyes and her face. Slowly her smile faded, even from her eyes. "AND?" was all she said.

"I looked at Lee Ann and shrugged my shoulders, 'Guess Janice has fallen for me.' Lee Ann smiled and said, 'Great pun.' The whole story was much funnier today, than when it actually happened."

That evening, Renée and I decided to walk to the storytelling since St. Dominic's Church was not far and I had already delivered the ice cream and sundae fixin's earlier. Stars twinkled in the sky. The blanket of snow on the ground sparkled in the street lights. Even though it was a chilly night, the church doors were open, spilling out light as a bright welcome. People streamed into the sanctuary. A half hour before the program was to begin, seats on the main floor were filling up. There were even a few people in the balcony. I saw Richard and his two friends, the dissenters from the pub, come in and sit down together. Almost immediately, Tom Long sat down beside Richard. Fred Williams, and another policeman sat at the other end of the threesome. Richard leaned over to Tom and said something. Tom nodded and smiled. Good, I thought.

Janice squeezed into the pew right in front of us. By 7:00 the place was nearly full. David Sims and the local TV station's camera crew had set up in the far corner. Regardless what happens, we're making history tonight.

Mayor Handel opened the proceedings and thanked all of us who had a part in the planning. "Before I introduce any of our speakers," he said, "I want to acknowledge and offer our sympathy and prayers to Dr. and Mrs. Siddiqui. In the midst of their grief, they have come tonight because they too want to support the Ahmadis and they are grateful for your support of them. Dr. Siddiqui has cared for and loved our children for many years. Rashimi is a blessing at the Catalpa Creek women's shelter. They are both treasured members of our community. Many of you knew and loved their son, Harrar, an excellent student and an accomplished artist. We will all miss Harrar. Let's take a moment of silence to express our love and our prayers to Rashimi and Kasun."

Good, Bob, I thought. You always manage something appropriate.

After the silence, Bob introduced Tracey as the catalyst for the evening. Renée looked at me, smiled and squeezed my hand. That girl will be a politician someday, I thought. Tracey spoke about the kids' concern for the Ahmadis. “We are happy to have you in our community. We hope tonight will help us understand your journey from Syria. We welcome you.”

Eleanor spoke next, thanking the community on behalf of our committee for their generous response of gifts, money and friendship. She reminded us that our support and our friendship will continue to be needed. Eleanor is a wonderful public speaker. She told the story of meeting the Ahmadi family when they first arrived in Catalpa Creek. When Eleanor finished, the room was totally silent.

Wisely, Bob suggested, “Let’s sing a song.”

We watched the big screen gradually descend from the ceiling. The words to “You’ll Never Walk Alone” appeared. David Tompkins slipped up to the organ and flicked the switch. Richard climbed onto the stage. I saw Bob look down at Tom. Tom nodded a yes, so the mayor let Richard step up to the microphone.

“Hi, everyone, if you don’t know me, my name is Richard Wallace. I own the town’s only laundromat. I know I have been very open with my opposition to bringing the Ahmadis to Catalpa Creek. There are two things I want to say. First, I had nothing to do with the fire in their home. I would not do something so underhanded. In my mind, whoever started that fire was just plain mean and cruel. He was no better than the suicide bombers we’re all afraid of.”

Richard took a deep breath and nodded over at the Ahmadis. I watched their Mustafa nod right back. Good.

He continued. “Second, when I spoke out in opposition, I spoke out of fear. Now that I have met the Ahmadi family personally, I know they are people just like you and me. Yes, we have to be cautious, but we can’t let our fear take away our generosity and our hospitality, and most of all, our humanity. I’m glad that our community didn’t listen to me. I welcome the

Ahmadis. We need both a doctor and a nurse, and we need their children, Mustafa, Hassan and Thuraya. I'm glad you're here, all of you."

Well, he's had a conversion experience, I thought as I watched Richard bound down the steps and almost run back to his seat. There was a huge burst of applause. As it diminished, David played the introductory strains of "You'll Never Walk Alone." We all stood up and sang. It felt like I was making a pledge to the Ahmadis and to our community. We sat down and the Ahmadis came forward. Khalil stood at the microphone, his family around him. He opened his notebook and read, his accent thick, but the words came through clear and strong.

"Thank you…Thank you for welcome. Tonight, we tell story. We learn English better each day. We happy here." He took a deep breath and lifted up two fingers. "We leave Aleppo, Syria, two years tomorrow. In Aleppo, Nazira and I help freedom fighters. Government kidnap our Saliyeh. Demand ransom. We pay…" He paused, wiped his forehead on his sleeve. "They kill her anyway."

The crowd gasped.

"They send picture of body…awful." Kahlil's voice faltered. "Awful," he said, tears poured down his cheeks. He looked back at his family. Mustafa jumped up and took his father's arm leading him to his chair beside Nazira.

"Oh my God," Renee whispered, her eyes overflowing.

I put my arm around her and pulled her close. I wished she wasn't hearing this.

Mustafa returned to the microphone and began to read. "We left for Turkey, the night the picture come. We carried only backpacks. We walked to station, along back streets, keeping in shadows. Not take car, too dangerous. Police stop cars, check papers. We joined with others. All the same, afraid. At train, no seats left. We stood in aisle all the way. Train stop kilometre from

Turkish border. Soldiers command us off train. When train empty it pull away. Soldiers yell, walk, walk and wave guns. They fired bullets in air. We run. Soldiers laugh and keep firing."

Mustafa paused. His family joined him at the lectern. He leaned against his father. Khalil reached up and put his arm around his much taller son. Their eyes met.

Silenced reigned. I held my breath. Renée squeezed my hand so hard it hurt.

Mustafa turned back to the paper, took a deep breath, looked up at all of us and said, "Stray bullet hit my brother, Zahir. He just five years old."

A murmur of anguish coursed through the crowd.

"My father carry him across border, but it not matter. He dead." With tears streaming down his face, Mustafa crumpled into his father's arms. Bob stood up and hugged both of them. We were all crying.

Renée sobbed uncontrollably, her head against my chest. My tears dripped into her hair.

Bob turned to the microphone and announced, "We're going to take a break now." He motioned to Eleanor. She led the family out through a side door. Reverend Linda and Father McGarrity followed. Bob remained at the microphone. "This is a tough story. The Ahmadis are very brave to share it with us. They may not be able to continue tonight. For sure, they need some time. And we do too. We will take a twenty-minute break. In the church hall, there is coffee, tea, juice and refreshments. Please be back here by 8:00"

No one moved. After about five minutes, a few people stood up and a quiet murmur spread throughout the crowd. Gradually, some people filed out to the adjacent church hall.

Renée turned to me, "Oh Dad, how awful…"

I nodded. There was nothing to say.

Harrar's parents stopped at our pew, their faces white, their cheeks glistening with tears. We stood. "You're our friends," I said. "We want to support you."

Kasun nodded. "Thank you." He turned to Renée, "Thank you for the friendship you gave Harrar. We will always be grateful…"

Renée nodded and reached out with a hug for Rashimi.

"Now, we want to offer our support to the Ahmadis." Kasun said."Steve, can you take us to them, please?"

I looked at Renée. "I'm okay, Dad." Susie and I will go to the hall."

At 8:00, people began to file back into the sanctuary. Bob didn't hurry us. I guessed what was coming before he spoke.

"Folks, I'm sure you will understand that the Ahmadis have gone home. They have asked me to give you their apologies. They would like to continue their story. The planning committee has had a quick meeting. St. Dominic's is available in two weeks' time. We will reconvene on Sunday, November 26 at 6:30, here. The Ahmadis will finish their story and answer any questions you may have as best they can."

I checked my phone. The 26th… that works.

Bob continued. "I want to thank the committee for their efforts, and all the people who brought refreshments for this evening. I ask you to keep the Ahmadis and the Siddiquis in your prayers and thoughts over the next two weeks. Grief is a tough journey. Our community has two families that need our love and compassion. Thanks so much for coming. See you here, same time on November 26th."

Chapter Twenty-Two

In the Dark

Friday, November 17

Renée

Mostly, the school had recovered from Harrar's death, even if the four of us hadn't. We had pledged to get together once a week at one of our houses, just to talk and ask either a parent or Reverend Linda to join us. So far, we'd managed to meet twice, once with Dad and once with Reverend Linda. It helped. I hadn't had another nightmare, but Antonio kept reliving the whole thing in his dreams. Reverend Linda suggested he talk with a counsellor. He said he's on a waiting list.

Tracey said very little at our meetings. She seemed okay at school. I hoped she was. And Susie was just resilient, effervescent Susie. She talked, she hurt and she coped. I'm so blessed to have Susie as a friend. I thank God for her every day. I think it helped that there were four of us. With Mom, I felt so alone at first. I didn't realize that Dad and Susie and all our friends were grieving, too.

Mustafa seemed to be doing better with the kids. I think he must have understood me, because he settled a little. Of course, he was still a bit over the top, but he seemed more real.

Rachel, Susie and I worked with Thuraya after school, at least three days a week. With the extra help, her English improved. It felt good to be able to help the family in a very real way. Dad and I were beginning to feel that the time for trouble had passed.

I worked away on my project a little each night. On Friday, I stopped into Dad's office. After talking for a few moments about our day, I said. "It's time to get back to Nana's diary. I've written up some things, but we need to finish the diary before I can go any further on my essay. Could we work on it Sunday afternoon? Susie says she's free.

Dad looked at his schedule. "Yup, Sunday afternoon's good."

"Great," I said. "Are you home tonight?"

Dad frowned and hesitated. "Tony and Angelique, Lee Ann and I, and Tom and Eleanor are going to the Christmas play at the town hall tonight. I thought I'd told you."

I groaned. "Yes, Dad, you told me. I forgot. I'm having trouble focusing."

"That's all part of it. Hang in there, sweetheart."

"I know, I know." I swallowed the big lump in my throat. Think about something else, I commanded myself. "You are certainly seeing lots of Ms. Hamilton lately. Wouldn't you like to branch out a little? There must be more women around besides her."

"There's always Janice Lawson."

I grit my teeth. "Oh, Dad, really. I thought you'd…" I stopped when I saw the twinkle in his eyes. "Okay, you're teasing."

"She's not even a possible."

"Good."

Dad looked toward the clock on the wall, frowned and then turned back to me. "I thought you were getting used to Lee Ann and me. We're friends, Renée. We enjoy each other's company."

I grabbed a chair and pulled it over to his desk.

"Oh, oh," Dad said, "I feel a lecture coming." He grinned.

I didn't. "Don't get serious, Dad. It's much too soon. It's only been two-and-a-half years since Mom…"

Dad stopped the bantering. He leaned toward me. "Renée, you'll have to trust that I know what I'm doing and can take care of myself. At the moment, Lee Ann and I are friends. I'll let you know if our relationship becomes more serious."

I remembered saying the same thing about Harrar. I sighed, "Okay, I'll try. It's not easy, especially now."

Dad let silence rest between us for a bit. He leaned back in his chair. "While we're talking about relationships, what about you?"

He's shifting to me. Okay. I can do that. "Lately, Susie and I have been too busy to worry about boys. I do have a date for the Christmas dance. When he came to pick up Thuraya today, Mustafa asked me if I would go with him. I'm not sure about him but he's always polite and sincere with me. He's more outgoing than I'm used to. It won't be like going with Harrar. A date with Mustafa will involve a lot of laughter and people. I won't have to say much. I thought I'd risk it."

"Guess I don't have to worry about you with Mustafa, at least not on this first date."

"No, Dad. If he's anything like Harrar, Mustafa will treat me like a princess. I miss Harrar. He was a good friend. I keep telling myself that it was good to respect Harrar's confidentiality. He was my friend and he knew it…I keep repeating Dr. Sampler's advice, 'There are no reruns. I had no control over Harrar's decisions.'"

Dad got up and came round the desk to give me a hug. "Renée, I'm proud of you."

"I learned with Mom that God is my companion giving me strength, not Mr. Fix-It. I wish God would step in and keep us from doing terrible things."

"I'd like God to have a magic wand that conjured up miracles, too," Dad said. "I don't understand the why of things, Renée. I wish I did. I just keep plugging along and trusting that God is in charge. What I can do is give thanks for the good that I receive."

"Yeah, I know, Dad…I'll try giving thanks that Ms. Hamilton is your friend, though that's a mighty big leap for me."

Dad smiled. "Sounds good." He looked at his watch. "It's five o'clock already. Time to pack up. Let's pick up a pizza for supper on the way home. The play starts at 7:30 tonight." He stuffed papers in his brief case. "If you've nothing else to do, maybe I can call and get a ticket for you."

"No thanks. Susie, Rachel and I are taking Thuraya to a kid's early movie. Afterward, we're going to Rachel's to hang out. Rachel's Dad will bring me home by eleven."

The house phone was ringing when we opened the door. I stepped out of my boots, dropped books and coat on the floor, and ran for it. I clicked talk and heard nothing, only breathing. Oh no, not again. The breathing was replaced by a deep male voice, "Tell your father and his committee to get rid of their terrorist friends. They're not wanted in Catalpa Creek." The connection broke with a sharp click. My hands trembled as I replaced the phone on its stand.

Dad took one look at my face and asked, "What is it?"

"It was one of the troublemakers. A horrible man's voice ordered me to tell you and your committee to get rid of your terrorist friends."

Dad gave me a hug and pulled out his cell. "I'll call Tom." He talked a minute and turned to me. "He'll be right over."

We sat at the island and stared at the pizza. "My appetite's gone," Dad said.

"Mine, too…Why do people have to be so mean? I'd hoped they'd given up."

"So did I," Dad said. "I'm not so sure you girls should be taking Thuraya out tonight. Let's ask Tom."

"Maybe we could have a police escort. It might be fun for Thuraya—no it wouldn't. The police in Syria were the enemy. They are just getting used to feeling safe here."

"We're not going to let fear control us. We both need to eat." He opened the box of pizza and handed me a slice.

I took a bite and chewed. It tasted like wood. Obviously, my taste buds felt my fear. We had both choked down a piece and a few bites of salad before Tom rang the doorbell. I filled him in on the few details of the phone call.

"We're pretty sure we know who this group is," Tom said. "Unfortunately, we have no proof."

Dad told Tom my plans for the evening.

"Is Rachel's dad driving you to the movie?" Tom asked.

"Yes," I told him.

"Good. We'll have an officer keep you under surveillance. You'll be fine. I wouldn't want the four of you walking on the street without an adult, just in case." Tom stood up to leave. He looked straight at me. "Stick together. Don't look for the police presence. You won't recognize them anyway."

We followed Tom to the door. As he was going out, he said to Dad, "See you at the play."

Nothing happened all evening. Thuraya had a fine time at the movie, and so did we. I like kid's movies. They help me feel good.

Rachel's dad delivered me home at 11:05. I had just stepped into the kitchen when I heard a car drive up. No sound from the garage door. I came out into the hall and listened for Dad's key in the front door lock. Silence.

I checked the peephole. An eye stared back at me, and then darkness. What…? Tape? Fear shot through me like an electric current.

Shizzzzzzzz – something hissed – silence – a car door slammed followed by the squeal of tires as the car drove away. I stood frozen. A few seconds passed. Car lights flashed through the living room window and the crunch of gravel told me another car had pulled into the driveway. The garage door rumbled. That's gotta be Dad.

I ran into Dad's arms for a hug when he stepped through the door between the garage and the kitchen. "A car stopped out front just a few seconds ago. I thought it was you. When you didn't come in, I checked the peephole. An eye, that's all I could see, an eye staring back at me." Dad went straight to the front door. "Good thing you locked the door when you got home," he said, and untwisted the latch. I just nodded.

When Dad pulled the door open, the smell of fresh paint filled our lungs. The porch lights illuminated the one stark word – Terrorist – written in black paint across our door. Dad slipped his arm around my shoulders. "It's all right, Renée. This is just vandalism. We're safe. I'll call the police."

A squad car with two officers arrived within minutes. They checked out the yard and surrounding area. While they were taking down our story, two more officers arrived. They checked the door frame and knob for fingerprints. They took a sample of the paint and the duct tape. They left us with the assurance that there would be a squad car in the area checking over the next few days.

"Let's go to the kitchen and talk. I'll make us a cup of tea," I said to Dad after the policemen left.

Dad smiled. "Your mother will always be with us as long as we can have tea together."

"I know. Her words are written on my heart and I'm glad."

We sat at the kitchen island, our cups steaming. "We can't let this frighten us." Dad said, "but we can't ignore it, either. I'll be glad to talk to Tom about it in the morning. I need his wisdom."

"It brings back the fright I had when Russell Carding was harassing me, especially when he told me he had watched me buy my dress for the Christmas dance. The thought of someone else stalking me is…"

Dad reached out and took my hand. "Just remember, we're not alone. We have each other, our friends, the police and God. We will be fine."

"I'm worried about the Ahmadis. What if these people terrorize them again?"

"We have to trust that the police will be vigilant. Tomorrow, I'll tell our committee about tonight, in case someone else is targeted." We sipped the rest of our tea. "Renée, we need to go to bed. It's already one a.m. Whoever is trying to frighten us won't be back tonight. The police will patrol our neighbourhood and the Ahmadis'."

I nodded and slid off the stool. As we carried our cups to the sink, Ebony sidled through the kitchen door. "Okay, friend," I said. "It's time for bed."

Dad turned off the lights and the three of us climbed the stairs.

Sleep was a long time coming.

Chapter Twenty-Three

Invitations

Saturday, November 18

Renée

Saturday was a slow day. Exhausted from so little sleep and so much worry, neither Dad nor I felt like doing much. After breakfast, we sat in the living room, trying to read, waiting for Tom. I knew I should be doing homework, but I didn't feel like even trying to focus. I kept hearing that man's gravelly voice on the phone and seeing the eye staring into mine through the peep hole. Tom arrived shortly after ten. He called the paint on our door vandalism. It felt more like harassment to me.

"We'll have the fingerprint report this afternoon," he said. "There's not much else to tell you. We'll keep your house under surveillance. It looks like they don't want to harm either of you, just frighten you."

"They're succeeding," I answered.

After Tom left, I went upstairs for a nap. Sleep eluded me. Finally, I got up and turned on my computer. Might as well work on this project, I thought. At least I'm having lots of firsthand experience with being terrorized.

Supper was Thursday's leftovers. While Dad and I were cleaning up, my cell phone chimed. *Mustafa Ahmadi* flashed on the screen. "Hey," I said when I answered.

Mustafa laughed. "Hey," he said. After a short pause, he continued as if he were reading, "Renée, my family invites you and your father for traditional Syrian supper Saturday evening, December 5, 6 p.m. I am inviting whole committee. We want to thank you."

"Thank you, Mustafa. Let me check with Dad." I turned to Dad and repeated Mustafa's invitation. He dried his hands and pulled out his phone to check. He lifted two thumbs up. "Sorry for the delay, Mustafa. Yes, we will come. Thanks so much. Can we bring anything?"

"Bring anything?"

He sounded puzzled, so I added, "To offer to bring something is traditional. Sometimes, the offer is accepted, and we bring a salad or dessert. Sometimes it's not, and people say, 'No thank you.' Sometimes we say, 'Just bring your smile'."

Mustafa laughed. "Just bring your smile," he said. "It's beautiful."

It was my turn to be embarrassed. I swallowed nervously, "Thank you, Mustafa."

"See you at school on Monday." He sounded relieved.

"Yes. Thank you for the invitation. Bye."

"Bye," he said and clicked off.

"Now, isn't that nice?" Dad said as he put the last plate in the dishwasher. "Having the whole committee is quite an undertaking." He wiped down the counter and hung the dishcloth over the tap. "Maybe I'll call Tom and tell him. This dinner would be a perfect opportunity for someone to make trouble."

Dad retreated to his study.

I was opening a can of cat food for Ebony when I heard faint music from Dad's phone. A few minutes later he returned, phone still in his hand. "It's Lee Ann. She's inviting us both to her place for an impromptu crokinole tournament tonight."

Anxiety flowed through my veins. I pointed to my chest and mouthed "Me?"

"Just a moment, Lee Ann," he said, and pushed hold. "That's what she said. She's having some friends over and is including us."

"No, I don't think so. You go. Tell her thank you but no, for me. I'll come another time."

He frowned.

"Tell her I have homework. I do, scads of it. Besides, I'm not ready. It feels too much like we're becoming family." I could see the hurt on his face. "Sorry. It's just that I need time. I'm still not used to the idea of you and Ms. Hamilton dating. Maybe at Christmas, we could have a party and invite my friends and yours. Then you can invite Lee Ann as one of the group."

Dad's face cleared. "Okay, honey. We'll go at your pace."

He took the phone off hold. "Sorry for the delay, Lee Ann. Renée says she has scads of homework, so we'll take a rain check."

"What?" I mouthed.

"Talk to you soon. Goodbye."

"Dad, why aren't you going?"

"I'm not leaving you here alone. I know Tom assured us we are safe, but I'm worried."

I opened my mouth to argue. Dad shook his head. "No arguing. You don't feel good about our going to Lee Ann's together. That's valid. I'm worried about someone causing trouble here. That's valid too. End of discussion." He turned and headed for his study.

"Okay," I yelled and stomped up the stairs to my room. This time, my emotions seemed to spark creativity. I laid out the structure for my essay.

At ten, Dad and I had hot chocolate. Back in my room, I turned on Mom's candle on the window sill. I needed her close. I settled on the floor and stared at the flame. "Come to me, Mom," I said. "I know we're working on our third year without you, but

I still need you." I tried to make my mind go blank. It wouldn't. "Okay, Mom. I'll talk. There's been so much. I miss Harrar's comfortable friendship. I'm afraid here at home. I'm worried about the Ahmadis. There's too much going on without Dad and Ms. Hamilton. They're getting closer and closer." I shifted my weight and turned my gaze to the blackness of the window. "My world feels so dark. I wish he could be satisfied with just the two of us. I know that's not fair. Help me, Mom."

Once again, I cried—not wild sobs, just slow silent tears spilling down my cheeks and dripping off my chin. I stared at the candle. My legs got stiff. My back began to hurt. Peace finally crept in and cradled my heart. I prayed, "Thank you God, for this candle-lighting ritual. It helps." As I flipped the candle's switch to off, a light went on in my head. Ms. Hamilton, suggested this ritual in the first place. I groaned. "Thank you, God for that reminder. You do have a sense of humour."

Chapter Twenty-Four

Freedom

Sunday afternoon, November 19

Renée

We had finished lunch when Susie rang our door bell and walked right in. "I'm here," she yelled. "Let's get started."

Dad opened his study door as I ran down the stairs. "Be with you in a minute," he said.

Susie and I made tea and got out the squares. "I'm glad there's some left," she said.

"Was everything quiet here last night?"

"Yup, at least no unwanted visitors, if that's what you meant?"

"What else happened?"

"Ms. Hamilton invited Dad and me over to her place for a little spur of the moment party with some of their friends. I refused to go, mostly because I don't want to be her friend. Dad stayed home, too.

"So, you did homework all evening? That must have been fun."

"Not quite. I turned on Mom's candle for us to have a chat. I must have sat there for an hour, complaining, trying to listen. When I felt a little better, I shut out the candle. Right then I heard it."

"Heard what."

"It felt like a real voice."

"Heard what, Renée?"

"The question?"

"What question?"

Susie actually stamped her foot. I grinned. It was fun to tease her for a change. I don't often do that. "I heard, 'Who gave you the candle idea, Renée?"

Susie frowned.

"I've decided it was God talking."

"God?"

"I think God has a quirky sense of humour. It was Ms. Hamilton who told me about the candle ritual."

Susie's frown cleared. "Guess you're just going to have to get used to the idea of having Ms. Hamilton around. Let's look on the bright side. It won't hurt to have a private *in* with the vice principal."

We both laughed.

Dad stepped into the kitchen. "I'd like to read tonight if that's okay."

"Sure," Susie and I agreed at the same time. Once our ritual was finished, Dad began.

October 10, 1911

Thanksgiving Day at Hazelbrae is wonderful. They cooked four big turkeys. There was lots for all of us. We went to church this morning in a big cathedral downtown. The music was wonderful. Tilly was there too. I sure hope they never find another place for me. I've been working in the kitchen here at Hazelbrae. One thing I learned at MacDougalls was how to cook. I think that's what I'll do when I'm eighteen. I'll get a job cooking in a restaurant. At least I won't have to worry about having enough to eat or being warm either. The kitchen here at Hazelbrae is mighty warm.

November 3, 1911
Dear Diary, Well, it's finally come. I knew it would. This was really too good to last. They don't usually send us out just before winter but tomorrow I go to Mrs. Caroline Brown. They say she lives in town and there was no mention of a Mr. Brown. I sure hope there's no dirty old man in this household.

"I do, too," Susie interjected.

November 5, 1911 Sunday
Dear Diary, God, you've finally answered my prayers. Mrs. Brown is sweet. She has 5 children and no husband. She runs a bake shop. She was thrilled to learn that I knew how to cook. She told me to call her Miss Caroline. It's such a pretty name. I'm on my feet all day in the shop. My leg hurts a lot but it's different when Miss Caroline works beside me. She actually says thank you at the end of the day. She's paying me too. She gives Barnardos $4.00 a month and a dollar a month to me. I feel rich and in a few years I'll have all the money that has built up for me at Barnardos.

Already I feel like one of the family. I eat with them. It's pretty noisy but the kids are fun. I'm not lonely here. When Miss Caroline notices that my leg is hurting, she gives me a job I can do sitting down. There's lots of water for washing up. She says we have to be clean because we are selling our cooking. We wouldn't sell much if people got sick on our food. It feels so good to be safe and clean. I want to stay here forever.

I reached out and put my hand over the diary page. "Finally, Nana has found a home. Thank you, God,"

Dad smiled.

Susie piped up with, "It's about time. I don't think I could have withstood another McDougall."

Dad fanned the remaining few pages. "Nearly done. Looks like good news from here on."

December 25, 1911

Dear Diary, It's Christmas night. We've had a wonderful day. Yesterday, we decorated a big pine tree for the living room. This morning there were presents under it. There were even three for me. The first was a box with five pencils, a pen, ink, a whole pad of paper, envelopes and ten stamps. I can write to Tilly. The second was a new dress, not a hand-me-down, a dress made just for me. And it isn't a work dress. It's a pretty, party dress. Miss Caroline said it's time I had something nice to wear to church, and when we go visiting. She actually takes me with her. I'm part of the family. The third box was huge. Inside was a lovely warm coat, hat, scarf and mittens. I feel like I'm in heaven. I made my gifts for them. I wrote a story for each one of them. Miss Caroline cried when she read hers. Her story is about a girl like me. At the end of it I thanked her for loving me.

"I'm so glad Nana finally had a good Christmas," Susie said.

"I'm happy that she could give gifts as well as receive them," I said. "I wish we had some of her stories."

"I can imagine Nana and the Brown family sitting around the tree, reading her stories," Dad said.

"Our Tomchuk Christmas Eve family tradition," Susie said, "is to gather around the Christmas tree while Dad reads the Christmas story." She turned to me and asked, "Are you going to get a Christmas tree this year?"

Dad shook his head. He looked so sad.

The words just burst forth. I don't think they came from me. Maybe Mom, I don't know. "Let's have a Christmas tree this year, Dad. We can tell stories about Mom as we decorate it."

He looked as surprised as I felt. He paused a moment, brightened up a bit and said, "Okay, sure."

Susie joined in. "Get a tall tree that touches the ceiling. It would look amazing in this old house."

Dad looked at me. I nodded. "We'll see," he said.

I poked Susie and added ,"That's always Dad's stock answer when he thinks something is a bad idea."

"Now Renée," he started. He caught the gleam in my eye and stopped. "Okay," he said.

Susie and I chuckled.

Dad picked up the diary. "Almost done, girls. Let's finish it." He read:

July 1, 1912 Canada's birthday,

Well diary I haven't written in you for a long time. In fact I just found you down at the bottom of my Barnardo trunk. I guess I haven't needed you, since I came to live with Miss Caroline. It's wonderful here. I even have time to read. I go to the library every week. I'm a member of the family. I love them all and the best part is that they love me.

For some reason, I am no longer stupid, careless, untidy. I willingly work hard. I'm 17. I've had a raise. Miss Caroline says I'm worth it. Since all my needs are met, I use very little of my money. My bank account is growing. I've graduated from grade 8 and I have a trade. I can work as a cook. My dreams when I first came to Canada are finally realized. Yesterday I sold a story to a magazine. I received a cheque for $5.00, a whole month's wages just for one of my stories. Maybe someday I'll be a writer. I have a family. I'm grateful. I go to church every week and give thanks to God. I still don't understand why I had it so tough for so long or why God lets people like old man MacDougall exist.

July 21, 1912. Sunday

Dear Diary, My heaven has been invaded. Miss Caroline has a hired a man to do deliveries. He stays in a room at the back of the shop. I don't like him. He emanates meanness. I don't want to desert the children but I have no choice. Until I'm 21 I'm not truly free of Barnardo's, and I can't access the money they have saved for me. I will have to take another place. I talked with the Barnardo's inspector, Miss Kennedy today. She said that I am old enough to seek my own position. She will help me find one if I need it, but I don't. Miss Caroline helped me get a job in a restaurant in Port Hope. That's where Tilly lives. I'll be able to visit with her lots. I have rented a room at Mrs. Duncan's boarding house. I'll find friends at church just as I have here. Maybe I'll even fall in love.

I'm 17, old enough to be on my own. Miss Caroline asked me how I survived at those other places where the people were so cruel. I said, "I guess I'm a strong woman."

I've grown up. All those tough experiences are part of me, yes but they are in the past. I can learn from them. I'm free now. I can begin again. From here on in I will follow the advice Tilly gave me long ago when we were on the ship to Canada. I will count my blessings. Here they are:

1. I have a family now with Miss Caroline.
2. I've learned to cook.
3. I have a job.
4. I'm independent.
5. When I'm 21, Barnardo's will give me my money. I will be rich.
6. I have my whole life ahead of me.
7. I'm free.
8. I can begin again.

Dad carefully closed the diary and laid it on the table. We just sat there, not saying anything. Reverently, I placed the precious book back inside its box. Safe and comfortable. I wondered how many times Nana had taken it out to reread it, especially that list of blessings. I let my fingers slide over her name carved into the lid.

Life is about choices and letting go. You did it, Nana. You survived.

After a few minutes, I said. “At least Nana’s story has a happy ending.”

“Are you sure?” Susie asked. “We don’t know what lies ahead for her. Yes, she got married, but who did she marry? Was he good to her?”

“I guess we’ll never know,” Dad said. “Unless, of course, you find something more in Grandma Rushton’s trunk.”

“I don’t think so. The diary was in the bottom box. There’s no one to ask. They’ve all died, even Mom.” My words fell into the midst of us like lead. Dad heaved a sigh. So did I.

Susie broke in, “You never know. Maybe somewhere else in the attic. Maybe someday, in a box of old stuff, at the back of a drawer or somewhere. Wouldn’t that be exciting. Her eyes danced with the mystery.”

“Yeah, maybe.” I couldn’t join in her imagining. “At least I have lots of stuff for my project.”

Susie wasn’t going to let us drag her down. “And you can be very proud of your Nana. Wow, she was a mighty strong woman.”.

I tried for a smile but didn’t quite make it.

“Let’s have another cup of tea?” Dad said. He picked up the teapot. “Empty.”

I dragged myself up from the table and put on the kettle. Ebony wandered in from the laundry room, meowing as if he wanted to be included in any treats.

Sunday evening, November 19

Steve

Susie invited Renée to her house for supper, which was good, because I hadn’t planned anything. They said they were going to do a homework marathon together. They both had tests Monday and could help each other study. We arranged that she would text me when she wanted to come home. Shortly after Susie's dad picked them up, Lee Ann called. When I told her Renée was out for the evening, she invited me for supper. Grateful, I put the still-frozen TV dinner back into the freezer, locked up the house and left.

No crazy drivers came peeling around a corner trying to force me off the road. Slowly, my mind let go of all my worries. I pictured Lee Ann. I kept my focus on her eyes and her peaceful spirit.

She answered the door wearing a frilly apron over her slacks and bright red sweater. "Interesting apron," I said.

She blushed and answered, "It's definitely not me, is it? It's a gift from Eleanor."

"Of course, only Eleanor would give you something like that. Mind you Eleanor isn't frilly, either."

We both laughed as I untied her apron strings. "We're just having leftovers from the party last night.

"Sounds good to me," I said as I pulled her close and nibbled on her ear lobe.

She kissed my cheek and pulled away slowly.

She took my hand to lead me in by the fire. "Let's have a glass of punch while the hors d'oeuvres get hot and you can tell me about the attack at your house."

"It wasn't really an attack, exactly," I said as we settled down together on the couch, our thighs touching. Her closeness felt exciting. I breathed in her scent as I slipped my free arm around her shoulders. "Someone spray painted 'terrorist' on our door. That was all, but it was scary for Renée. He obviously doesn't like our close connection with the Ahmadis."

"Renée's sure having a rough time. First, Harrar, and now this. Is there anything I can do to help?"

"Just your presence helps…at least me and that's good for her in the long run."

Lee Ann smiled.

"Now, let's set that aside. I've other things on my mind." I drew her into a long, slow kiss. "Let's try that again."

The buzzer went on the stove. Lee Ann giggled. "Even the stove is our chaperone." She stroked my cheek. "We'd better eat those hors d'oeuvres before they dry out totally."

"After supper, for now, just one more" Our lips met. My whole body responded. Lee Ann very gently pushed me away.

"Later," she said her eyes sparkling. "Later."

In between main course and the coffee, I thought. "Shall I put on some music?"

"Of course. I'll set the food out on the coffee table in here, so we can enjoy the fire as we eat." Lee Ann walked briskly into the kitchen.

While we cleaned up on the party sandwiches, I told her the latest about Nana Sinclair's diary. Lee Ann asked lots of questions. We sat quietly for a while, enjoying being together and thinking our own thoughts.

Lee Ann wriggled a bit and said, "Let's clean up and start the coffee."

"No rush."

A shadow crossed her face. Her eyes lost their sparkle. "Can we clean up first?" she asked.

"Of course. Remember, I will never try to take anything you don't want to give."

"I know that, Steve. It's just, I'm not as resilient as I would like to be." A tear slipped down her cheek.

I pulled her to her feet and wrapped my arms around her suddenly stiff shoulders. Laying my cheek against hers, I said, "This is for two of us. It's not beautiful if both of us don't enjoy it." I felt her relax a bit. I drew my arms away and turned to stack the dishes on the tray.

"I'll get the coffee on," Lee Ann said.

Well, Steve, I thought, you have to go slowly. She's lovely, and she's worth it.

When she returned with cookies and coffee, I had already taken down the crokinole board and set out the disks. She smiled. "You missed the big competition last night. Eleanor was our champion."

"I'm not looking for a champion tonight, Just a fun relaxing game, but first dessert." I picked up a chocolate chip cookie and dipped it into my cup.

She turned to me, her eyes full of mischief and held up the one lemon square on the plate. "Want a bite?"

"Sure. Thanks for offering."

She broke off a piece. I opened my mouth wide.

"Wow, that's really the Grand Canyon," she said as she dropped it in.

I laughed, a deep belly laugh splattering the whole front of her shirt with lemon square. I swallowed what was left. "I'm sorry." I grabbed my napkin and started to wipe off her blouse. By then we were both laughing. I patted away till I got to her long beautiful neck. Our laughter disappeared when our lips touched. I pulled her close. Lee Ann…I love you, I thought – no I can't say that yet, I don't even know if it's true. "Lee Ann, you are such fun," I said, looking deep into her eyes. We kissed again. She wrapped her arms around my neck. I could feel her heart beating as she moulded her body closer and closer.

The insistent strains of the William Tell Overture emanated from my telephone. I tried to ignore it but lost the battle. It's just a few minutes past nine. That won't be Renée.

Lee Ann pulled away an inch or two. "You'd better pick it up," she said, her voice thick with emotion.

I groaned, reached into my pocket, glanced at the screen and clicked the talk button. "Hi, Tom, what's up."

"I'm sorry to disrupt whatever you're doing, Steve, but you need to know that we just caught the Rembrandt who painted your door. He was standing on your doorstep holding a dummy with a hangman's noose around its neck and a sign saying *Muslims go home*. A buddy held a drill and screws in his hands. A spray can of black paint lay on the seat beside the driver of their car. We got all three of them. Tonight, two other officers intercepted two more people—a man and a woman—trying to break into the Ahmadi's apartment. I think we may have the whole gang."

"Thanks for letting me know. I'll tell Renée when I pick her up tonight. She'll be relieved that you've caught them."

"We all are. I'll drop by in about an hour to give you more details. See you then."

"Thanks again." I clicked the phone off and turned to Lee Ann. "Well, that's a big relief. They've caught the gang that were trying to terrorize Renée and me. I'm glad I took the call even though…"

Lee Ann grinned, "I'm glad too, Steve, even though?" She leaned over and touched my cheek. Her slim gentle fingers reignited the fire within me.

I sighed. "I have to go. Tom will be at my house in an hour. I need to text Renée that I'm coming for her."

Lee Ann placed her lips on mine. That kiss spoke volumes for both of us. She settled back into the sofa. "There will be another time. This is only the beginning. Thank you, Steve. You've been so patient with me. That means a lot. I feel safe with you. I've needed that."

I wound a stray curl around my finger and thought, soon I'll have the privilege of loosening the pins and setting those curls free. Thank you, God. I am—we are truly blessed. I sighed again and dragged myself off the couch. “Thank you for this wonderful interlude. You find safety with me, and I find peace with you. What more can we ask?”

When I pulled on my boots, I remembered Renée’s compromise. “Lee Ann, Renée and I have decided to have a Christmas party with some of our friends. You are on the top of my guest list, and she has agreed that it would be a good way to have you over for an evening. Please understand it’s not that she dislikes you. She’s just struggling so with our friendship.”

Lee Ann nodded. “I’d be honoured to come, Steve. Have you set a date yet?”

“Oh… no. We haven’t got that far.”

“Okay, let me know as soon as you have. I will bring some Scottish shortbread. I use my grandmother’s recipe that she brought with her when she came to Canada.”

“Before I go…”

Late Sunday night, November 19

Renée

Dad and I arrived home about ten minutes before Tom knocked on the door. I put on the kettle. Dad welcomed him and brought him through to the kitchen. “Hey, Detective,” I said. “Are you ready for a cup of tea?”

Tom’s face relaxed into a smile, “Sounds good, Renée. It’s been a long evening.”

“Tell us all about the arrest,” Dad said.

“It really wasn’t very exciting. We’ve kept a patrol car making extra rounds in your neighbourhood. About 8:30 tonight two of our constables turned down your block in their cruiser. They saw a car with three men in it stopped just down the street from your place. They had a hunch that the car didn’t really belong, so they computer-checked the license plate, turned around about halfway down the first side street, and came rolling back." He took a sip of tea and continued. "By then, two of the men were standing at your front step trying to hang on your door, a dummy with a noose on its neck and a sign saying, 'Muslims go home.' The constables pulled up, turned on the spotlight and ordered the men to freeze. They dropped the dummy and ran. The constables followed and caught them easily. These two were not very fit."

Dad refilled Tom's cup from the pot.

"The wheel man drove off. From the vehicle registry plate, we found the home address of the owner. A cruiser was despatched to that address and picked him up as he drove in his driveway."

Tom cupped his hands around the mug of tea. After the second big sip, he said, "The other two were caught cutting a pane out of a bedroom window in the Ahmadi's apartment. The man had a packsack containing a hand grenade. The woman was carrying mace and a spray can of black paint. Already, they had sprayed the message, 'Go home terrorists' on the back wall of the building under their window. All five are in custody at headquarters."

Renée, touched his arm. "A woman! There was a woman in the group?"

"Yes. We've run her picture, but far as I know, no identification yet. She's not talking without her lawyer. Someone else is doing the interrogation. My shift's over, I think you can rest easy tonight. The surveillance detail is still in place and will be till we get all the loose ends tied up. I'm glad you weren't home."

Dad put his hand on Tom's shoulder. "Thanks for stopping here on your way home. It helps to know what's happening."

Tom nodded. "Time I got going. I need to get some sleep. It's been a long day."

Dad saw Tom to the door. I gathered up Ebony and was on the stairs when he returned.

"I'll just shut off the lights and lock up."

"Okay."

"Good night, Renée."

"Good night, Dad." I ran back down the steps and gave him a hug. "We're a team and I'm glad."

"Me too," he said.

Chapter Twenty-Five

The Ahmadi's Story Part 2

Sunday, November 26

Renée

My phone startled me awake. I lifted it from my night table. Yikes! It's 8:45. I swiped the screen, "Hey, Susie."

"Renée, could you and your Dad pick me up for the storytelling tonight? My family doesn't want to go early. Joey and I need to practice our song."

"Sure, Dad needs to be there about an hour ahead. Is that soon enough?"

"Yup."

I rolled over and pulled the covers back up to my chin. "You've written another song. Where do you find the time?"

"I haven't been sleeping a lot.

"You okay?"

"Yes, it's just the Harrar thing. I'm doing better. Writing this song has helped. Besides, it will go in my portfolio for the music program at university."

I snuggled down to talk for a bit. "Maybe we need another group meeting amongst the four of us."

"Maybe. Let's set a date when we're together at school. Have you thought any more about university?"

"I'm thinking about your suggestion of journalism or at least something that involves writing. I'm loving my Nana Sinclair project even if it is bleak. I've decided to take your advice and sign up for General Arts – English and History."

"Where?"

"Same places you applied."

"Great!!!"

"I think so too."

"Guess, I'd best get back to work. Mom's declared war on the state of my room. At least, next year my mess will be my problem."

I envisioned Susie's room, the floor carpeted with discarded clothes and books. Posters on the walls hanging at crazy angles, tacks missing, and smiled. Rooming with her would be interesting. "Okay," I said. "Guess I'd better do something, too. See you at church."

I clicked off, dragged myself from my bed and made a list: breakfast, yoga, church, homework. Not very exciting. At least the Ahmadi's storytelling tonight will be interesting.

Throughout the day, the outside temperature dropped steadily. The clock said 5:15 as we dumped our supper dishes into the sink.

"They'll wait for us," Dad said. "I'll get the car started. See you in five. Make sure you lock the front door."

We picked up Susie and were at St. Dominic's by 5:35. I had brought my iPad so I could work on my project while Susie and Joey practiced.

By six-thirty, the church sanctuary was full. Dad slipped in beside Susie, Joey and me. Janice Lawson appeared and squeezed in beside Dad.

He leaned over and whispered to me. "Okay if I sit over there with Eleanor and Tom?" I chuckled and nodded. Dad stood and excused himself to Janice as he escaped.

Susie squeezed my arm. "Why'd your Dad move?" she asked.

I smiled. “He needed to talk with Tom.” A few minutes later Lee Ann came in and sat beside Eleanor. Susie looked at me and rolled her eyes. I pointed to the pulpit. Mayor Handel had stepped up to the microphone.

“Good evening,” his big voice boomed out over the crowd. He waited for everyone to settle. After he had welcomed us, he said, “Let’s start the evening with two of our young people. Susie and Joey have written a special song for this evening.”

I pulled my feet back under the pew to let Susie and Joey out. Janice wasn’t any more polite for them than she was with Dad. Poor Joey tripped over her feet and staggered into the aisle. He did well not to yell at her.

Their song was beautiful as always. When they finished, Mayor Handel turned the microphone over to Dr. Ahmadi. He opened his notebook and began to read.

“Thank you for returning tonight. I start where Mustafa left off two weeks ago. We buried Zahir. We walked long time. When we stop to rest, people streamed past. At villages, Turkish citizens offered food and clothing. Exhausted and hungry, we arrived refugee camp at Killis. People everywhere.” He spread his arms wide to show the enormity of the place. Then he shook his head and read, “No tents, no supplies for us. UNHCR had nothing.” He shrugged his shoulders and gestured the nothing with his hands. “They said, ‘Go north to Gazientep. Smaller crowd. Only fifty-six kilometers—maybe only three days walk.’”

Dr. Ahmadi paused. He took a sip from the glass of water on the lectern.

“Only three days walk!” I whispered to Susie. “For Thuraya that would be forever.”

“Well, they had no choice. They couldn’t go back,” she responded.

He began again. “Volunteers from a Christian church gave us food. Thuraya not strong We walked five days. We slept at road side, afraid of other travellers. Everyone hungry. Last day, we see young couple with two-year-old and small baby. Baby cried and cried. Mother, hungry, thirsty, exhausted, little milk. We shared last of our food." He took another sip of water.

"Poor baby. This is worse than Nana Sinclair's story," Susie commented.

"I don't think so. They were together as a family. That means a lot."

Dr. Ahmadi continued his story. "We smell camp before we see." He held his nose. "Tents in rows. Narrow, muddy pathways between. When it rain, pathways flood—sewage." Once again, Dr. Ahmadi shook his head, held his nose. His body drooped. "UNHCR gave us tent, sleeping mats, blankets, five plates, cups, spoons, knives, forks. One sharp knife, and two water pails, one for wash, one for drink. Each morning, we line up for small ration of food."

Silence filled the church. No one wanted to miss a single word. Once again he took a swallow of water. My throat felt dry, too. Thanks to my research, I could visualize the scene in detail.

Dr. Ahmadi said, "We live at Gazientep two years. At first, enough food for all. More people arrive every day. Last few months, only strong, healthy receive food. Some days, Thuraya turned away, she young, not strong. We shared ours with her." decided

I just shook my head in despair.

His story continued. "Canadians come to camp." They say, 'Come to Canada.' Many were afraid. They say Canada cold. Shake their heads. We decide cold better than refugee camp. I fill out papers in French. When Canadian official see I, doctor, Nazira, nurse, he… Kahlil made a thumbs-up sign. I hoped that mean we be near top of list. We gave thanks to Allah. We would survive."

Susie turned to me. “We have just one family. There are so many.”

“One is better than none,” I said. “We better do a good job with our one.”

Kahlil continued, “We grateful to be in Canada. I study hard. My English improve. I volunteer at hospital. I do residency. We work. We support family.” He turned and smiled at Nazira and the kids. We promise to be good citizens.”

Dr. Ahmadi looked exhausted. He stumbled on the last few sentences. He turned to Mustafa and nodded. Mustafa stood, gave his dad a hug and stepped forward to take his place at the microphone.

God, give him strength and wisdom, I prayed. I wouldn’t want to speak to this crowd.

“We are Muslim,” Mustafa began. “Muslim not terrorist. We believe in God, same God you believe. We have one prophet, Mohammed, peace be upon him. We have Qur’an, our sacred book. Your Bible sacred too. We pray formal prayers five times a day.” He paused and looked out at the crowd.

He’s doing fine, I thought. Yet, I know he’s afraid. He wants so much to be accepted.

Susie leaned over and whispered, “I wish he was like this all the time.”

He continued, “Suicide bombers not true Muslim. They brainwashed by people who twist faith to justify violence.”

He gripped both sides of the pulpit. The passion in his voice was so strong it was almost frightening.

“Our faith teaches human life is sacred. Our faith teaches women are to be loved and respected. Our faith requires us to care for others, to give alms to the poor. Our faith values children. Please understand our faith is good. We want to be accepted.” Mustafa turned to his father. The whole family stood and joined him at the microphone.

Susie nudged me. "He's doing a good job, isn't he?"

I nodded. I tried to catch his eye, but we were too far away. I sent him thoughts of support and friendship, hoping he could feel my caring.

Someone started applauding. Almost immediately, everyone joined in. Well, everyone but Janice. She was staring straight ahead. Finally, Mayor Handel stepped up to the mike.

"Okay, folks, thank you for your response. Now, we will take some time for questions."

There were lots. Don Lakey asked, "One of the news reports said that the refugees had cell phones, as if that meant they were rich. Can you explain about the cell phones?

Mustafa answered him. "It's true many refugees have cell phones. In Syria cell phones cheap, and Wi-Fi free everywhere. Only way to connect with family in Syria. On journey need cell phone to survive."

Mayor Handel let the questions continue for nearly a half hour. Then he ended the question period. "You have all learned a great deal tonight. The Ahmadis will be among us for a very long time. You can invite them to your homes. You can ask them questions and answer theirs on an individual basis. They've done a wonderful job tonight. Now they deserve a rest. Let's end the evening with all of us singing Susie and Joey's song. It's up on the screen. This will be followed by Father McGarrity giving us a blessing. We will close with 'O Canada.'"

I felt relieved. They did it and did it well. I watched their group hug. I am proud of our response tonight. As a community, we did well, too.

Our national anthem finished. Eleanor spoke, "One last word, folks. I have instructions around the refreshments. The crowd is huge. We'll do shifts. I'm going to flip a coin. Heads those on the right side go first. Tails the people on the left." She threw a loonie up and let it land on the floor. Mayor Bob shouted. "Lefties go first."

Dad and I had the responsibility of picking up the overflowing donation baskets. Susie scooted out the back way. Her job was serving coffee.

I struggled through the crowd to Dad. "Where's Ms. Hamilton?" I asked.

"She's on kitchen duty."

Good, I thought. For once she's not tagging along with us.

Eleanor appeared just as we dumped the last basket into a black garbage bag.

"Wonderful," she said. "It's nearly full. That should help with Dr. Ahmadi's exam fees. Father McGarrity gave me the key to his study. We can count and record these donations in there."

We opened envelopes and read off cheques. Eleanor recorded everything.

Dad turned the garbage bag inside out to make sure it was empty. A last envelope fluttered out onto the carpet. As he opened it, he said. "What's this? Gingerly he extracted a note and laid it face up on the desk.

My stomach dropped. The message was composed with cut out letters. The three of us stared in silence:

<u>LIES CAN'T HIDE A SUICIDE BOMBER.</u>
<u>YOU'RE ALL RESPONSIBLE FOR WHAT COMES NEXT!</u>

"I thought the police had caught the entire gang," I said.

"Obviously not," Dad replied.

Eleanor pulled her phone from her pocket. "I'll call Tom." A few seconds later she said into the phone, "Please come upstairs to Father McGarrity's office. We've found an anonymous note among the donations." She turned to us, "He's on his way."

We sat in silence while we waited. Anger boiled in the pit of my stomach.

He was only a few minutes, although it seemed like an hour. When he opened the door, Eleanor pointed at the note. He reached the desk in two strides. "Which of you has handled this?"

Dad raised his hand, "Just me."

Tom turned to us, "Neither of you?"

Eleanor and I shook our heads.

"Excellent," he said.

He pulled a pair of tweezers and a plastic bag from a case he carried in his breast pocket.

Always ready, I thought.

Carefully, he slid the paper and envelope into the bag, using the tweezers. "Please keep this to yourselves for now. Let's go downstairs and you'll announce the total collected. People are waiting to hear. Right after, we'll go to Police Headquarters to take down your statements. ."

I won't be able to tell Susie, I thought, as I followed the rest down the stairs.

Before entering the hall, Tom turned to us. "Okay, everyone, we need a smile. Eleanor, you make the announcement about the total. We'll just do all the regular stuff, get some coffee, etcetera. If the author of the note is still here, we won't give him the satisfaction of seeing us stressed. I'll meet you at police HQ after you've finished up here. Park around back and give the Desk Sergeant your plate number."

With that, Tom gave Eleanor a quick hug and left. Dad and I looked at each other and nodded.

"We can do this," he said.

I opened the door and followed Eleanor and Dad into the noisy hall. Eleanor clapped her hands together sharply and called out, "Could I have your attention, please?"

I looked for Susie. Couldn't see her. Guess that's best. I won't be tempted to tell her.

Eleanor pushed through the crowd to the stage. By the time she'd climbed the steps, silence reigned. With all eyes turned on her, Eleanor began. "First of all, I want to thank everyone who had a part in planning this storytelling—the high school committee, the refugee committee, Father McGarrity and St. Dominic's Parish and especially, the Ahmadi family. We have been truly blessed."

Everyone applauded loud and long.

I whispered to Dad, "She remembers everything."

She lifted her hands to bring it to an end. "Now, I'm sure you'd all like to know how much was collected in the donation baskets. The final total was $10,678. Wow!" The entire room erupted in a cacophony of approval and celebration.

Dad and I knuckle-bumped.

When the noise had settled again, she continued. "This tells me our community is behind the Ahmadis. We are not ruled by fear or prejudice. We're just caring people who want to help." Again, the cheers erupted. She paused and waited for quiet. "Thank you to everyone who came and offered their support." In the midst of the applause this time, she rejoined us and led us to the refreshments table.

"Good job Eleanor," I said. When I checked out the dessert table it was bare.

"We'll get to our treat later, at home," Dad said.

For the next half hour, I hung out with my friends. Joey told me that Susie had gone home with her parents right after Eleanor made the announcement. When the crowd began to thin, Dad tapped me on the shoulder. "Tony says he'll take charge of clean up. Let's go. We'll do the night deposit on the way."

Steve

Tom was in his office waiting when we arrived. I glanced at the clock, 11:15. This had turned into a long night. Tom asked one of the constables on duty to take notes as we talked. He also received our permission to record the session. It really didn't take long. There wasn't much to tell. I reiterated the story of the donation baskets. Yes, they were part of the master plan for the evening. Yes, we had advertised that fact. When his questions were answered, Tom sent me with the constable to have my fingerprints taken. That done, he sent us home.

"Eleanor's coming to our house for a bit," I said. "Would you be able to join us?"

Tom smiled, "I'd love to, but I'll be here for two or three more hours. I'll have to take a rain check."

Back in the car, Eleanor said, "Steve, I think I'll take a rain check, too. Tonight, has left me totally wiped."

"Of course," I answered. "We're all tired." Renée nodded in agreement. We dropped Eleanor at her place and went on home.

Ebony greeted us at the door. His agitated "Meow" told us we'd forgotten to feed him before we left many hours earlier.

"Yes, my friend," Renée said as she scooped up her cat. "Food in two minutes."

I followed them to the kitchen. While Ebony enjoyed his late supper, we had our treat.

"I'm glad Mom made chocolate sauce," Renée said as she licked her spoon. "It feels as if she has stepped into the room every time we eat it."

"Yes, I miss her, too." I gathered up our dishes. "

"That was pretty weird, finding that note."

"Sure was and disappointing too.

"Creeps me right out."

"Tom said they're watching our house. Guess we'll just have to let the police do their job." I gave her a hug. "We're together in this. We're going to be fine. Let's go to bed." She gave me a weak smile, finished her milk and headed for the stairs.

"Good night, Dad," she said.

"Good night, Hon."

Chapter Twenty-Six

New Traditions

Wednesday, December 6

Renée

The next two weeks were busy. With no more disturbances from the dissenters, fear had faded into the background of our lives. I stopped in at Dad's office on the way home from school on Wednesday. He was buried in papers. "Hey Dad," I said to announce my arrival. "What's all this?"

Dad raised his head looking weary. "It seems that the RRSP run is starting early. And I've been planning our ski trip for after Christmas. I thought we'd do the same as last year. How does that sound?

"Oh yes, I had a great time. We said it was going to be our new Christmas tradition. Can I invite Susie again?"

"I've been talking with Susie's parents, and they want to come, too. Tony and his crowd will come as well, I'm sure. It should be a great party." He picked up a folder labelled "Ski Trip" and laid it on his briefcase.

I grabbed it. "Okay if I look?"

Dad grinned. "Sure, you might as well know what this trip will cost."

As I flipped through the pages, I said, "Speaking of parties, Dad, we talked about getting a Christmas tree and having a house party before Christmas. Have you forgotten?"

"No, of course not. Do you remember that I was going to invite Lee Ann along with the rest of our friends?" He looked up, checking out my reaction.

I endeavoured to keep all expression from my face. "Yes, I remember Dad. I want you to be happy, and if that requires having her on our team, then …"

Dad sighed.

"It won't be easy, but I can do it. Right?"

"Right. Thanks, Renée. I promise you that I won't embarrass you. Well, at least not on purpose."

I reached over and grabbed a notepad and pen from his desk. Using the folder for support, I wrote "Christmas party" on top of the page and said, "Now, let's make up the guest list. I'd like to invite Mustafa and his family, as well as Susie's family, Tracey's and Rachel's, and the Siddiqui's."

"Well, along with Eleanor and Tom, Tony and family and Bob Handel and his family, we'll have quite a crowd. Do you think we can handle that many?"

"Sure, we can. We're a team, remember? Let's go for the tree this Saturday morning. We can decorate it on Sunday. Let's have the party on the 16th."

"Right. I sure miss your mother. She would have loved this, and the skiing too."

I took a deep breath. My head whirled. "How do you do that, Dad? One minute you're talking about Ms Hamilton and the next you're missing Mom." I shook my head back and forth. "I don't get it."

Dad just shrugged. "I don't know," he said. "It feels okay to me, but obviously, not to you. I'll try not to do that again. Maybe that's something we can discuss with Dr. Sampler."

I sat there, doodling on the notepad, trying to get my feelings under control. I drew a Christmas tree. Stabbed the pad with the pen, swallowed hard and said, "Back to the party plans. We'll have munchies and some of those store-bought hors d'oeuvres and end the evening with ice cream sundaes. When Mom's chocolate sauce is there, she'll be there."

Dad looked at his watch. "It's just four o'clock. I'd like to work for another hour and then go to Lakey's for supper. Making party plans will be more fun on a full stomach. Don't forget to add Don and Dorie to the guest list, and Eunice Logan and Reverend Linda."

I scribbled down the names. "Supper at Lakey's sounds great. Think I'll just cuddle up on your couch with my laptop and do homework."

Chapter Twenty-Seven

Surprises

Saturday morning, December 9

Steve

It was still dark when I woke on Saturday morning. I stretched and looked at the clock. Seven a.m. I wonder how cold it is outside? Checked my phone. -2 C. I lifted my eyes to Serena's candle. "Well, Serena, we're making headway, slow, but sure. Today is Christmas tree day. It's early for us to be putting up the tree. We're trying to do things differently, so it doesn't hurt so much.

I rolled out of bed and stretched. Better wear long johns and that heavy bright red sweater my brother Richard sent me for Christmas last year. I might as well look like Christmas, I thought. Besides, no one will see the crazy colour under my coat.

After breakfast, we made the ten kilometer drive out to O'Donnell's Christmas Tree Farm. The parking lot was nearly full. "I guess lots of people get their tree early," I said, as I pulled in beside a bright yellow half-ton truck.

"Well, that's quite the colour," Renée remarked. "At least it won't disappear in a snow storm. I bet it belongs to a woman."

I grinned. Now, that's a sexist remark she'd complain about from me.

The wind made the -2 degree weather feel like -10. After receiving our instructions at the sales shelter, we tramped down the lane and back through the field of trees.

I heard the welcome sound of her laughter before we saw them. Lee Ann and a young man in a bright yellow parka stood two rows ahead, pointing at a tiny tree. She was shaking her head. I looked over at Renée expecting to see a scowl. Surprise, surprise, she had a smile, but not for Lee Ann.

"Look at that cool yellow jacket," Renée said. "Bet he owns the yellow truck."

I nodded and greeted Lee Ann with, "Have you picked out your tree already?"

She smiled. I felt the warmth travel through my body.

"No, not quite. She put her hand on the shoulder of the yellow jacket, John thinks I need a little tree, but I'd like a tall one, so the star nearly touches the ceiling."

Ignoring our conversation, Renée spoke directly to John, her voice confident, "Hey, your jacket matches your truck. Neat."

He grinned, "Good guess. Glad you approve. I like to be seen…in a snowstorm that is."

Renée never missed a beat with her response, "In a crowded field, too, I think."

His smile widened to fill his face. "Well, I've got the attention of a beautiful young woman, so I guess it worked."

Lee Ann joined the conversation with, "Steve, Renée, I'd like you to meet my son, John. He's home for the weekend and has agreed to risk a little dirt and pine needles to get my tree."

"Good lad," I said. "You know how to take care of your mom."

"Since you three know each other," John said, "let's search for our trees together. It'll be more fun."

Renée nodded and the two of them started on ahead. I heard John ask her, "What kind and size of tree are you looking for?"

I looked at Lee Ann and said, "It's amazing what hormones can do to build a bridge over discomfort."

She laughed. "Obviously, God is on our side today."

I took her hand, and then dropped it. "Sorry, that was my heart acting."

She laughed and blushed, her face alight.

She is so lovely, and she understands. What more could I ask?

We followed the two young people as they wandered through the trees. They stopped at a row of long needled pines, all of them splendidly tall. "Pines keep their needles longer," John said. "Surely, we'll find two that we'd like in this row."

Renée walked right to the tallest in the row. "How about this one, Dad? It should be great with our high ceilings."

I walked all around it. "Looks good to me. It's a good shape, has no gaps."

John motioned to the third one down. It was considerably shorter but was still quite bushy. "What do you think, Mom? Your cottage has regular height ceilings, but there's lots of space. I think this one would be good."

Lee Ann followed my example and walked round the tree. She held up her hand to measure its height. "I think it will be just about right once it's cut. We can take some off the bottom if it's too tall."

John and I made quick work of cutting them down. He picked hers up to carry it himself. I lifted the butt of our tree. "Renée, it will take the two of us to carry this one."

"If you wait," John said, "I'll take Mom's to the truck, and come back and help you with yours."

Determination radiated from Renée's entire body. "I think Dad and I will be just fine," she declared.

John just shrugged and headed back towards the truck. Renée grabbed the trunk about two feet from the top. I picked up the base. That tree must have weighed at least 150 pounds and I had the heavy end. With every step it got heavier. This tree was definitely a poor choice.

At one point on the journey back to the car, Lee Ann said, "Once we're loaded, let's get some hot chocolate and pancakes at the sugar shack."

"Great," Renée said.

By the time we reached the parking lot, my scarf and collar were soaked with sweat. John looked from the tree to our Prius and said, "How 'bout we put yours in my truck, too. It will be easier than crushing the roof of your car."

Oh, oh, I thought. That may get a rise from my independent daughter. As usual, Renée surprised me.

"Sounds good to me," she said, "Just as long as I get to ride up in the cab and keep an eye on it on the way home."

She's flirting outrageously. Is this my daughter? And what happened to all her reservations about Lee Ann and me? Lee Ann is going to think I've been making it all up.

As we walked to the sugar shack to pay for the trees and have our hot chocolate, Lee Ann spoke to me, her voice quiet, so only I could hear. "I'm glad she's fascinated by John. He's a great kid. You don't have to worry about him. He has a girlfriend, and he's 23."

"Not to worry," I said, "Young women love older men, at least to look at and dream about."

We had a great morning. There was lots of talk and laughter. John obviously loved to tease and totally enjoyed Renée's attention, and well he should. We issued our invitation to our party for the following Saturday. Lee Ann quickly agreed.

John paused, and said, "I'll have to look at my work week. I don't think I can take another Saturday off. Thanks for the invitation, though." He looked at Renée and saw disappointment settle over her face. "I'll be back for Christmas. Maybe we can get together then."

Yes, he's a nice young man. He's charming and knows how to care for others. Too bad he has a girlfriend. Well, no, he's at a different stage in his life. Renée has years of school ahead of her. She's best to just dream for now.

Lee Ann and I enjoyed the unexpected opportunity of extra time alone together as we drove back to our place. John and I lifted the tree out of the truck and leaned it against the wall inside the garage.

"Thanks a lot for the free delivery," I said.

"You're welcome," Lee Ann and John replied as one.

"I'll watch for your flash of yellow when it gets closer to Christmas," Renée said.

John grinned. "Just call me old yeller. No—Flash—that'll be great."

As the truck disappeared around the corner, Renée said, "Well, that was nice. I guess, having Ms. Hamilton around might have some benefits."

I put my arm around here as we walked into the house. "Thanks, hon, you were very gracious with Lee Ann. I'm pleased."

"I'm pleased, too," she said. "We wanted this Christmas tree thing to be different. Well, we've certainly succeeded so far. I'll remember today, for sure."

"Let's leave the tree in the garage to dry and decorate it tomorrow."

"Sounds good to me. I'll spend the afternoon on my project. I've got a stack of pictures I found on the internet. I even have one of the Barnardo trunk the kids received." Her smile faded. "I wish Harrar was here to help with the layout."

"You miss him, don't you?"

"Yup, and the guilt still creeps in, too."

I gave her a hug. She sighed and climbed the stairs to her room.

As I watched her go, I wished I could fix it for her. She's so young to carry so much grief.

When we arrived at the Ahmadis apartment later that evening, Thuraya rushed into the hall straight to Renée, her arms open wide, obviously ready for a hug. From Renée, she went to Eleanor, and then Bob's wife. I heard her tell each one, "I love you." Children have no barriers.

Nazira stepped forward, hugged Renée and reached out to shake my hand. That was a surprise. I didn't expect the physical contact.

Kahlil came next, followed by Hassan. "Please come in," he said.

"Thank you," I said, and offered the young lad my hand as well. Hesitantly, he shook it.

"Thank you for coming."

It was a magical evening. The Ahmadis had obviously worked hard, and probably spent their whole week's food budget on a wonderful feast. It was quite unlike anything I had ever eaten before, all delicious, laid out to impress the finest gourmet.

Renée asked Nazira about a dish that looked like meat balls but tasted distinctly different. She said, "Kubbeh – made with semolina, meat, onion, nuts, fried in oil."

I asked and learned that the funny looking little sausages were called Yabrak and weren't sausages at all. They were grapevine leaves stuffed with rice and meat. Loved them.

Eleanor picked out a dish that looked and tasted like lamb. By this time, Thuraya had joined us. She called the tasty mixture of lamb, rice and pine nuts, *mensaf*. She said, "Mensaf best" and rubbed her stomach. She pointed to several salads and vegetable dishes. "All good."

I agreed and filled my plate to overflowing.

After dinner, I asked Hassan what traditional games they play in Syria. Immediately, he pulled a box from beneath the coffee table. Inside was a game that he called Mancala. Carved from a piece of olive wood, the board was stained, sanded and painted with many coats of varnish. The surface was indented with two rows of six grooves, similar to an egg carton. Coloured stones nestled in the grooves.

"Beautiful," I said. "Did you make it?"

He pointed to Mustafa, Kahlil and himself and said, "We work together." He ran his hand over the board. "Slow work." He held up two fingers. "We make two." He smiled, "I show you play."

Mancala was easy to learn and lots of fun. Renée and I played with Hassan and Thuraya, then Mustafa. Eventually, everyone else joined in, taking turns with the game. We talked a little and laughed a lot.

When we got to the car, Renée said, "Great party."

"I loved the food."

"Dad…"

"And the family too. They're wonderful, a blessing for our community."

"I wish there wasn't this cloud of fear hanging over them and us," Renée added.

I turned the key in the ignition. "I wish it too. I'm glad Tom's team is doing the investigation."

"I'm sure Tom will have the rest of the creeps arrested soon," Eleanor added.

"I hope so," Renée said.

We delivered Eleanor.

As I pulled into the driveway, Renée asked, "Dad, will it be safe for Mustafa to be my date for the Christmas dance?"

"I think so. I'll talk with Tom and ask him if he thinks we should take any extra precautions. We're not going to be intimidated."

Once inside Renée said, "I'm not sleepy. Think I'll design an invitation to our party. We can deliver some at church tomorrow."

"Good idea. We'll deliver the rest after church."

"Will we have people bring finger food munchies?"

"Sounds good.

"Love you." She said and ran up the stairs.

I went 'round the house checking all the doors and turning off the lights. Think I'll read in bed a while.

An hour later, I heard Renée's printer spitting out the invitations. Time for sleep. Turned out the light, but my mind kept right on running. I reran the storytelling and finding the note among the donations. My mind jumped to the car trying to run me off the road, the men with the effigy, the paint on our door, the fire at the Ahmadis.

I tossed and turned. I thought about the Siddiquis and their pain. I prayed. I considered going downstairs for hot chocolate. I looked at the bedside clock. 1:40 a.m. I have to go to sleep. I tried forcing my eyes to stay open. That's a trick my father used to do when he couldn't sleep. It didn't work. I decided to focus on Lee Ann. I pictured her in that frilly apron when she greeted me at the door. I relived holding her close, kissing her. That must have worked, because I didn't see the clock again until morning.

Chapter Twenty-Eight

I Don't Believe It

Sunday, December 10

Renée

The next morning, while Dad and I sat waiting for the church service to begin, Mrs. Logan came in and stopped for a hug. There was no room left beside us, so she sat down across the aisle with Susie's family. I'm glad Mrs. Logan is part of our church. She's a good friend and neighbour.

When the organ music swelled, we stood. The choir processed in singing "O Come, O Come Emmanuel."

Well, Mom, Advent is with us again. I'm glad you gave me your love for it. Dad and I are doing fine, most of the time. Wish you were here. You'd like the way they've decorated the sanctuary. The angel we gave in your memory looks down over the manger scene. I like thinking about your presence there. I miss you, Mom. Tears slipped down my cheeks. Dad reached out and covered my hand with his. He smiled. His eyes were extra bright. I saw a tear sneak out. He must be thinking about Mom, too. I can feel your presence, God. Thank you for our church family. Thank you for loving us. I'm so glad I have faith.

Reverend Linda looked out over us. Her smile felt meant for me. "In the name of our Lord Jesus the Christ, welcome to God's house. This is the day the Lord has made. Let us rejoice and be glad in it. Let us worship God."

The service has begun. Thank you for your peace, I thought.

After church we delivered the invitations. By the time we pulled into our driveway, big fluffy flakes of snow filled the air. It felt like we were inside my snow globe. Dad pushed the button to open the garage.

"Think I'll get my camera and get a picture of this. It feels too special for my phone." I grabbed my Canon DSLR from the shelf just inside the back door. After snapping a picture looking down at the creek, I ran down towards it, so I could take one looking up toward the house. At the creek bank, I stopped entranced. He was there, on the hill across the creek. Dad's stag stood absolutely still, outlined by the snow. I turned on the video. A branch cracked. The stag jerked his head and ran. Five long strides and he had disappeared.

From behind me, Dad said, "God, he's beautiful."

I clicked off the camera. My Christmas present for Dad, I thought. In this video, there will be a snapshot to enlarge and frame for him. Thank you, God.

Happiness radiated from Dad. I snapped his picture too.

He reached out for a hug. "Glad you saw him."

"Me, too…I'm hungry."

We trudged back up the hill to the house. Once inside, Dad stamped the snow from his feet. Ebony waddled into the kitchen.

"Hi there, friend," I said as I picked him up. "Susie suggested I come over there to do homework this afternoon. Okay?"

"Sure."

As we sat down to our soup, I decided to tease Dad a bit. "By the way, what happened to Janice…can't remember her name? You haven't mentioned her lately. I thought maybe she was providing some competition for Lee Ann."

He frowned. "Not likely. She's makes me nervous."

I swallowed my spoonful of soup too quickly. It burned all the way down. I gulped some water.

"Besides, I don't like her attitude towards the Ahmadis."

"Why? She came to the fundraiser and the storytelling."

"Oh yes, she comes to the parties, but it feels like she's there mainly to harass me."

Well, that bit of teasing sure wiped out. I concentrated on my soup. When we had finished and were clearing up, I could still feel the tension coming from Dad. I was glad his phone rang. He disappeared into the study to get it. In a few minutes he returned, a big smile on his face.

"That was Tom. He's on his way over with good news about the investigation."

"You were taking me to Susie's."

"Tom won't be here long."

"I'll just run upstairs and get my stuff, so I'll be ready to go as soon as he leaves."

Steve

Less than ten minutes after he called, Tom knocked on our door. "Come on in, friend. We'll sit in the kitchen." I called up the stairs, "Renée, Tom's here."

"Coming, Dad."

Tom was all smiles as we settled down in the breakfast nook.

He opened with, "I can talk more freely in your home than on the phone from headquarters. We made a sixth arrest this morning."

"Another one?" Renée and I said together.

"Someone from Catalpa Creek?" Renée asked.

"Yup, and she's a woman. Her name is Tamara White."

We both frowned. "I've never heard of a Tamara White. Have you, Renée?"

She shook her head.

Tom smiled. "Well, you know her. I know you know her. In fact, from what I saw at the fundraiser, she's fascinated with you, Steve. Her alias here is Janice Lawson."

"Janice Lawson? That pushy little woman, who pretended to sprain her ankle?" Renée said.

Tom nodded.

"Really. No wonder I didn't like her. Though I'll have to admit that at first I rather enjoyed the extra attention."

At that, Renée groaned.

"It will all be in the news tomorrow. We found explosives, guns, and hate literature in her apartment.

Oh, my God, guns, explosives. I shook my head, trying to make sense out of Tom's words.

And we found the costumes."

"Costumes?" Renée asked.

"Yes, the clown costume worn by the person who set the fire at the Ahmadi's and…" Tom paused for emphasis. "and the ski mask, the wig, and the outfits worn by the bank robber. At the moment, we're thinking the gang did the robberies to finance their hate campaign." Tom paused and shifted his weight in the chair.

"Hard to believe. She's pushy, but a gang leader, a menace? I'm glad I wasn't sucked in."

Ebony jumped up on my knee, purring like a motor boat. Automatically, I rubbed behind his ears.

Tom smiled at me and the cat. "Looks like that cat likes you just as much as Janice."

"I prefer the cat." That brought a giggle from Renée.

Tom continued his story. "Tamara White is fairly well known out west among the white supremacists."

"No wonder she didn't applaud at the storytelling." My mind struggled to believe Janice could be the source of hatred among us. To think I was tempted.

"The important thing is you, Renée and the Ahmadis don't have to worry any more. There may still be some disgruntled citizens, but we think we've got the violent ones in custody."

"Thanks, Tom. The Ahmadis are wonderful people. I want them to feel safe."

Tom stood up. "Time to go."

We followed him down the hall. "On a lighter note, Renée and I are having a party on the 16th. You and Eleanor are on the top of the list. We delivered the invitation to her this morning."

"Great. I'm starting a month's holidays on the 16th. I'll be able to come."

"Fantastic," Renée said.

"By the way, the week after New Year's, Eleanor and I are flying to Vancouver for a week. Nazira has agreed to run Lights Out while we're away. Business will be slow. If she has a problem, Dora Lakey has promised to help her out. She wants to try, and Eleanor thought it would give her confidence."

"That's great," Renee said, her eyes shining. "Eleanor is the best."

"What a wonderful message for the community," I added. "Renée and I will be skiing in Vermont. We won't be able to drop by and see how she's doing."

When Tom straightened up from pulling on his boots, his smile stretched wide. It was obvious he was proud of Eleanor. "Not to worry. Your neighbour has volunteered to stop in every day. She wants to get to know Nazira better. Bye now. Have a great time skiing," he said as he closed the door behind him.

Renée started to giggle. "Oh Dad, really. What did you call her… pretty little Janice?"

Her giggle intensified. I just had to join her.

When Renee found her breath again, she continued, "Well, Dad, I'm glad your heart's not broken. Now, let's get going. I want to tell Susie."

While I watched her gather up her books and laptop. I thought, she should be grateful for Lee Ann. After all, if I wasn't so interested in Lee Ann, I just might have reacted differently to Janice. Guess I'd better not say that out loud.

Chapter Twenty-Nine

Party Time

Saturday, December 16

Renée

Susie spent Saturday helping me get ready for the party. We rearranged the furniture to make room for our thirty-six guests. Once everything was set, we relaxed on the couch.

"Hey, you're looking mighty serious," Susie said. "What's up?"

"I was thinking about Harrar. I wish he were here. I miss him and Mom, too." I rubbed my eyes but I couldn't rub away my thoughts. I got up and walked over to the mantel and picked up a picture of Mom and Dad and me at Myrtle Beach. I stared at the picture. "I used to get so impatient with Mom. I'd give anything to have her say, 'How about a cup of tea and a cookie?' Mom was the queen of tea breaks." I looked over at Susie, my sight clouded with tears.

"The day she died, I refused to sit down with her. I took my tea to my bedroom so I could keep working at my science or history or… I can't even remember what it was, yet it was more important than time with Mom."

"Oh, Renée…"

"And Harrar…I let him pull away. I didn't push hard enough…"

Susie hugged me. "No reruns, remember. That's what Dr. Sampler told you. We said. But we can do better. Ever since…Harrar, I've tried to be more patient with my brothers." She wiped her eyes. "Although sometimes…C'mon Renée." She took my hand and dragged me to the kitchen. Handing me the box of tissues that always sits on a corner of the island, she said, "Let's mop up and have tea. We're supposed to be getting ready for a party. That's what your Mom would say."

We both wiped our eyes and blew our noses. Susie plugged in the kettle. I automatically reached for Mrs. Logan's cookie tin. We had finished our treat by the time Dad got home. He surveyed the living and dining rooms. "Great job, girls. Guess, we're ready."

"Are you kidding Dad?" I handed him another list.

As he skimmed down it, he said, "Three trips. Should have borrowed Tony's truck." He turned and headed back out the door.

"Your dad's neat."

"Susie, I'll need your support to deal with Ms. Hamilton tonight."

"Sure, but you'll be fine."

"I wish...

"No reruns, remember. Besides it's a Christmas party. We're going to have fun. Deal?"

"Deal."

Our first arrivals were Don and Dorie. She came in with a huge slow cooker full of honey garlic meatballs. I lifted the lid and inhaled. "Yum!"

"We ordered Halal meat from one of our suppliers, and I made a sign so the Siddiquis and the Ahmadis will know they can eat it."

Dad smiled, "Thank you," he said. "You are very caring."

The Ahmadis arrived next. I was glad they came early. Thuraya greeted me with her customary hug. With a wide grin, Mustafa handed me a platter and said, "Yabrak and a smile."

As I took it from him, his eyes met mine. I blushed. He's certainly turning on his charm to me.

Thuraya pulled at my sweater. "Where cat?"

Thankful for the interruption, I set the platter on the table. "Let's go look," I said and led her off to the kitchen.

By seven, the place was crowded. With everyone talking, it was frightfully noisy. Ebony had deserted Thuraya for the peace of my bedroom.

Tony climbed up on a kitchen chair and clapped his hands for attention. "Well now, everyone. This is quite the gathering. We've some announcements. On behalf of Steve and Renée, welcome, all of you."

I looked over at Dad. Thank you, I mouthed. Neither of us like being up front. Tony is a natural emcee.

"We're setting up card tables for games. The Ahmadis brought mancala, Lee Ann, crokinole. We've Wizard, euchre, and dominoes as well. Try one for a while and move on. There are no prizes so just relax and have fun.

I checked out people's faces. They looked enthusiastic about the games. I hoped they were.

Tony wasn't finished. "Help yourselves to food, there's certainly plenty of it. Punch, etcetera is in the kitchen. Oh yes, before we start, there is a bathroom off the front hall, and one on the left at the top of the stairs."

That's helpful, I thought.

Tony continued. "A little later, we'll get Dorie to play the keyboard and we'll sing some Christmas carols." Head's turned toward the Ahmadis. I drew in my breath.

Tony must have noticed. He added, "We're going to share some traditions tonight. The Ahmadis told us they want to learn about ours. We want to learn about theirs, too." Everyone applauded.

The Ahmadis raised their hands in victory signs. Thank you, God, I prayed.

Tony added, “Guess that’s it…No, Tom is waving his hand.”

Tom shouted, “I brought my guitar, so if Dorie doesn’t know a song, maybe I will.”

Tony concluded with, “If you have any questions, just ask Steve or Renée. Have fun.”

As Tony jumped down from the chair, the noise erupted again. The scraping of chairs meant that people were already settling into games. It was a grand evening. I taught Mustafa how to play euchre. He learned fast.

At one point, I was filling empty platters on the serving table with desserts and Ms. Hamilton appeared at my side.

“You’re a wonderful hostess, Renée. You’ve thought of everything. This is a grand party.”

“Thank you, Ms. Hamilton,” I said, keeping my eyes glued to the food.

She touched my arm and said, “Do you think you could call me Lee Ann when we’re not at school?”

I bit my lip. In my head I heard, *You knew this would happen when you agreed to invite her*. Mom spoke up, I’m sure it was Mom, *Renée, it’s time. It’s time.* I looked around the room. Where’s Susie?

“Renée, I’d just like us to be friends.” Her voice was gentle, not exactly pleading but not demanding.

I lifted my head and looked into her eyes. She’s nervous, I thought, as nervous as me. She must really care for Dad. I managed a weak smile. “Okay, I’ll try. Thank you…Lee Ann.” I heard Mom respond, *That’s my girl. Thank you.*

Lee Ann’s eyes sparkled. “Thank you, Renée,” she said. “You must love your dad very much.”

She slipped away, leaving me with my thoughts. She’s really nice, and she’s beautiful, different from Mom. She’ll never be

Mom. Mom's words interrupted my thoughts, *That's right, Renée. It's okay for you to like her. Your Dad is wise. He's making a good choice.* I closed my eyes. Oh Mom, it feels like I'm saying goodbye but I'm not, am I? You will be with me always. Friends, Ms. Hamilton…Lee Ann and I can be friends. "Thanks, Mom," I whispered.

At nine, Tony climbed back up on his chair and clapped his hands once more. "Time for music. Dorie and Tom, would you please come lead us. Renée and Susie have set up the digital projector, so we will have the words. We have lots of variety here."

We clapped. Tony climbed down, and Dorie took over at the keyboard. We spent another hour singing Christmas carols, winter songs and favourite pop songs. At one point, Rachel's family taught us an Israeli dance step.

Best of all for me was the moment when Mustafa sang, unaccompanied, a traditional Syrian melody. He has a fabulous voice. He sang first in Arabic, then in English. His love for his homeland shone through. When he finished, the room was absolutely silent for about 20 seconds, then the applause was deafening. All in all, it was a grand party.

The last of the guests left about midnight. Lee Ann stayed behind to help clean up. I was glad. Even though we had encouraged people to take their leftovers home, the fridge was packed with food.

"We'll never eat all this," Dad said. "Tomorrow, we'll take most of it to the Catalpa Creek Family Shelter."

Lee Ann looked at him. I could see the pride in her eyes. "You are a blessing to this community," she said.

"I agree, one hundred per cent," I said, and gave Dad a big hug.

"Now, it's time for me to go home. Would it be okay if I join you two at church tomorrow?"

"That would be nice." I said.

Dad just smiled and nodded. He walked her to her car. I didn't watch. I didn't want to see him kiss her, but I knew he would. I poured a saucer of milk for Ebony and climbed the stairs to my room.

Steve

We stood by Lee Ann's car. I pulled her close. We kissed, long and slow. My whole body responded. Slow down, Steve. I leaned back just a little. "Something happened tonight. Renee has shifted. She's…more at ease with you or something."

"We had a few minutes to talk. She's agreed to call me Lee Ann, away from school. She is trying hard, Steve. She wants you to be happy. She's taken a step. She's a wonderful young woman."

"Thank you. Thank you for your patience with her and with me."

"Oh, Steve, what you've done helped me heal. I was broken. Thank you."

"I love you, Lee Ann. Yes, I'm sure. I love you."

Tears streamed down her face. "I love you, too," she said. "Yes, I'm sure I love you."

We stood there. It felt like time had stopped. The night was cold and clear. Stars twinkled in the velvety sky. "Look," I said, and pointed at the sparkling stream of a falling star. "Let's make a wish."

She closed her eyes and whispered. "I wish that everyone could feel the happiness and love that I feel tonight. Thank you, God for the gift of Steve and Renée in my life."

I kissed the tip of her nose. "I wish that our love will grow stronger and deeper each day. Thank you, God, for the gift of Lee Ann in my life and in Renée's life. We need her."

We kissed again.

"I think it's time to leave the past behind," I said and watched her face. "We can choose a new life."

She nodded and smiled, "Yes, we can." A car drove past. She sighed. "It's late. I must go home."

I opened the car door for her. She started the car and lowered the window.

"Text me when you are home and safe inside," I said.

"I will."

I watched her drive off. "Thank you, God, for Lee Ann. Nana Sinclair counted her blessings. I've so many to count tonight—Lee Ann, Renée, our friends especially the Ahmadis, Tom and the police force, a grand evening, and more. Thank you, God. I pray for those six who have been arrested, especially Janice. Give them opportunities to learn to love all of your people. Oh, and thank you for Nana Sinclair's diary. It's brought Renée and me closer. Thank you. Amen."

Chapter Thirty

It's Time

Wednesday Evening, December 20

Renée

The night of the Christmas dance, Dad picked up Mustafa and brought him back to our house. I tried to tell him that it wasn't necessary, but Dad was sure it was. "It's not Mustafa's fault that they don't have a vehicle. I want him to feel good about himself."

Getting ready for the Christmas dance was fun. I loved my new azure blue dress with its filmy, swirly skirt, perfect for dancing. As I slipped it over my head, I gave thanks for Mrs. Logan. We'd had a grand time shopping for it. I'm glad she's my friend. Maybe next time, Lee Ann will…No I don't want to think about that tonight. I've taken a step in accepting her. That's enough.

I twirled round the room, my blue dress flying free. My picture of the ducks swimming through the morning mist, stuck in the corner of my mirror, reminded me of Russell Carding. He was my enemy. Now, he's just another kid like me. I wondered if his school was having a Christmas dance, too. Was he going? Did he have a date? I'm glad I talked with him down by the creek, I thought. It feels good to know he's back on track, he has hopes and dreams just like me.

I sat down in front of the mirror. Mom's precious opals flashed fire around my neck and at my ears. That girl staring back at me from the mirror has done a lot of growing up, and I'm glad Russell has, too. I wish Harrar had had more time. The eyes in the mirror filled with tears. Can't do that now. I made myself smile. Took a deep breath.

I like my hair down around my shoulders, I thought. The loose curls look sweet. I hope they last all evening. Having one shoulder strapless is neat too. I hope Mustafa doesn't think it's too…Oh well, he'll have to cope. I'm not Muslim.

I reached into my closet for my new matching blue pumps that rested among my runners, sandals and others. I looked up at the jeans, shirts, skirts and dresses. I thought about Nana Sinclair and those ugly huge dresses that protected her from Mr. Renwick. Nana was so pleased to have that little trunk full of clothes. I remembered Mustafa's story to Susie about wearing the same pair of jeans for months in the refugee camp. I must never forget how blessed I am. Nana had a rugged life but she left it behind. When she got the chance, she chose to begin again. That's what Mustafa is doing. His escape from Syria was terrible. Yet he is also choosing to begin again. My life has been different but I have my own misery, my pain. Still, I too am free to count my blessings and choose to begin again.

I flipped on Mom's candle. "Yes Mom, I am blessed. I miss you. I miss Harrar, but life continues, doesn't it? We can't go back, but we can remember. We can learn. We can be grateful. We can begin again."

I heard Dad and Mustafa talking downstairs. Guess it's time.

He stood at the bottom of the stairs looking very flash in a jacket and tie. He is handsome, I thought. He watched me come down the steps, his face serious. Oh dear. He doesn't approve. When I reached the bottom, he held out his hand.

"Beautiful, Renée."

I took it and smiled. His eyes danced. "Flowers, I have flowers," he said.

Nestled on a wrist band were three exquisite red roses.

"Thank you, Mustafa. You are a gentleman." I pulled the corsage onto my wrist and held it out to show him. His whole body relaxed.

"I ask Antonio. He had flowers for Susie. I told store lady, red roses, for a beautiful woman."

I blushed.

Dad handed Mustafa my coat. As we stepped out the door I thought, well, Harrar, I wish you had felt accepted in this world. I wish things were different. I wish no one had to be afraid… I'm sure you're accepted now. With God, you've found peace.

Susie and Antonio arrived at the school right behind us. "Hope you enjoy Mr. Gorgeous tonight," she whispered. "Do you think he'll know how to dance?

I looked at her and laughed. "Of course, he will. They dance in Syria. We'll manage."

And we did. Mustafa was a wonderful dancer.

The Greatest Commandment

One of the teachers of the law came and heard them debating. Noticing that Jesus had given them a good answer, he asked him, “Of all the commandments, which is the most important?”

“The most important one,” answered Jesus, “is this: ‘Hear, O Israel: The Lord our God, the Lord is one. Love the Lord your God with all your heart and with all your soul and with all your mind and with all your strength.’ The second is this: ‘Love your neighbor as yourself.’ There is no commandment greater than these.”

(Mark 12:28-31 NIV)

Gram, circa 1958

Nana Sinclair

With the exception of Nana Sinclair, all of the characters in this story are creations of my active imagination. Even Nana's story is sprinkled with imaginary detail. Margaret Sinclair was my biological grandmother.[1] She was born in England May 10, 1896.

Like many Barnardo children, Nana did not talk much about her younger life. When asked about it, she would reply, "Like Topsy, I just growed."[2] All of the records from the town where we think she was born were burned in a church fire. The few stories she told of her earliest years in Britain often contradicted themselves. Sometimes she spoke of her parents being killed in an accident. Sometimes she said they died along with other siblings with the flu or some other epidemic of the time. She gave no details. They were just statements of fact.

Barnardo records from England do say that she went from the Gateshead workhouse to one of the Barnardo villages for girls and that she was in the village only a few weeks Their records tell us that she came to Canada on the SS Dominion, arriving October 2, 1903 and that she was eight years old.

She did speak of having a little brother. Sometimes, she said he died in the epidemic with her parents. Other times, she spoke of him dying on the ship to Canada. She called him Wilfred and named one of her sons after him. Nana had a friend named Tilly whom she met either in the workhouse or on board ship. They remained friends for many years after they both were married.

Because this is a work of fiction, I chose the accident story as her beginning and kept Wilfred with her, even though I changed his name. I just couldn't send her out all alone to that workhouse.

There is no diary, only a few closely written, hard-to-read Barnardo records kept by the supervisors who visited the children here in Canada. Those records tell us that she was in several homes. Each time a placement ended she was returned to Hazelbrae. Depending on the home, some supervisors reported that the family said Nana worked hard. Others said she was lazy and untidy. There is a report that she took the green rat poison and made herself very ill.

I chose to tell Nana's story with a diary because of this supervision report from December 12, 1905:

> *Barnardo worker reports M. strong robust girl, good conduct. Teacher says Margaret is best writer in class and good reader.*

As an adult, one of Nana's leg was misshapen and discolored and she walked with a limp. She said she had broken it at work.

My sisters knew nothing more. I created the accident. In fact, I created the homes in which she stayed. The reports give us a few details. Like many Barnardo children, some of the homes were awful. The reports show that the supervisors encouraged her to remain in her placements. They warned that changing homes would not be good for her.

> "I trust you will be able to remain there a long time, as it always seems a pity to see girls moving about too much. Sometimes, of course, a change may be advisable for all concerned, but to be continually moving is generally not to a girl's credit. One must guard against a spirit of discontent and a love of change. It is by doing well what lies nearest to us that we become fitted to do work more difficult and take more responsibility."

Many of the other details attributed to Nana's life, I learned through my research into Barnardo children and their stories. Building Nana's story was a challenge which I was happy to undertake. Although I never met my grandmother, she cared for my half-sisters throughout their growing-up years. They speak of her with love.

Dr. Barnardo wanted to give the children an opportunity for what he believed was a better life. All around him in England, he saw the problems of homelessness, hunger, unemployment that were a result of the industrial revolution. He hoped that as immigrants, the children would be able to begin again in a new country. At the time, he didn't understand the loneliness that immigration entailed. He didn't see their vulnerability to what I call our inhumanity.

Dr. Barnardo expected the children to be accepted into the pioneer families with respect and love. He didn't consider the fear that "street kids" would engender, nor the effect that a little power can sometimes have on people. He thought he had safeguards in place. Some of the children were welcomed into loving homes when they arrived. Others like Nana were eventually loved and accepted. Some suffered degradation and abuse. Some died. The amazing reality is that many of these child immigrants grew up to become good responsible citizens like Nana. Their stories are a tribute to the inner strength God has given to humanity.

If I were writing Renée's essay I would say that today there is hope for a better tomorrow. We have taken some tiny steps. Many, but not all of our refugees today come with a group of sponsors who care about them. They come as families so they aren't one child alone. There is some government support in learning the language and culture of our land, and for the first year some financial support as well. Many of us are better able to see immigrants as people, like ourselves. People like the Ahmadis who come with dreams and skills, willing to learn and heal. Prejudice, hate and fear still raise their ugly heads, but I think, I believe that the numbers are fewer.

There is hope for a better tomorrow. Our new friends can *begin again*.

You will find pictures and links concerning Margaret Sinclair, a Barnardo child, at www.janetstobie.com.

[1]For my personal story "Twice Blessed", you can read the short, polished version of the story in the May/2015 issue of the United Church Observer: www.ucobserver.org/opinion/2015/05/spirit_story/

[2] From a quote by Topsy in *Uncle Tom's Cabin, or Life Among the Lowly* by Harriet Beecher Stowe.

Book Club Questions

1. From your experience would her grief journey be different if Renée was five, twenty-five, or fifty?
2. What wisdom would you give Steve as he thinks about beginning again?
3. In your mind, how would the situation change if it had been Renée's Dad who had been killed, and her mom who was starting over again?
4. What learning did you receive from Harrar's story?
5. What faith questions would you have had Reverend Linda?
6. As they journey through their difficult times, Renée and Steve believed that God offered them help through people, animals, books etc. What examples of this do you see in the story? And in the world around you?
7. What are your thoughts about welcoming large numbers of refugees to your country?
8. If you were writing Renée's essay, how would you compare Nana Sinclair's experience with that of the Ahmadi's?
9. What signs of hope for a more loving world do you see happening today?
10. When we read a story, we tend to identify with one of the characters. Which character in *To Begin Again* felt most real for you?
11. The story is told from two viewpoints – Renee's and Steve's. How was this helpful for you? Did the two viewpoints present any difficulties for you?
12. What will you remember most from *To Begin Again?*

With Gratitude

I need to acknowledge and thank the following people for their contributions to the creating of *To Begin Again.*

My editor, Ruth E. Walker of Writescape, has been wonderful. She treated my work with respect. As I endeavoured to follow her suggestions, my writing ability grew. It feels as if she has led me through an entire course in creative writing. When my friend Nancy finished reading the final draft, her comment was that Ruth's help had enabled me to make an already good novel so much better. I give thanks for Ruth, for her support and commitment, and her wisdom. She's amazing.

My loving husband Tom, who patiently supports my dedication to answering God's call to write. Tom is my frontline editor of ideas, grammar, spelling and punctuation. He has spent hours reading and rereading *To Begin Again* with me.

I am truly grateful to Nancy Miller, my friend of over forty years, who has hung in there with me through all of my books. She read the first draft of *To Begin Again* three years ago, plus all the subsequent drafts as well. I count on her for her opinion of rewrites, emotions, ideas, titles and covers. Her friendship is a precious gift in so many ways. Sharing in my writing projects and especially the anguish that comes with writing a novel is a priceless gift of friendship.

I say thank you to my mom and her sisters, and my sisters and cousins, all of whom have shared information about my grandmother, Margaret Sinclair. Over the years, they researched and gathered all the information available from the few records of Grandma's life. They will recognize the parts of Nana's story that are based on fact and the details that I filled in from my imagination and from my own research into the stories of Barnardo children in Canada.

I also offer my gratitude to Gail H. Corbett for writing *Nation Builders: Barnardo Children in Canada* and Kenneth Bagnell for writing *The Little Immigrants.* Their work helped me with crafting Nana Sinclair's diary.

The Ahmadi's story is fiction, yet it is also inspired by reality. I give my thanks to Shining Waters Refugee Resettlement Group and our two refugee families. My experience with you helped in crafting the story of the Catalpa Creek refugee resettlement committee and the Ahmadis' response. I am also grateful for the magazine articles about the many refugee families coming to Canada, and the experience of world aid volunteers working in refugee camps in Turkey and other places.

I give thanks for Raheel Raza, author of *Their Jihad...Not My Jihad!: a Muslim Canadian Woman Speaks Out*, and advocate for women's rights. Raheel shared her time and resources willingly. She answered my questions on the Islamic faith with patience and wisdom. Raheel's information was essential for the writing of Harrar's story.

I give thanks for my friend Stephanie Richmond. She has always taken the time to listen and make suggestions concerning the marketing decisions for this book.

I give thanks for Sue Reynolds. She is a gifted graphic artist. Her patience and willingness to work to my deadlines made it possible for me to get this book printed in time for the Bay of Quinte Conference of the United Church of Canada.

I give thanks for Lisa Coulombe. As the representative of Marquis Books she went out of her way to accommodate my schedule. Marquis Books do excellent printing at reasonable prices.

Rev. Janet Stobie,

B.A., M.Ed., M.Div.

A writer, spiritual director, and ordained minister, Janet is welcomed as an inspirational speaker at fundraisers, group meetings and Sunday morning church services. During her nineteen years in parish ministry, Janet was particularly appreciated for her storytelling and her pastoral care skills with young people and children. Janet writes a blog and has a column in a local newspaper.

For Janet this book carries a message of the need for us all to learn and practice the lesson of acceptance on an individual basis. She believes this is God's call to discipleship and is a path to peace.

Janet is married to Tom and together they have five children and nine "amazing" grandchildren. When Janet is not writing, or fulfilling speaking engagements, she and her husband Tom enjoy their blended family of five adult children and their spouses. In between, they have fun square dancing with their friends, travelling and volunteering at their church.

For more about Janet Stobie check out her website.

www.janetstobie.com

NOTES

FIREWEED

by Janet Stobie

First Book in *The Catalpa Creek* Series

With compassion and insight, Fireweed explores the complex relationship between father and daughter. Fireweed offers a feast of mystery, tears, and laughter for the reader. Janet Stobie has created for you a community of very real and intriguing characters living in the small town of Catalpa Creek.

The secure life of Renée Grenville crumbles when a drunk driver kills her mother. Consumed by her grief, she's skipping school and avoiding her friends. Home has become a battleground of daily fights with her dad. When a stalker turns her telephone into a tool of terror, she feels totally lost and alone.

Steve, in the midst of his own grief, is struggling to learn how to be a single parent, and carry on at work and in the community. Encouraged by his friends to have a social life, he begins a friendship with Lee Ann Hamilton.

Searching for new life in the midst of this tragedy, they both turn to their faith community for support. Together they journey from their "Mr. Fix-it God" of childhood, to a "Companion God", who walks with them through life's pain.

Fireweed is available from www.janetstobie.com and www.amazon.com and www.amazon.ca

ELIZABETH GETS HER WINGS

by Janet Stobie

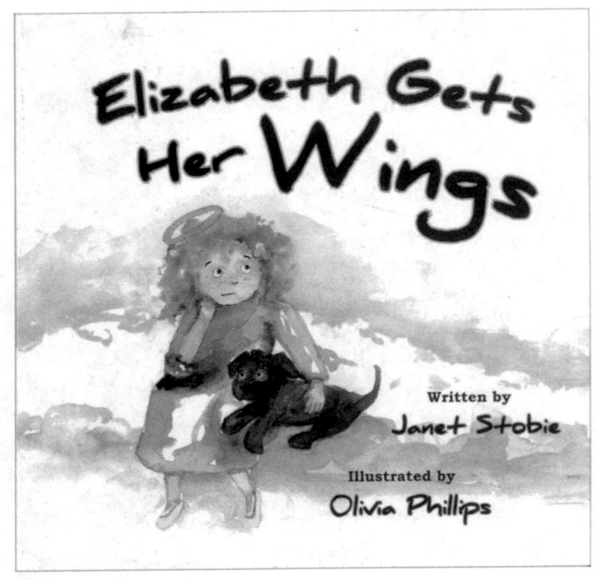

Energetic, enthusiastic Elizabeth doesn't want to wait another three years to get her wings. "Pick me," she cries when God asks for a helper.

Maybe Elizabeth can earn her wings early. The task sounds easy. Will Elizabeth be successful?

Janet Stobie invites you to travel the Earth with Elizabeth as she searches for volunteers for a mysterious journey. Enjoy this new approach to the story of the three king's and their visit to Bethlehem.

Olivia Phillips has captured the Spirit of Elizabeth's adventure in her delightful watercolor illustrations.

Elizabeth Gets Her Wings is available from www.janetstobie.com and www.amazon.com or www.amazon.ca

SPECTACULAR STELLA

by Janet Stobie

Created in God's pottery studio, Stella is left on the window to dry. Along comes the wind and carries her away for an adventure. Suddenly the wind drops baby Stella and disappears.

Stella is lost. She knows only her name. What she is and where she belongs is a mystery. She looks up from her bed of autumn leaves and sees only angels crisscrossing the sky above. Must she become an angel to get home? Will anyone help her find her way?

Parents and children the world over will respond with delight to Janet Stobie's engaging story, and Marion Hill's gentle illustrations. Spectacular Stella carries a message of personal affirmation. In today's world it's important to hear, over and over again:

"You are special just as God created you."

DIPPING YOUR TOES

in Planning Small Group Devotionals

by Janet Stobie

Dipping Your Toes contains everything you need to lead the devotions for your group, or for Sunday worship leadership. Inside you will find 44 complete devotional services including scripture, reflection, discussion, hymns and prayers, organized by the calendar year. Leaders can download the color picture and add the unique "Tweet/one liner" for focus and advertising.

Part 2 invites you to "Wade in a Little Deeper" in your devotional planning as you learn to create your own service.

"Janet's faith shines through every page as she calls us to respond to the voice of the holy in our lives in many different ways." Betty Radford Turcott

Dipping Your Toes is available from www.janetstobie.com